HALF A REASON TO DIE

HALF A REASON TO DIE

HALF A REASON TO DIE

CHIP DUNCAN

SELECTBOOKS, INC.
NEW YORK

This edition published by SelectBooks, Inc.

For information address SelectBooks, Inc., New York, New York.

First Edition

ISBN 978-1-59079-408-1

Library of Congress Cataloging-in-Publication Data

Names: Duncan, Chip, author.
Title: Half a reason to die / Chip Duncan.
Description: First edition. | New York : SelectBooks, Inc., [2017]
Identifiers: LCCN 2016029892 | ISBN 9781590794081 (softcover : acid-free paper)
Subjects: LCSH: Reporters and reporting--Fiction. | Journalists--Fiction.
Classification: LCC PS3604.U5263 A6 2017 | DDC 813/.6--dc23 LC record
available at https://lccn.loc.gov/2016029892

Text design by Pauline Neuwirth, Neuwirth & Associates, Inc.

Manufactured in the United States of America
10 9 8 7 6 5 4 3 2 1

For Ron Wallace

CONTENTS

ACKNOWLEDGMENTS

I'm grateful to Crystalyn Glover, Patricia Ostermick, Cathy Ryan, Cynthia Flynn, Stevie Ballard, Muna Shehadi Sill, Astrid Vaccaro, David Barrett, Karen Tredwell, Kurt Kleman, Elaine Joli, Tom Matthews, Jeanette Yoder, Molly Stern, Nancy Sugihara, and Heather Mitchell for their intelligent review, thoughtful criticism, and encouragement.

A NOTE TO THE READER

The stories in this collection are told in the first person. Each includes a different narrator who possesses some knowledge of print journalism or documentary filmmaking, crafts with which I have long been associated. All of the stories are based on interviews I was never able to conduct, though each features real places or personal events I've experienced during my travels. That all the stories happen to reveal a guarded secret or reflect the deeply held beliefs of a particular character is intentional, while the circumstances around those revelations are pure fiction.

HALF A REASON TO DIE

TELL ME WHAT TO BELIEVE, STEELY DAN

GARLIC. MUSTARD. MY HANDS REEKED from pulling the thick weeds that invaded my two overgrown acres. For the first time in years I thought of Randy, and the way his breath always smelled of gyros. The way lamb grease and garlic tzatziki merged with 10W-40 and dried paint just above the knees of his old green camo pants.

It put me back there, back to things that mattered a long time ago. State Street. The student union. The perfect tear in an old pair of jeans. The occasional protest still riled campus police, but coed dormitories captured the imagination of incoming freshmen. Recession was taking its toll, and jobs were scarce for recent graduates. I had my self-inflicted afternoon gig, standing on the corner near Rennebaum's Drug Store and nodding at the passersby who threw quarters in my open guitar case but rarely stayed around for the song.

There we were, the streeters in Madison, Wisconsin—musicians, jugglers, unemployed refugees from the Mariel Boatlift, and homeless veterans with bad dreams. Ronald Reagan was in the White House.

In my attic room on Mifflin Street, I kept an old Nagra tape recorder, a cheap mono microphone, and four rolls of bootlegged, one-pass audiotape that I used to record interviews with unlikely suspects. I didn't have a client, but it felt like I was in production. And there were challenges. It wasn't as simple as someone with time on their hands saying "yes" to an afternoon of questioning. A person had to be special. In Randy's case, his brain was in and out, and clear thinking seemed rare. I'd heard him channel snippets of wisdom during a few of his street rants. But with Randy, timing was everything.

"Where's your guitar, Carlos?" he asked, approaching me with his hand extended. Randy had a thing about not using real names. So on any given day, I was Carlos, Clapton, Jeff Beck, or B.B. If someone asked for folk music while Randy was standing nearby, I was Woody. With a slide in my hands, I was Bonnie or Ry. Gender didn't matter to Randy. Crafting his own reality did.

"This Sunday," I said. "It's you and me at a picnic table in Tenney Park. Noon, right?"

"Right Joni," he said. "I'll be there."

\\\\

It wasn't until he approached me two days later that I was certain he'd show up. It ranked as a small miracle.

"Hope I'm not late, Mr. Bee Gee." Randy high-fived me as if we were old friends. "A guy's got things to do."

Like what, I wondered. But Randy was right on time. Some part of him remembered that we were meeting to talk about him. His life. Things that had happened, things he might want to remember, things he might want someone to know. The idea of an actual interview, of opening up about something besides sports, girls, or flat tap beer had him trapping sand under the heel of his black Army boots.

"Duct tape holding your boot together?" I asked.

"Where would we be without it?"

"Indeed." Indeed? Why that word had come from my mouth was a mystery, albeit a short-lived one. Waves from Lake Mendota were crashing over the fake rock wall, and I took a step back to escape the spray. The west wind was so noisy that I pulled a white gym sock over the microphone.

"What's that thing?"

"Microphone," I said. "I tried to borrow a stereo mic but this was all I could come up with. So we're *mono-a-mono* today."

Randy didn't get the joke. He usually didn't.

"It's a sock over my microphone," I said. "Keeps out the wind noise."

Randy dug deeper. His left foot was now anchored by ankle-deep sand.

"If you're not sure about this, it's okay, really. We don't have to do it."

Caution was like a trigger to Randy, his cue to get with the program. He pulled his foot out, shook off the sand, and sat down at the table. Then he slowly, and very deliberately, rolled up the sleeves of his secondhand shirt, leaned across the table, and pushed the pause button on the Nagra into the record mode.

"You know how this thing works?" I asked.

"Two years of technical school," he said. "I wanted to be a television engineer."

No reason to stop, I thought. Randy probably knew more about the machine than I did, and he was already talking.

"What made you quit?"

"I didn't quit. I graduated."

First revelation. Randy was an unemployed Marine veteran, but he had a degree in television engineering from the technical school. Everything I thought I knew about him went out the window with a question I'd not even planned to ask him. When a college kid landed a Frisbee on our table, Randy didn't flinch. He rose to toss it back, and when he saw the guy's beautiful girlfriend, tossed it to her instead.

"Never miss an opportunity," he said. "She might just drop the fratboy before dusk and make some room for old Randy Gianelli."

Not likely, I thought, but yes, why not keep his options open.

"I dated a girl like her once," he said. "Sharon. Started out as one of those born-again types who hung around at the campus ministry. Prayed for me when I got drafted for Nam. Rode old Randy hard the night before I shipped out. Yeah, Sharon Sharon, Sharon."

"Better to play the field, right?"

"Really?" he asked. "Who wants a lot of lovers when you have the right one, right there in your arms. She was the one for me, Donovan. Really, *the* one."

Revelation number two. Randy had been in love before he shipped out, and he held on to the idea of monogamy.

"Something happened to Sharon?"

"Something, yeah. Like Dear Randy John something. Dear Fuckin' Randy John."

Revelation three. Sore subject. True love says good-bye while Randy's in the jungle.

"I'm sorry."

"Sorry? For what? Sorry. Yeah, well, Ms. Pearly White Teeth Tiny Boob Christian Country Club Republican Sharon got what she came for. Guilt, man. Guilt. Can you imagine what it's like to look in the mirror fifteen years later and think 'Wow, I screwed up that guy? I left him when he was crying his eyes out in the freakin' mud over in Nam to be with some son of a rich dude Ivy League phony. Yeah, sorry.'"

I avoided eye contact with Randy by pretending to monitor the VU meter on the Nagra. It had sliders instead of knobs, and I slid an unused channel up and back as if I had a special reason to reset the levels.

"Am I pinning your needle?"

"Nope, everything's fine, actually. I was just checking levels."

"You were just done with her. Sharon," he said. "Not a problem. I'm done with her, too."

"What year did you go to Nam?"

"'68."

"Served until '71?"

"Yes."

"You were drafted?"

"Yes."

Never ask a yes/no question during an interview. I reminded myself of journalism school rule number one. Yes/no answers would get me nowhere.

Suddenly, the wind lifted the Frisbee. But this time, it brushed the backside of Randy's ponytail—close but harmless.

"You want your nuts in your mouth?" he yelled.

"No, sir." The kid looked genuinely scared. "Maybe it's time we quit, what with the wind and all."

"Maybe it's time you quit?" said Randy. "Do I look like a nice guy to you? Do I look like someone who could care less if a Frisbee hits him in the head? Or do I look like someone who might just ram your head so far up your butt it's back on your shoulders?"

An answer wasn't necessary, but it was implied when the kid and his girlfriend turned and headed toward campus. As the young woman looked back to wink at Randy I realized for the first time that he had that thing. Charisma. A hint of danger. The allure of the unexpected. It explained my own desire to interview Randy. He was better than good-looking. Even with all the wear and tear on his face and the beat-up clothes, Randy could have won the Robert Redford look-alike contest.

"How's the interview working out for you?" he asked as he sat back down. I couldn't tell if he was being sarcastic or trying to regroup. The reels were still turning, though it was hard to imagine I'd ever use the last interaction.

"Were you in engineering school before or after being drafted?" I asked.

"Do I look like a television engineer to you? Of course not. I was a sophomore studying philosophy at Oberlin when I got my lucky number fourteen. Can you imagine? Fourteen. That's a death sentence. It was about as much fun as reading *The Stranger* during an acid hangover. Does life have meaning? I'm asking you, Bo Diddley, does life have meaning?"

Randy was asking me. A street corner musician with just enough cash on hand to buy a used tape recorder, eat cold pizza for breakfast, and pay cheap rent for an attic apartment on the east side of Madison, Wisconsin.

"I thought I was asking the questions today."

"Good answer." Randy reached around for his ponytail, pulled the rubber band out, and let the wind carry his mane back across his shoulders.

"Yes," he continued, "life has meaning. And yes, I could have had my daddy get me out of the draft. And yes, I could have gone to freaking Canada or Sweden. But what kind of philosophy major would that have made me? What kind of a guy uses his privileged little life to get away and avoid conflict while leaving the poor and uneducated to fight the losing battle? I didn't have a welfare mom. I didn't need the GI Bill to get an education. It wasn't right to make us fight an unjust war, but it was worse to walk away and force someone else who didn't have the connections to take my place. What kind of man would that have made me, Sid?"

Sid. Hmm. Sid Vicious? The reference couldn't have been a coincidence, and I was searching my mental database for anything symbolic. I opted to be a punk.

"Maybe you can answer that?" I said.

"Touché. Maybe you have a career here, Phoebe. What kind of man would that have made me? What kind of a man?"

The Phoebe Snow reference came from nowhere and we both knew it. I'd never covered her songs on the street, and as a player, she didn't hold a candle to Carlos or B.B.

"So I went. I did boot camp in San Diego and then got assigned to a nice little regiment out of Pendleton. First in, last out. Etcetera. Are you getting this?" Randy looked at the spinning reels knowing full well that we were getting it. When he tapped on my headset gesturing for an answer, I blurted "yes" loud enough for the folks at the next table to look our way. They were having a full-on Sunday picnic, and when I signaled that everything was okay, the mother put her toddler on her lap and looked the other way. Randy grabbed the front of the sock-covered microphone, brought it close to his mouth, and said "Testing, testing, one two three, testing," and then started laughing. I hit the pause button.

"Maybe we can pick this up another day," I said.

"Or not," he shot back. "Old Randy Hambone Gianelli just knows how to have a good time. Unless you're in some kind of hurry to get to your day job?" He laughed again, but this time we both knew he was bordering on nasty. A Vegas slot machine took more quarters in five minutes than I did in an hour on the street.

"Come on, let's do this thing." With that, he pressed the play button again, looked me square in the eye and said, "If you think I'm gonna talk about killing babies, you got me wrong . . ."

I twirled my forefinger in circles, the insider's cue that we were rolling tape.

"It wasn't *Apocalypse Now*, okay? There were some people who thought what we were doing there was important. I wasn't one of them, but that didn't mean I shirked my duty to my guys. I was there for them. They were there for me. Not one of us gave a damn about McNamara or that bunch. It wasn't like they were in the trenches. You think Kissinger ever got his hands dirty? No way, because he never had to carry the money. Kissinger never did shit. The funds were wired through a hundred back channels before they ever got to Saigon. The Saudis probably washed it along the way. And while you fruit loops were back here sniffing tear gas and getting high, we were doing what soldiers have been doing for three thousand years—wielding the sword for some numb nuts politico with a warped sense of moral high ground whose only hope for the future was a bigger piece of the McDonnell Douglas pie."

"What about the day-to-day?" I asked.

"What about it?"

"What'd you do?"

"What do you mean what'd we do? We soldiered. Pretty damn boring. Move here, move there, dig this, carry that, get drunk, get stoned every chance you get, read the same goddamned paperbacks over and over until someone new shows up with a three-month-old issue of *National Geographic*. You gotta get more specific with your questions, Sly."

Randy popped the machine into pause mode and got up suddenly.

"Buy me a gyro." It wasn't a question, or even a suggestion. Greasy lamb on a chewy pita was what it would take to keep the interview going. By gyro, Randy meant we should head to Café Acropolis on the corner of Gilman and State. The café was a hangout for the less fortunate because the owner, Dino Tsakopoulos, would let a homeless guy sit inside for hours during winter months as long as he bought just one bottomless cup of coffee. It was also a well-known fact that Dino would put a plate of leftovers on the back step when he closed up at night.

Randy shook sand from his boots as I packed and wrapped cables. On the sidewalk a few feet away, a retired greyhound caught our attention as he paused for his morning movement. His owner, a lean, tired old man, pressed the leash between his aging knees, shifted a bag of groceries and bent to retrieve the deposit. Knowing an opportunity when he saw one, the greyhound jerked free and bolted toward freedom, recapturing the glory of his days at the track.

In short order, the angry greyhound pounced on a terrier puppy curled up at the feet of Abby, the same woman at the picnic table who'd scorned us earlier with her tepid gaze. With her obese husband screaming Abby's name in fear as he tried to maneuver himself past the wailing kids, Abby pulled frantically on her puppy's hindquarter in an effort to free the pup from the clamped jaws of a greyhound with a depressing past.

The elderly owner was still scooping poop into a baggie when Randy's Camp Pendleton training kicked in. He shortened a distance faster than anyone I'd ever seen. Randy knew the hound would move for the jugular the first chance he had, and as the woman lost her grip on the screeching terrier, Randy launched into a horizontal dive, his right hand extended, his gaze fixed on the mouth of the greyhound.

Time recollected never seems quite real, but my memory is that in the instant Randy left his feet, everything became slow motion. He pushed the woman and her puppy sideways with his left hand just as the greyhound chomped down hard on his right hand. Randy had the momentum, and with the hound's firm grip, both flew across the table, sending fruit salad, a platter of croissants, ham slices, and a Tupperware filled with Door County cherry pie flying onto the chest of the trapped husband.

By the time the duo hit the ground, I'd untangled my audio cables and was standing over Randy wondering what the hell I was supposed to do. Before I could ask if he needed help, Randy grabbed a cable from my hand and wrapped it around the neck of the greyhound, pulling tightly until the aging beast was immobilized. Within seconds, the dog let go of Randy's hand. Any fear I had of him strangling the sad dog as an act of vengeance went out the window when Randy got on his knees, pinned the hound's head to the ground, removed the audio cable from its neck, then gently called out to the elderly owner to come and leash his pooch.

"Grab me your sock, Arlo." It was then that I saw how badly Randy's right hand was bleeding. "Battle scars," he said, laughing.

I handed Randy the sock and he slid it over his hand, then helped the owner leash up his greyhound. When the old man tried to tip Randy, he politely refused. He was just following orders, he said. As I brushed mashed cherries off his back, Randy looked over at the picnic table to see whether his help was needed. The husband was mopping up his shirt, the kids were cuddling the spooked terrier, and Abby was trying to restore order by putting brunch back in its proper place. There was no acknowledgment of Randy or his heroic actions.

"Ma'am?" I said, "Maybe you oughta . . ." Randy interrupted me with the wave of his hand. Whatever offense I felt by her prickly behavior was overruled. He grabbed me by the arm, helped me pick up my audio gear, and we headed off for a gyro. When we were a block away and out of earshot, I asked him about his quick course of emergency action.

"Puppy's got a right to live," he said. "He didn't start it."

"You could have killed the greyhound if you wanted to."

"Why? For doing what dogs do? That dog means something to the old guy. They're related. Who knows what his situation is? His wife could be dead, she might have cancer, or maybe there's never been another person there for the guy. That dog serves a purpose, gives him company, brightens up his day. We don't know what we don't know, Marshall Tucker. Now that woman's a different story: she's got a lot bigger problems than ignoring Randy Gianelli."

\\\\

By the time we got to Café Acropolis, all Randy wanted was fries and a Coke. There was an alley behind the place that Randy knew pretty well so we sat on the stoop of the back door and he helped me re-rig. The park had been my idea, but Randy seemed more comfortable now that the only people who'd be in our way were either moving on to something else or had a job to do. We weren't spoiling their picnic.

"Just roll it, Leo, and let's see where things go."

"Maybe the reason I want to keep coming back to the idea of Vietnam is because of your pants," I said. "They're part of your old uniform, right?"

"You wanna talk about my pants? My time's valuable, Jethro Tull."

"I want you to talk about your pants . . . if they mean something."

"They don't."

"Are you unemployed and homeless because of your Vietnam experience?"

"That's what I'm talking about, Jerry Jeff, direct questions. I like that, even though, yes, you should try to avoid yes/no questions. The answer's no." Randy took a long drag on his straw. I could see the Coke going down in the cup, inch by inch. Then he let go of a very long, deep belch.

He caught me rolling my eyes and slapped me hard on the back. "You'll laugh later when you transcribe that part."

"Because?"

"Because no matter how often guys do it—and only guys do it—they still get a laugh when they belch out loud or fart up a storm. Makes no sense, does it?"

"So your answer is no? Nam has nothing to do with your life on the street?"

"You ask the question like it's a problem for you. I don't think it is. Sometimes people like being unemployed and homeless. It's not like I come to your corner asking for things. I don't ask you to share your tips with me. I don't beg."

"You mentioned your father earlier. Tell me about your father."

"Now that I think about it, I did ask to use your shower that one time," he said. "And I was grateful. As for my dad, there's not that much to know. Or maybe not that much that I know. He seems like a good man. And his pants mean something to him, at least on the days when they match his jacket and complement his tie. He takes care of my mother in a way she seems to appreciate. They both seem to enjoy cribbage. And I never saw them fight . . ."

Randy stopped abruptly, his voice trailing as if he wasn't ready to complete the sentence. Still, I could tell that Randy was telling the truth about his parents. He seemed to have little emotional connection to Mom and Dad. His clipped sentences also suggested he hadn't really thought much about this before. Whatever his parents meant to him, they didn't seem the cause of anything in particular. Or they simply weren't that important to him.

"Anything else? Siblings?"

"Twin bro, dead. And a half-sister from Dad's first go-around."

Revelation number twenty-seven, Randy had lost a twin brother. The next question was a risk no matter which way I went. So I took the safest route possible.

"Your dad was married once before. Did the half-sister live with you?"

"Nope. I met her just one time. Her mother wasn't the healing kind, and wasn't wild about family ties, but if you want to read more into her than that, you'll have to ask her yourself. We were maybe thirteen when the kid came camping with us up on Lake Superior near Bayfield. We had a good time."

"Only that one time?"

"No one told us the girl was our half-sister and she was cute as all hell. My brother and I figured we'd just won the lottery. We did everything we could to get a real peek at her breasts, rub shoulders when we were swimming, maybe something more than that. It was kid stuff. We were staying in this cabin that was close to the Amnicon River. I remember the river because there were these big pools under the waterfalls and we could swim behind the falling water. It was like being in a *Tarzan* movie. Anyway, we were all three sharing a room that had two sets of bunk beds. There was a fish boil on the Friday night and the folks decided to go on their own and get a little time together, just the two of them. When they came home, they found the three of us playing spin the bottle."

Randy dipped a handful of fries into my ketchup, stuffed his mouth, and wiped a dab of grease from his lips using the sock on his injured hand.

"You could say it didn't go well because that trip was the first and last time I saw her."

A sprinkle of rain had been falling for a while, and without a clap of thunder for warning, it became a downpour. As quick as he'd been to save a puppy's life, Randy reacted slowly to the rain. He seemed to welcome it and, warm as it was, he removed the *"What is Art?"* t-shirt he'd been wearing for the past week. With my arms full of audio gear, I opted to hover straight as a pillar under the tiny overhang on the back stoop of Café Acropolis. I remember muttering "Shit, shit, shit," as I closed the plastic cover to keep water off the reels of audio tape still attached to the Nagra. I turned to face into the wall, and with my head half-turned toward the alley, I could see Randy laughing, dancing, and soaking in the hard rain. His camo pants clung to him, and with water rolling off his muscled upper body, I thought of a shirtless young Stallone doing a Gene Kelly alley dance. Or better yet, Brando before the attitude.

A stream several inches deep began rushing down the crevice that carved out the middle of the alley, and the sound of pelting rain was almost deafening as it banged off the lids of tin trash cans, car roofs, dumpster lids, and the tiny sheet metal roof that barely covered my head.

"Tell me what to believe," shouted Randy.

I tilted my body sideways, still cradling the Nagra and covering the reels with my right forearm.

"Tell me what to believe, Steely Dan!"

"I don't know what you mean," I shouted back.

Randy stopped moving and crouched with his feet ankle-deep in the crevice, water rushing high over his boots. The duct tape that held the top rim together had peeled back and was flashing like a fish gate.

Randy just sat there, his empty eyes staring up at me. His brief bout with joy was gone. Streams of water rolled down his face, braiding his long whiskers. His arms were stretched wide as if he was searching for something, anything, to bring him some safety. Maybe some comfort. Maybe something to mend the cracks. For the first time since Randy had met me at the park, the next move was mine. I checked the handle on the back door to see if I could put the Nagra inside, but it was locked. The strap had worked a painful groove into my right shoulder, and it felt good to take it off. I set it upright, as close to the door as possible, removed my own shirt to cover it, and then turned toward Randy and took a tentative step toward him. He didn't move. I sat on the top step and took in his stare, knowing that whatever discomfort I felt from the pain in his eyes was a one-way street. Randy was looking past me into something that had happened a long time ago. He was beyond discomfort.

The downpour eased to a steady shower.

"You should go get yourself dry," he said. "You should find your little attic apartment and make yourself into something."

The fast flow of water in the middle of the alley was subsiding, but his boots were full to the rim.

"I'm not messing around, Kid. You should pack it in and head out of here. Put on some dry clothes, some pants that mean something." It was the first time he'd ever called me by anything except a musician's name, and I imagined him participating, for however long, in what seemed real to me. I sensed shame in his tone. When I didn't move, he filled the pregnant pause the way he did with the hundreds of strangers that passed him on the street corner every day—a meaningless statement except for the acknowledgement, the confirmation that he existed.

"Looks like it's letting up a little."

Randy stopped crouching and sat down in the middle of the alley, his bottom just above the crest of drainage water. He pulled the sock off his hand, washed it in the stream, and then removed his boots. He emptied them slowly, one by one, into the stream.

"Ya gotta know why you're snoopin' around in people's lives."

"You didn't have to accommodate me," I said. "I don't even have a buyer for the article yet."

"You're right. I didn't. Maybe that was wrong of me. I mean, look, now you're sitting in the rain in a dirty alley, you're soaking wet, and your fancy audio gear is probably all crapped out on you."

"Maybe it wasn't wrong. Maybe you do have something to share."

"I needed the shower. Makes it easier for the shop owners when we're cleaned up a bit and don't smell so bad. The customers don't get so scared."

"Do I look scared of you?"

"You never have. But you've never looked comfortable either. More like, it's like you've got curiosity but no confidence in yourself. If you want to interview people, don't be shy. You can talk to rock stars if you just ask. People wanna talk, Stevie Wonder. People wanna be listened to."

"If I had more confidence, maybe I'd try to get a real gig instead of playing music on street corners filled with people who stare at the sidewalk or cross the street to avoid eye contact."

"I think it takes more confidence to be ignored," he said. "Not that it matters, but I like your work best when you're singing for yourself, when there's nobody paying any attention at all. You think a big crowd is what makes Springsteen the boss?"

"It's hard for me to know, not having been there."

"If you just do what works for you, then I'm pretty sure you got a chance at happy."

The stream had waned with the rain, but a reservoir had built up near Randy's feet. He used the heel of his left boot to break up a tiny dam of debris—a popsicle stick, the cellophane wrapper from a cassette tape, the lid from his cup of Coke, the runt end from a loaf of garlic bread.

"Your twin brother, right?"

"Touché, Otis. Touché. You're really getting right to it."

"How'd he die?"

"Behind door number one, suicide. Door number two, accidental death by use of a needle. Door number three . . ."

"You don't have to make it funny, Randy. I'm not recording. There's no one to hear you but me."

There was a long pause as Randy used the popsicle stick to push a gum wrapper down what was now a canal of slow moving water no more than two inches wide.

"The problem, Hendrix, is that I wasn't there to hear him."

"Would it have made a difference?"

The wrapper was floating so slowly it was driving me nuts, so I got down on my knees and blew hard against it. It picked up with the gust of wind, and the notion of a throwaway sailing a back alley brought a smile to Randy's face.

"We think it would have, don't we? We think that if we'd been there, asked the right question, skipped the last drink, used a condom, put the money back, swerved a second earlier, we think it would have made a difference. All I know is, I wasn't there."

"Does it matter?

"What'd you major in, anyway?"

For the first time, I started laughing. Whatever I'd studied in college had never mattered, it didn't matter now, and answering the question wouldn't matter. Randy knew that as well as I did. He wadded up the soaked, bloody gym sock, dipped it for good measure in the last puddle he could reach, then threw it at me. I tried to duck, but he'd anticipated my move and it hit me squarely in the upper chest with a thud loud enough to make us both roar with laughter.

Cued by the street gods, there was a crash behind us as the owner opened the back door of his café and sent my Nagra falling sideways, off the stoop, and into a soaking pile of cardboard boxes. Two shirtless guys playing with trash in a wet alley might have been cause for suspicion. Or concern. Not to Dino Tsakopoulos.

"You guys want gyros?" Dino nodded, it was a rhetorical question. "My crazy brother, he bought more lamb than we can sell this week and a whole lotta garlic. I don't want it goin' rotten."

Dino set two paper platters on the top step, mopped his hands on the greasy towel that hung over his shoulder and walked back inside.

WAITING TO LIVE

THE HILL AT THE END of the cul-de-sac was a garbage dump until ten years ago. Julia said kids played on heaps of grayish silt until their bike trails became gutters for the winter rains. That's when a neighborhood boy discovered a tiny array of decayed fingers jutting up from the mud. Now it's Huaca Pucllana, Lima's oldest archeological site known for mummies and sacred objects that pre-date the Tiahuanacan culture. High wire fences keep the locals out, but tourists with a few soles in their pocket are always looking for something to do in Lima during the layover flights they're forced to endure while en route to Cuzco. The four desiccated mummies that recline in glass-enclosed caskets now draw enough attention to help fundraise the dig.

It was my fourth visit to Lima since 2000. Julia picked a restaurant within walking distance from Miraflores. The bistro overlooking Huaca Pucllana serves overpriced dishes like lomo saltado and coy, sea bass, and chupe. The ruins are lighted at night, she said, a selling point for tourists in a competitive market.

"And you want to know the best part?" I knew she'd answer before I could. "The first pisco sour is free. It's *always* free." Julia had schooled me in pisco and I acknowledged that while the first one is usually free everywhere, not all pisco sours are the same. "That's my point," she said. It wasn't her point, but that didn't matter to Julia.

We walked north under cover of the same dreary skies Lima is known for, with the sun little more than a rusty ball on a horizon confined by inversions. This is Lima, I thought—this is always Lima. It's never warm. It's never cold. There's no identity, nothing to embrace, nothing to recommend. Lima is not about heritage or culture, or even history. Like all harbor towns, Lima is about work.

Or finding work.

The descendants of the Spanish here are mostly rich. Even after 400 years, they still enjoy the trappings of colonial conquest. The Quechua and Aymara descendants who came first are mostly poor. Like the gringos who visit from the north, the people who live in Miraflores and Barranco never see the edges of town. They never see the shanties built of tin and mud bricks that overflow with children and tired parents. Julia and I were not exceptional in so many ways, including the fact that we restricted our movements in Lima to the least interesting and safest parts of town. We enjoyed our evenings by indulging our cowardice and our gluttony. We were impervious to guilt and usually spent more on dinner than most Peruvians make in a month. We resigned ourselves to the things we understood. We lived on our per diems. We were entrepreneurs, self-indulgent, living largely in denial, and just curious enough to land our next gig. We complimented each other for hiring local freelancers for the occasional need of an assistant, and while we didn't actually roll up our sleeves and work in the poor neighborhoods, we did what we could to refer to their problems so others could work toward their solution. We weren't idealistic; we were utterly typical.

Julia Marie Garcia grew up in Miraflores and had long ago donned the air of entitlement and a flair for righteous indignation. Her English was perfect, but she went out of her way to let others know she was Peruvian, through and through. For Julia, it wasn't about Bush versus Gore, it was about President Fujimore. It wasn't about NAFTA, it was about the Truth and Reconciliation Commission. It wasn't about Iraq or Bosnia, Iran or North Korea, it was about the plight of oppressed coca farmers in Bolivia. For Julia, life was about things she could criticize from arm's length, just beyond the personal drama of two former husbands and the recent betrayal by her twentysomething lover. Javier had been her student, and he had learned well. A month before my visit, he'd run off to Italy with "a girl his own age" and left Julia to discover her feelings about middle age.

It was October and finger-sized cockroaches covered the sidewalk at the end of the row houses. We tried to sidestep them as we walked, but eventually they outnumbered our good intentions, and we could hear their tiny shells crunching beneath each grizzly footstep. It was like a death march as their armored bodies crackled under our shoes. I looked up from time to time just to make sure they weren't falling from the canopy of old trees.

That's when I saw her window.

The row house where she lived wasn't Spanish or Andean. It was more like something from Georgetown or London, I thought, a British influence—a half level down, and a half level up. I could hear music coming from her open window, an old German anthem somehow in sync with our funereal procession. It wasn't a sophisticated sound system or a recent recording, but more like a Victrola playing a 78 rpm of Wagner from the Berlin Philharmonic.

Julia motioned to me to keep walking, but I was already leaning across the iron rail and hedges for a closer look through the half-opened curtains. That's when I saw the small German flag hanging above the fireplace. There was no mustachioed Bruno Ganz commanding a salute. No Rolf or Maria or Captain Klink. No cascade of fire swallowing life in Dresden. It was simple but odd—old German music and an outlawed flag in residential Lima. To my surprise, Julia had no more curiosity than the other pedestrians. Huaca Pucllana was only a hundred yards further and she was hungry. Besides, she said, she hated Wagner and anything that sounded militaristic, or worse, evil.

"All that old Nazi stuff," she said. "It's—" She grabbed my hand and we were off. For Julia, tyranny and atrocity weren't far away or long ago. She'd lived it. Loved ones had disappeared. Classmates were in jail. Julia didn't want to live in the past, she wanted to celebrate freedom—all the way, every day.

After chilled ceviche and the first pisco sour (which, I told her, was too heavy on the egg whites), I ordered the national dish, lomo saltado. My vegan days were behind me thanks to the microscopic critters that loomed with digestive malice in the otherwise beautiful salads. The "salty beef" came broiled medium rare with light brown gravy over a mound of sticky white rice and fried potatoes carefully molded into the shape of an Andean cross. The waiter, a body builder from Trujillo, recommended a Chilean Malbec that carried us through dessert.

Julia went on and on about the emotionally strenuous "work" she'd been doing with a horny shaman from Porto Maldonado who'd changed her life forever. She'd spent four days fasting in a rain forest hut with only ayahuasca to sustain her. The shaman had administered half a cup of the hallucinogenic liquid once or twice a day. She'd vomit, then sit in meditation and explore the sacred plant's power to connect her to the God force. She'd even experienced death, she said, or at least what she imagined death to be, a fact that would remain mostly rhetorical for lack of descriptive verbiage beyond her energetic pantomime of the geometrical patterns she'd witnessed in her inner cosmos.

"It wasn't nothingness," Julia said. "I don't have words for it, but it was peaceful, and I felt connected to a oneness—God, I guess. And there were shapes, lots of shapes, dense shapes but not thick. Just patterns. It made me happy even when I was weeping. Or vomiting. You should try it."

"I should try vomiting?" I was half joking, half not.

"You're not listening."

"I should try death?"

"You like hearing me say it, don't you?"

I did. It was part of our game.

"You should try *a y a h u a s c a*!" Julia said it slow and loud as if I had both a language and hearing problem. "The shaman is there to guide you on your sacred journey. They monitor every part of the ritual and only let you drink an amount you can handle."

"I've read the psilocybin studies from Harvard Medical School," I told her. "It works. So maybe I should try it."

Julia had no idea what I was talking about, and wasn't likely to admit it. Academic research on sacred plants confirms what shaman and healers have said for centuries—peyote, magic mushrooms, wachuma, ayahuasca—they work. Under a healer's watch, the active ingredients do more than just send users on a round-trip to the cosmos. The plants help people open a spiritual portal of some kind that allows the user to confront or explore everything from their God to their origins, even their death.

"Death is the next generation," she said. It sounded profound, but like the rest of her ayahuasca journey, it didn't make much sense. We'd been friends for years, and colleagues for nearly as long. We'd had a one night stand that neither of us had been able to discuss the next morning. But we were always there for each other, true friends. Julia was rationalizing her need to kill off memories of Javier and move on with her life. It wouldn't happen quickly, there would be a few more men, and a few small traumas of her own making to overcome along the way, but eventually Julia would find her way.

"I can't get my head past the vomiting stage," I said. "It seems like such a waste of good avocado."

"Ayahuasca!" She wanted none of my teasing and reinforced her dismay by gnawing a bite too big to chew from her Argentinean filet.

"Purging is part of healing," she said. "You have to get rid of the bad energy." Julia continued the story about her week with Rodrigo in the rain forest. She'd even lost eight pounds, which wasn't her intention, but she was glad of it. An ayahuasca journey was a mildly entertaining notion, but I couldn't stop thinking about the odd little row house we'd passed on our way to dinner.

\\\\

An hour later, I sat in the dimly lit bar at the Hotel Ariosto and tapped their free Wi-Fi. Google: Nazis in Peru. Bing: SS on the run. Yahoo: Nazi communities in South America. I knew that more than a few SS and German generals had fled with their families to avoid war trials. Some escaped to Paraguay. Some found safe haven in Uruguay or Argentina. A few found a village in Brazil or Chile where they went unrecognized by people unlikely to care. Some brought along their stolen jewels or classic artwork lifted from museums and wealthy families all over Europe. Some just carried cash.

But I had no idea Nazis had relocated to Peru after the war. I searched for more than an hour, but there was nothing online to suggest I'd walked past anything more than the home of a disgruntled skinhead with Hitleresque fantasies. After all, Peru has its share of fascists like anywhere else, along with plenty of teenaged Shining Path wannabes stuck on the glories of faded tyrants. So, I asked myself, why not some nut job conducting a little worship of the Third Reich on a dead-end street in Miraflores? Still, why was Julia so casual about it? Why were the neighbors so nonchalant about a renegade Nazi in their midst? It didn't add up.

\\\\

It was just after ten the next morning when I arrived at 27 Simon Bolivar Lane. There were a few people around, some walking dogs, some seeing children off to school, some meeting their secret lovers. An Andean housekeeper was trimming hedges, two workmen pushed and pulled a broken refrigerator to the sidewalk, and a DHL driver bumped the cars on both sides as he tried to squeeze his van into a spot on the narrow street.

The curtains of the home were closed, and there was no sign of activity. I had no idea what to expect as I walked up a flight of eight cut stone steps and knocked on the finely carved wooden door. I waited a good minute, smiled at a gorgeous neighbor half my age, and then knocked again.

The door opened a tiny crack but I couldn't see anyone.

"Por favor," I said in my horrible Spanish. "¿Es possible que yo hablo a madam o senor que viven aqui?" Clearly, whoever was behind the door would know I was a gringo.

The door closed and I could hear a dead bolt fasten.

"Por favor," I said again, louder. "¿Es possible . . ." I stopped as the curtains parted and the tiny round face of a very old woman stared out at me. I gestured that I wanted to speak to her, and she snapped the curtains closed. Then the window slammed down.

I could wait her out, I thought. Yet even I was uncertain of my intention. My curiosity rarely takes me this far. But it had. I was here. I'd already been spotted. So I sat on the top step and gave the appearance of settling in. After a few moments, I glanced at the curtain again and she was there, staring at me boldly, her eyes pierced with a blend of contempt and mild curiosity. She was hardly the person I'd expected to see. I looked back toward the street, wishing I had a plan. The inner voice that guides me, which I too often ignore, said that she would come to me when she was ready. I folded my hands behind my head and leaned back for a nap.

A half hour later, a delivery truck backfired as the driver over-revved the engine. I woke up to find my neck and left shoulder crammed tightly between the top two rails. Whoever she was, she'd won the first round. The wind had picked up enough to blow some seeds loose from the canopy of trees. They floated like cotton balls and covered the parked cars and sidewalks in a thin layer of white. I brushed them from my sport coat and jeans and stood up to stretch. Maybe it was worth another try, I thought. I knocked gently at first; then the ugly American got the better of me and I knocked again—shave and a haircut, two bits. Before I could drag up my lame Spanish, the door opened.

She may have been old, but she wasn't afraid. She leaned on a walker with her left hand and motioned me in with her right. I stepped inside and stood next to her. She couldn't have been more than five feet tall. Her shoulders drooped forward and her back curved hard from years of osteoporosis. Her long gray hair was pinned in a bun, and she'd made an attempt to put on some makeup. Her eyes were a striking blue, and she didn't seem to need glasses to see from a distance.

Now what? I thought. But she'd taken charge and motioned me toward the same living room I'd seen illuminated the night before. There was a tray of butter cookies with a candied center, tea, and a small pitcher of hot milk on a footstool between two formal chairs. I glanced up at the wall above the fireplace. There was no sign of the German flag. Had it been my imagination? But in my mental replay I recalled that Julia had seen it too.

"Would you like some tea?" Her English was accented with a hint of Scandinavian or North German. "The cookies are from a bakery in the far north, in the village of Caraz. They're delivered once a week to a small store one block from here. They're very rich, and very sweet."

"You speak English perfectly." Perhaps I shouldn't have been surprised, but I was expecting perfect Spanish. Or perfect German. Or broken English at best.

"I was a translator for the German embassy. One gets the job because one can speak many languages. In my case, I speak English and Spanish and enough French to place an order. You're American?"

"I live near Chicago. Well, sometimes I do." As I grabbed a cookie, I noticed she'd served me on nineteenth century Meissen porcelain. I'd written an article about tea sets for a British airline magazine and had learned enough to know that Meissen was anything but common outside of Europe and the Eastern US.

"Milk?" she asked. "It's steamed. What is your business?"

I should have been the one asking questions, but I was still getting accustomed to sitting in her living room. When I looked around, I could see that her home was full of memorabilia that had little to do with South America.

"Textiles. Import, export. The alpaca wool is exceptional here." I wondered whether she could read my lie.

"Alpaca. So you work in the mountains then?"

"Sometimes, when I can get out to visit the farms. I've been to Ariquepa, Huaraz, and Cuzco of course. And Chavin, even before they put in the new road. I'm sure it's easier now."

"Cuzco was once a great city," she said. "It's getting tired now. There's no more room . . . and too many ghosts."

She was right of course. I thought of my many visits to Cuzco and how much the city had changed during the past decade. The valley had limitations, but it was the infrastructure that put Cuzco at risk. There was too much sewage, too many discarded water bottles, too many daily tourist flights. Not what the Inca had in mind, I thought, but there were plenty of jobs, which is more than one could say for Lima.

"You've visited Cuzco often . . . for the ghosts?" I wondered what she meant by ghosts, but she didn't take the bait. She may have been referring to the death of ten million Inca at the hands of Spanish conquistadors, or maybe not.

"My first visit was after the second war," she said. "And of course, I've been back many times since. Every visitor to Peru wants to go to Cuzco. A few choose Colca Canyon or Lake Titicaca, but not so many."

After the second war. Now we were getting somewhere.

"But tell me more about your work . . . in textiles." She may have been old and frail, but there was nothing wrong with her mind. She played me beautifully.

"Really, well, it's, well, there's not much money in it." There was of course. Exports were thriving. But I hadn't planned my lie, and my ignorance rattled me. "The best part is the export business gets me to Peru. And I don't even know your name?" Fumble, punt.

"I must have forgotten to ask you—milk?" she asked, ignoring my question. She poured the milk this time, then politely stirred my cup as well as her own. She was very deliberate, her movements graceful but slow.

Her eyes did most of her talking and, in our silences, most of her probing. I guessed they were once a sharper blue, the kind that stops a person in their tracks.

"Your name?" I asked, hoping to take back the offense.

"Bettina Kohl." She sipped her tea as if considering what to say next. "Even my granddaughter calls me Bettina so you can as well if you'd like. What brings you to my house, Mister . . . ?"

"Svenson." Almost involuntarily, I stood up, my hand outstretched. I'd been raised to be polite, but Bettina giggled. She placed her hand over mine while pushing me gently back into my chair.

"David Svenson."

"You're a Swede?" she asked.

"My father's name was Gunnar. He grew up in western Nebraska, a place called North Platte. My mother was actually born in Göteborg but her family came to the US after the war. You were right about the cookies." I'd taken a bite that was too big and it crumbled across my chin.

"Yes, delicious. The spread in the center is like molasses, but sweetened with a fruit from the Andean tundra. Would you like another?"

I was still trying to swallow the one in my mouth. The center was as sweet as Bettina said, but also chewy. She offered me another cookie and I lost the upper hand again. I'd been chewing for a while when she fired another question.

"You've been to Huaca Pucllana?"

"Yes."

"Recently?"

"Not the ruins, but the restaurant. Last night. It's lovely." Lovely? Lovely isn't a word I'd normally use, but Bettina brought out my best job interview behavior.

"I had the lomo saltado," I said. "Good, but too salty for my taste. I'm more of a spicy type. Chilies, that sort of thing."

The visit wasn't going well for me and as my mind raced, I could barely remember what had inspired me. Nazis. Yes, Nazis. I'd let my curiosity get to me. But she was just smiling and listening, stirring her tea, and looking at me with her cool blue eyes and tight little bun, and offering very little.

"You've eaten there, I presume? I mean, it's just a block away."

"No. I haven't," she said. "But I walked on top of the ruins when I was younger. We didn't know they were ruins then. The kids played there and you could see the ocean from the highest point. We thought it was a dump."

"They had an avocado soup," I said. "I didn't know you could make an avocado soup but they had one." Now I was babbling, giving her every card in my hand. I watched her slowly stirring her tea until I had no choice but to fill the silence.

"Aren't most ruins surrounded by a dump of sorts? I mean, that garbage had to go somewhere," I continued. They are, of course, but it was a strange segue. "The Anasazi dumped their garbage right off the stone balconies of their desert homes. They even shattered ceramic objects as part of their rituals and left the potsherds behind. The Mayans let the jungle recapture their trash. And the old Buddhist monks at Tiger's Nest Monastery in Bhutan live so high up in the Himalayas that they dump their refuse right over the cliff. Why carry it down I guess."

Bettina was squinting, watching me question every thought I expressed.

"Archeology, if you think about it, really is nothing more than mining our past." I was, at least, in my wheelhouse. "And what better place than a dump to, well, to go mining. When you think about the Inca, were they really so different from us?"

"Why are you here, Mr. Svenson?" Answering a question with a question—never a good sign. Bettina's patience was waning. "Is there something I can do for you besides letting you use my front steps for a nap?"

Clever. Touché. Bravo. I'd been up half the night researching her fascist Nazi princess past, and I wondered if she somehow guessed this. It was time to come clean.

"Bettina, did you really work at the German embassy?"

"For twenty-four years, yes. But before that I was in the homeland." She said it with a teasing smile. The homeland? Who was she trying to kid?

"So you're from Germany . . . originally?"

"A small village near Hamburg. I grew up on the Baltic Sea not too far from your mother's home in Göteborg. You ask a lot of questions for an import export man."

It's always difficult for the self-absorbed to surrender, but Bettina was clearly the smarter of us and I wanted to wave my white flag. I caught a glimpse of myself in the dining room mirror. My hair was a mess from napping on her porch step, and there was a smudge of pollen on the shoulder of my dark sport coat. She looked at me over her cup, but her expression was more curious than judgmental. She seemed charming and harmless. I was the invader in the room.

"I think we both know I lied to you," I said.

"Yes."

"I'm a travel writer. I write for those airline magazines that live in the seat pouch next to the airsickness bag."

"That must be a noble profession, David, but it hardly explains why you're here."

I sat back in the chair and could feel my shoulders sink in. It was as if the chair was slowly increasing in size and I was getting smaller and smaller with each breath. In my mind, I shrank completely, and Bettina leaned over with her duster and flipped me into a pan. I screamed for help but my voice came out as a high-pitched whistle audible only to dogs.

"I don't think you came for the cookies," she said, bouncing me back.

"Were you a Nazi?" I get direct when I'm nervous, and the question was so blunt that even I was surprised. "In Germany, I mean. Were you part of it?"

And with that, I'd rebounded. I'd taken real control of things, but at what cost? Being direct ruined our game, and Bettina sat deflated. Silent. She was tiny again. Now the chair dwarfed her. I could see the bones in her hands, the tiny rolls of skin across her forearms, age spots above her right eye, strands of pale gray hair hanging loose from her bun. Her print dress was belted tight to a waist that disappeared into the folds of torso and hips.

Her shoes were black with a tarnished bronze buckle, the heels about two inches in height. But her feet barely touched the floor. There was a wedding ring on her finger, a classic design of diamond and silver that reminded me of the ring passed on to my sister when my own grandmother died.

Bettina reached for her tea but her hand was shaking, and before she could bring it to her mouth, it rattled back into the porcelain saucer. She folded her handkerchief evenly across her belt. It was white with a pink lace edging around tiny lilacs. The monogram read "BK."

The room was suddenly quiet, and I could hear the clocks. There were at least two, plus an old window fan in the dining room rumbling on its slow setting. Bettina wheezed just a bit as she breathed. On the hall table near the kitchen, I could see six or seven prescription bottles. Spanish language newspapers were stacked in a pile near her chair with a dog-eared copy of Luis Borges' *Labyrinth* folded open near the middle of the book. Bettina reached toward a tray and grabbed her pair of reading glasses. She held them almost defensively, as if they'd protect her from me, her hand nervously rubbing the bridge.

"I'm sorry. Maybe I should go." When I stood, I seemed to tower over her, and I sat down again.

"You saw the flag?" she asked.

"Yes, I saw the flag. Last night. When I was walking to Huaca Pucllana."

"And that gave you the right to come to my house?"

"Really, I can go. I didn't mean to create a problem for you." I stood up again, even more aware of my size.

"What is it you want, Mr. Svenson? Be honest with me."

Bettina looked up at me with eyes demanding the truth.

"Not everything is about wanting," I said. "It just felt like more of a need. I needed to know."

"You need to know what? You need to understand my story so you can hurt me? So you can judge me? So you can do what with it, Mr. Svenson?"

"I'm sorry, Bettina. Mrs. Kohl. The last thing I want is to hurt you. Or judge you. I don't even know you. It was stupid of me to come here. I had no agenda but following my curiosity, which I'm sure must sound stupid to you."

As I turned to go, I could feel Bettina's tiny hand pull at me. I realized the uncomfortable feeling of being a giant wasn't about my size as much as the symbolism of looking down on her. I surprised myself by falling to my knees so we were eye to eye. She put her hand on my face as if forgiving me. And then, a smile. A peaceful smile. Bettina, it seemed, was careful, but she was past judging herself. Whatever shame she felt was buried deep, or gone.

"Come tomorrow," she said. "For lunch. You may bring something to write with."

\\\\

The claustrophobic gray skies along the bleak coastline shrink at night, tightening the cocoon until it seems there is nothing but the urban feel of Lima and the heavy breathing of sixteen million souls. The ocean winds die, and the only natural sound comes from hungry insects. In the barrios, smoke from cooking fires hangs over the tin roofs, wrapping its way through the alleys and footpaths. Children crowd around whatever house or shop has a television, and the light flickers, illuminating smudges on their cheeks and stringy hair. Their skateboards are worn, their soccer balls light on air. The older kids are scouts and guardians, never more than an arm's length away from their charges, a younger brother or sister, gleeful toddlers in recycled t-shirts caked with a week's worth of dirt. The bitter smell of urine and rotting garbage has mixed with spicy chicken and roasted corn for so long it's become normal. When the last of the long shadows are gone, the locals migrate toward the firelight or the occasional kitchen punctuated by strands of blue florescence.

A few miles away near the city center, the groomed walkways of Mira-flores are lighted for pedestrians, with each streetlamp planted a perfect thirty feet from the next. The outside dining has the feel of European cities with restaurants stacked atop one another. The tables and chairs are the same at each café, but the smells from the kitchen create a boundary the locals seem to comprehend. There are plenty of all-fare restaurants where ceviche and burgers share the menu. Garlic is the common denominator.

I couldn't wait to share my adventure with Julia over dinner. She picked Don Gusto's, a tight nook with a dozen white plastic chairs and a neon sign flashing "brick oven pizza."

"It was amazing," I told her. "I fell asleep with my head between the railing bars. I think she felt sorry for me because when I woke up, she invited me inside. I asked to use her bathroom and when I looked in the mirror, there were still indentations on the side of my forehead."

Julia had just taken a sip of beer and as she laughed, she managed to snort some deep into her nasal passage.

"Ouch, ouch, ouch," she squealed, still laughing. "You actually went into her house?"

"She's an old woman. There's nothing threatening about her."

"Yeah, except she's a freaking Nazi. I'm not big on tyranny as you know."

"She just seemed so vulnerable, almost like she needed me to be there. She gave me tea and some kind of molasses cookie from Caraz."

"You're a fool. You should leave her alone!" Julia was dabbing up beer when the waiter approached with our pizza.

Everything in Miraflores is orchestrated for tourists, and as the waiter approached, an Andean quartet came by to play another rendition of "El Condor Pasa" using a pan flute for melody. Blossoms had fallen during the past week and the scent of jacaranda softened the diesel fumes from passing trucks. I thought about Bettina and what she would think of us talking about her. Was there even a reason for her to care? If she had been a Nazi, what did it matter now?

Before he died, my grandfather told me he'd killed at least three German soldiers in the war. He wasn't proud of it, but he didn't feel guilty either. It was just something he'd done. People did things out of fear, things they wouldn't do otherwise. I'd asked him if he could still see their faces, and he said I'd been watching too many movies. But the question had made him wince slightly, so I knew he was avoiding the subject. He didn't want to lie. It was twilight, he said, and two men in his patrol had been shot first. He just fired and fired until three Germans were dead and the others had run away. Even if Bettina had been a Nazi, it didn't mean she'd killed anyone personally. But whose faces did she see at night?

"No mas, por favor. Yo quiero vino tinto." I'd known during college that languages weren't my forte, and I felt mildly proud when the waiter delivered two glasses of red table wine. Julia looked at me with a smile

"It's Kuelap that you need to write about," she said. "Americans don't know anything about it, and the government wants to promote it. I'm sure you can get free transportation and accommodation if you want. If the government won't fund you, a travel agency will."

With that, Julia and I reminisced about the many ways we'd found to get free travel around South America. Given her expertise with adventure outfitters and my fabled resource as a modestly dependable travel writer (I could deliver a thousand words on anything with a few hours of work offset by several days of free R & R), we'd managed to exploit barter agreements from Patagonia to Angel Falls. That we had no sustainable romantic chemistry for each other was a godsend as we became great collaborators.

Julia was full-bodied and outgoing, which appealed to a lot of the men we encountered during social outings. This had certainly appealed to Javier for a while, but Julia finally admitted that their problems ran deeper than another woman. Javier wanted children and marriage, but Julia had already tangled with both. As we discussed her continued melancholy over their tragic breakup, a table of middle-aged men sat down just a few feet to our right.

"They look Italian, maybe," she said. "Or Greek."

We put our bets on the table, fifty soles a piece, and I lost the coin toss.

"Excuse me, gentlemen," I said. They seemed annoyed at the interruption and pretended not to speak English until I explained that my female friend wanted to invite the single ones to join us for a nightcap. We were not a couple, I explained, and she was just past grieving the death of her fourth husband, Don Javier de Flores.

I was hardly believable, but two hungry Italians opted to join us. Julia played it like a champ and allowed them both to buy her drinks until past midnight. When she glanced at her watch, I knew it was my cue to move on. Though I didn't know which one took her home, I had seen Rocco remove his wedding ring and he had, no doubt, given a false name. Rocco was the less handsome of the two, but he was as feisty as Julia and he sported a new tattoo of a condor on his burly left forearm. As a team, they could last at least until morning.

\\\\

It was raining lightly when I returned to Bettina's house. I hadn't brought a poncho and managed to arrive at her house soaked. When I knocked, she ushered me in, then shuffled off for a hand towel. She was careful to put a second towel down on the same chair I'd sat in the day before. That she still cared about forty-year-old furniture was worth noting.

As Bettina poured me tea, I told her about my dinner with Julia and asked whether she knew much about Kuelap. Just a bit, she said. Her granddaughter from North America had talked about going there for more than a year, and the thought of it intrigued her.

"It's the only place in Peru that the Inca didn't conquer," she said. "In Kuelap they kept traditions that were unique to their people for hundreds of years. How wonderful to not be conquered. Even the Spanish were unable to penetrate their fortresses."

"You're right," I said. "To not be conquered. Even in this neighborhood the Spanish still control things five hundred years after Pizarro."

"So will you go there, to Kuelap?"

"There's some limited lodging, though nothing special," I said. "Julia's organizing a trip for us and we'll go part way by horseback. It may take a month or so to line up free transit and rooms."

Bettina poured milk in my tea, and I noticed that the shaking in her hands had disappeared. It could have been as simple as medication, but she seemed both calmer and inspired by seeing me again.

"With the rain, there won't be any tourists now," she said. "This is a place your airline travelers want to know about?"

"No, actually. There's not much interest in Kuelap. But sometimes I just write it and hope they buy it. Especially if it's someplace new and different. Someone is usually trying to fill space in their magazine." Bettina put a cookie on a small plate near her chair, then sat down very slowly. Suddenly, the back door near her kitchen flew open. A young woman burst inside, shaking the rain from her jacket.

"Bettina, I'm back!" she shouted. The woman hadn't seen me yet, but I stood as she entered, wondering how Bettina would explain my being there. She swooped in to kiss Bettina on the cheek, then shook the rain from her hair so deliberately that it hit both of us. This was clearly a game they played, and Bettina seemed to love the woman's informality and loose, fearless energy.

"You're a bit late," said Bettina. "This is David Svenson, the man I told you about." I extended my hand but she didn't take it right away. Instead, she paused and sized me up so blatantly it was uncomfortable.

"And David, this is my granddaughter, Marriam."

Marriam seemed to be waiting to hear my voice before deciding what to do next. She surveyed me with mild contempt.

"Nice to meet you," I said, pulling back my hand. "I hope I'm not an imposition."

Marriam was even less impressed with my lame politeness and lack of ingenuity than I was. With the energy of a cowgirl hot off a bull ride at a rodeo, she straddled the ottoman as she sat, then ripped open a bag of coca tea, filled her glass with hot water, and poured in a heaping spoon full of brown sugar.

"So you're the travel guy."

There was such a lack of enthusiasm in her voice it made me question my career choices. She seemed about as Peruvian as I was, which probably meant schooling somewhere far north of Lima. For that matter, far north of Mexico. There was no resemblance to Bettina except for her thick hair. Her skin was a soft brown color that hinted at biracial ancestry. Marriam was, by all physical standards, a beauty.

"I do some writing here and there to support my habit," I said. I was trying to pick up some ground, and perhaps incite a question worth answering. She was adding a third spoonful of sugar to her tea when Bettina stopped her with a gentle tug on her hand and a whisper, "Enough child." Marriam didn't seem interested in finding out about my habit so we wouldn't be talking about Kuelap or Cuzco anytime soon. Instead, she went right for the jugular.

"You want it in a nutshell, I suppose. Grams came here after the *big* war when anyone associated with the upper echelon in Germany took what they could and got out of Dodge. Most of them stayed east of here or down in Argentina, but a few trickled into Lima. Few enough to go unnoticed. She's not proud of what the Nazis did, but tell me what German is? My grandfather died fourteen years ago, unhappily I might add, and my mother and I have been doing what we can from Vancouver to help out Grams. One of us comes down every two or three months, not that she isn't just fine on her own."

Marriam took control of the room like an agitated midwife delivering triplets. I could feel the energy of a mother pushing and pushing as if trying to end it all as quickly as possible. Bettina may have been accustomed to the energy, but even she wilted a bit under Marriam's intensity. I tried to follow the action without taking my eyes off the curves accentuated by her soggy tank top. I hated being a typical guy, but then I always have been typical, and Marriam was distracting. Was her posture intended as a lure? I wondered. Did she know the rain had brought out the curls in her hair? Or was it always like that? What Marriam had also inherited from Bettina, on closer inspection, were her eyes—sharp, Aegean blue eyes. Yes, I was distracted, even enamored.

"Bettina is hardly a Nazi now, Mr. Svenson. She was barely one at the time. I'm sure you of all people, a writer from America—I'm sure you can see that!"

Tea can be a tranquil drink, but Marriam actually slurped hers as if she was in a hurry. She seemed to raise her voice with each gust of wind pushing the rain harder against the window.

"It was a different time and people made the choices they had to make, including Grams. What would you have done Mr. Svenson? What choices would you have made? I think it's a question we should all have to answer before we pass judgment."

Of course people had choices, but a Nazi? I wasn't trying to judge, I was trying to listen. Marriam had a way of discussing her grandmother as if she were not in the room, and I was beginning to wonder whether I'd hear from Bettina again. Using "Grams" had the familial touch, but she seemed equally armed with "Bettina," as if to reinforce their true bond, friendship. As Marriam defended her ancestry, I found myself gazing at every part of her as if information might help me through the conversation. Or attraction. Her hands were soft and so well-groomed I ruled out manual labor as a profession. The soft curve beneath her neck kept my interest as she went on about her grandfather's role in the bureaucracy of Berlin's city government. And when she talked about their Jewish ancestry, I found myself mesmerized by the fullness of her lips.

"Jewish ancestry?" I asked as if she'd had my full attention all along. "But it sounds as if your grandparents were part of the party."

"Yes, Bettina's mother was half Jewish, though nonreligious, and who's to say, really, what anyone's ethnicity is by looking at them? Who cares? But that makes Grams part Jewish and me about one tenth Jewish or something if you count Grandfather's Prussian grandfather who had several Jews in his history as well. And a few Italians. And at least one Tunisian of Arab decent. My father's father was half Spanish, half Andean, and he was born in Puno. He was part of a professional soccer team in the early 50s, albeit a not-too-well-known soccer team. All of which makes me a mutt, I suppose. A well-coordinated mutt. But aren't we all?"

"Coordinated?"

"Mutts."

"Is that a question you want me to answer? Of course we are."

"What I want you to answer is who are you, and why did you come barging in on my grandmother?"

"I don't need you to protect me, dear," said Bettina. I was wondering when she'd save me, and she managed to just in the nick of time.

"Mr. Svenson wasn't barging at all. He came to inquire about my taste in music and flags." For the first time in nearly forty hours we were getting somewhere. Bettina seemed inclined to open up and to set the record straight even for her granddaughter's benefit.

"I was just walking to dinner with my friend, well, my business partner, Julia. We were headed to Huaca Pucllana and . . ."

Marriam had a clear knack for interruption.

"But you're a writer. A freaking writer. Do you blog? Of course you blog because it's what writers do. Writers write. But here's the thing, I don't want you to hurt my grams with some hack story in the *Enquirer* about Nazi war criminals hiding out in Peru. Grams didn't do anything wrong!"

Bettina jumped to my defense again by reminding Marriam that I hadn't suggested that she had anything to hide. I watched them volley back and forth about the possible outcome of my dubious curiosity. It was resolved that I could stay and finish my tea. Marriam huffed off toward the upper level to change into dry clothes.

"She's a charming girl, isn't she?" Was it possible that Bettina understood both my attraction for Marriam and the aggressive personality that seemed unlikely to be reserved just for me. While she wasn't interested in matchmaking, Bettina seemed to understand that her granddaughter was magnetic.

"I love her dearly," she said, "but there's no stop button."

"Yep, she's a pistol." As quickly as sound could travel from mouth to ears, I was regretting another lame cliché. Bettina saved me.

"Where do we start, Mr. Svenson? What do you want to know?"

Due to the same nonchalance and lack of planning I'd long used when approaching the rest of my life, I hadn't worked out the details of how to interview Bettina. I wasn't even sure that an interview was my reason for being there. But Bettina had clearly made the invitation. I took a deep breath while asking for some inner muse to take control of me. Charlie Rose I was not.

"Oh, uh, where did you live, were you married, well, of course you were married, but that sort of thing. High school. Your parents. Ambitions, dreams." Could I have been any more vague? Fortunately, Bettina seemed to want a listener. She wanted to tell her story. She skipped childhood and launched right in to what mattered most.

\\\\\

Bettina had married Stephan Kohl when she was nineteen and he was twenty-four. He'd graduated from the University of Hamburg with a degree in economics and business administration in 1935 and had begun working for a village on the outskirts of the main city. She was working on a degree in romantic languages and had become well versed in English and French. They were, at the time, the two best languages for international commerce, and Bettina was already in demand. Stephan proved good at city management, and within two years, they'd moved to Berlin.

"It was the most dynamic city in the world at the time," she said. "But we have a way of killing such places when the opportunity arises because diversity and open-mindedness threaten people in power. It happened to Beirut, and Kabul too. Even to your New Orleans."

Bettina went on using broad strokes. They'd enjoyed a level of affluence afforded by two incomes and no children. Their social circle included nightlife with a sort of hedonistic freedom. Sometimes it was big dinners with friends; sometimes it was live performances—from mimes and puppetry to basement jazz clubs with artists from Paris, Stockholm, and New York City. For young people, Berlin was the center of the universe. No one cared about politics or the poor, she said. They were starched shirt professionals during the day, and they lived like Bohemians at night.

"Stephan's job gave us a bit of VIP status, which meant good seats in the clubs and no waiting in line. And because of my skill at translating, I was often the host for business engagements at the best restaurants. The business owners came to know me quickly. There were many Americans visiting then, and I helped manage deals on everything from automobile and airplane parts to weapons. We even sorted out some food distribution in Belgium, which as you know had been devastated after the first war. The French were interested in exporting fashion, perfumes, and art. People forget how much art was bought and sold in the thirties to the few people who had money."

I was lost in Bettina's story when I noticed that Marriam was sitting on the staircase, listening quietly. I had no idea how long she'd been there, but her energy had shifted. She was wearing blue jeans and a gauzy white blouse that brought out the brown in her skin. With her face perched between her hands, I could see a tiny tattoo on her wrist and part of her palm, what appeared to be a small butterfly. She had three piercings on her left ear, two studs of some kind and an inch long string of Andean beads that matched a single strand on the right. Her hair was pulled away from her face, and her round eyes were filled with love for her grandmother. But there was also sadness. She knew that Bettina had made choices she could try to defend, but would never fully understand.

"Would you like more tea, Mr. Svenson?" asked Bettina. I had no idea what she'd said before that, but I wondered if she'd been tracking my attraction for her granddaughter.

"I would, yes," I said. "Can I use your restroom? If I remember it's near the kitchen?" It was, and within seconds I was splashing water on my face. Marriam was more than a distraction. Her swing from distant and dismissive to attentive and compassionate was, to say the least, seductive. Though her charms weren't directed my way, my head was spinning. For a moment, I imagined the pleasures of Berlin nightlife and the enchanting energy Marriam had reserved for me. But there were boundaries, I thought. I caught myself in the mirror, took a deep breath, then splashed my face a second time.

When I returned from the restroom, Bettina was gone. Marriam was still sitting on the steps and informed me that her "Grams" had needed rest.

"You'll have to come back tomorrow," she said.

"Maybe you'd like to join me for dinner?" I suggested.

I considered her answer a triumph if only because she actually looked me in the eyes when she said, "No, I don't think so." Marriam led me to the door, shook my hand, and ushered me out without any additional pleasantries. I stood on the stoop and listened to the latch close on the door.

As I was walking back to the Hotel Ariosto, I passed my favorite café and stopped for a pisco sour. Julia rang on my mobile, and within minutes I was sitting with her and Rocco eating yet another brick oven pizza. Julia criticized me for eating more pizza than anyone she'd ever met, but I assured her it was only because the raw vegetables in most restaurants made me sick. Rocco was limited to about five words of English—enough to order Cusqueña lager and potato chips and to say "I love you" to Julia in every imaginable tone of voice. He was smitten and couldn't seem to get his left hand out of the back of her pants. She had it under control and kicked me under the table, then let out a squeal when he pinched her behind. Rocco was a smoker, and it didn't take long before I left them behind for the second night in a row. Something told me it would be the last time I saw Rocco.

Julia rarely spent more than a night or two with the men she was attracted to unless she fell in love. Men were a necessary evil for her, but little more. "A few are good for sex," she said. "Most are lousy at friendship, and all of them are boring on vacation." According to Julia, I was an exception among men in these ways. It helped that she found me physically unattractive and too culturally American, since we traveled together well, and with a certain style and level of experience. There'd never been an intellectual moment between us, and I was relatively certain there wouldn't be, given our desire to keep things as uncomplicated as possible. Perhaps, I thought, in another lifetime.

\\\\

Day three felt different. Bettina was less energetic, and she apologized that she'd run out of cookies. They wouldn't arrive from Caraz until the next day so we'd have to make it on tea alone. I asked about Marriam, but Bettina said she was on a long errand and wouldn't be back until late.

"I'd like to walk," she said. "Perhaps we can talk and walk at the same time?"

Given my height, walking with Bettina must have been an amusement for the other pedestrians. She took three steps for every one of mine. When we came to the first crossing, she tucked her arm into mine, forcing me to bend to hold it in place for her. Still, it seemed to comfort her that I was in no hurry and willing to play by her rules.

"I have been waiting to live for a very long time, Mr. Svenson. When I walk, it feels like there is the promise of something I left behind long ago."

A moped swung too close to the curb, and Bettina scolded the driver with her free hand. "That's an old woman's prerogative," she said, laughing. "We think we know things about right and wrong."

The cars along the street were marked with leaflets for the presidential race, and former president Alan Garcia's mug stared back at us from every windshield. A middle-aged neighbor named Mrs. Estrada grabbed one and crumpled it as she got into her car.

"Hola, Senora Estrada. ¿Como esta?"

"Hola, Bettina," she said, drawing out the "o" as if it added to the pleasantry. "¿La election es muy loco, si?" It wasn't a real question, and Bettina simply nodded as Mrs. Estrada revved up her aging Volkswagen Beetle.

"Do you think Mr. Garcia is different from Hitler?" Bettina asked the question in a nonjudgmental tone.

"Yes, Bettina. I think they're very different."

"Good, Mr. Svenson. But why is this so?"

"Hitler was a nut job. The guy killed millions of Jews, Gypsies, Catholics, the disabled, gays, and others—anyone he didn't think fit his bizarre idea of what a German should be. I don't see Garcia doing that. Not even Fujimore did that." I was, of course, speaking about the former Peruvian president known almost equally in Peru as a progressive and a criminal. After a brief exile in the homeland of his Japanese parents, Fujimore had returned to face trial, lost, and was sent to prison. As I thought of the number of political opponents of Fujimore who now lay dead in mass graves, I felt I should explain. But Bettina beat me to it.

"No ruler is without sin, David. May I call you David?"

"Of course." I was relieved by her familiarity. We were becoming friends.

"Many of us did not know Hitler was, as you say, 'a nut job' when he began. At first, some of the things he said just seemed patriotic. We thought he was for Germany when much of the world was still against us after the first war. If you were a patriot to your nation, you didn't question many of the things he was doing that seemed good for Germany. He promised jobs and prosperity. He promised to maintain our borders. He promised security. I saw his speeches more than once, and he could be an inspiration to disenfranchised people looking for a better life. It was the time of the Great Depression. And Germany had already lost a war. Hitler played off vulnerability and fear as if he were the only person who could protect Germany. He was the solution, and over time most of us believed him. I don't mean it as an excuse, but many of us were naïve. And many of us didn't care at all."

"We have made him into a caricature," I said. "But it's hard to attract that kind of submission and loyalty without genuine charisma."

"He had that, of course. But it was the fear, David. It began simply enough, with his suggested threats from outside nations. We were coerced to believe the military should be stronger in order to defend ourselves. We were persuaded that it was okay to sacrifice our liberties in pursuit of those who conspired against us. If we were law-abiding, what difference would it make as long as the government was finding the bad people and protecting the good? But we were wrong.

"By the late thirties, it was our lifestyle and our freedom of expression that were compromised, and by then it was too late. There was no room to protest, and if you did, you were a traitor. And they killed traitors. By then, he'd already started his grand plan and was exporting his ideas by invading other countries. Most of us had nothing against Jews. We'd lived together, had friendships over many years, and we knew each other long enough not to think about where we came from."

There was regret in Bettina's voice. She slowed her walk and looked up at me.

"We failed to see what was happening because we were living for the moment, you see. We are all self-centered, David, so if it wasn't me they were talking about, if it wasn't my store they were closing, my home they were raiding, maybe I would be fine. Most people don't react until something impacts them directly. I was no different from most Germans when I didn't resist."

Bettina hesitated, biting her lower lip.

"And in my case, I was very much in love."

With that, she smiled, and the blue in her eyes seemed to sharpen with the memory.

"It sounds like you and Stephan had what so many people strive for in marriage." If nothing else, I was the master of political correctness, and just shy of condescension.

Bettina laughed, more heartily than I'd seen before. There was a glimmer of hope in her. Even her posture seemed buoyed.

"It was not Stephan I loved," she said. "I was in love with another woman."

After a long pause during which no words came to me, Bettina asked if I would buy her a cup of tea. We were in front of a small café about two blocks from her house. I swept the purple blossoms off the table and we sat down under a jacaranda tree. The waiter had seen us coming. He brought a carafe of water with thinly sliced cucumber and greeted Bettina with a huge grin and his hand on his heart.

"Mi Amor," he said. "Buenas tardes. Siéntese por favor." And with that he helped her into her chair. Then he squatted near our table so they could converse at eye level. Bettina, in perfect Spanish, explained that I was a travel writer and that if the service was good, I might find a way to highlight his restaurant in an in-flight magazine. They laughed, and Faure introduced himself in passable English. It was quickly established that if I was Bettina's friend, then I was his friend as well. He brought Bettina green tea with honey and, given that I'd just experienced the unexpected surprise of Bettina's sexual orientation, I ordered a Cusqueña.

"Faure is the owner," she informed me. "He's one of the few in the neighborhood who grew up here. Most of the other shop owners came when the area was being gentrified for tourists."

"It seems to have worked."

"This has always been a quiet part of town. But it was not so exclusive until the past decade. Once Huaca Pucllana was determined to be an archeological site, the traffic and the tourists came."

Faure was quick with my beer and a small plate of sliced limes to keep the flies away.

"And your grandchild?" asked Faure.

Clearly, they'd made the choice to speak in English for my benefit.

"She will be here another week. Then back to Vancouver. I am going to miss that girl!"

I would too, I thought, but kept it to myself.

"Please give her my best. And tell her Miguelito still asks about her."

"After what happened, I may keep that one to myself!" Bettina laughed.

I sipped my beer and felt a small pang of jealousy, wondering whether Miguelito had scored in the contest I was longing to enter. The café was quiet in mid-afternoon, but another couple had sat down nearby and Faure left to greet them.

"Now where were we?" Bettina knew precisely where we'd left off but was back to playing me. Our game had a charm of its own so I took the bait.

"You and Stephan were married and living the high life in Berlin. Hitler was doing his fascist best to create fear in the German people at every turn in a sustained effort to consolidate his power, manipulate his citizens, and spread his ideology across Europe, including genocide. Civil liberties were eroding with each new threat to the homeland, and you were smitten by another woman."

"Precisely," she said, smiling. "And you're not even writing this down."

I didn't need to write it down because Bettina was giving me only the cliff notes. Plus, I wanted to watch her as she told it. She had a most expressive face, with eyes that conveyed more pain than anyone I'd ever met. Whatever her life had given her, happiness had been fleeting at best. So I listened.

\\\\

Emily was a teacher at the British school near the embassy. Her charge was third and fourth graders attached to English-speaking diplomats. She was, Bettina said, perfectly suited for working with children because she didn't have a bad bone in her body and could find hope in the worst of circumstances.

"We met at a Spanish nightclub called El Maestro," she said. "It was an underground place where people let loose with music and forgot about politics. Stephan had become conflicted with Hitler's grand plans. He was torn between being a good soldier in city government, and living the social life that felt natural to him. He was a joy when we were together because he had the innate capacity to simply enjoy life. But it was Germany in the thirties. We all remembered the devastation of the first war. And to be fair, Stephan wanted to be careful in his career. It may sound strange now, but I wasn't torn at all. I was young, and I wanted to have fun. I would drag Stephan out every chance we had. It was risky for him because of his position, but he loved me and we both wanted to feel independent. We were a bit deluded, but we both enjoyed feeling like we had some control over our destiny.

"Stephan was often the life of the party because he was kind and outgoing and easy with a laugh. The few times we ran into government officials at our night spots, he managed to turn it on them first by saying things like 'I came here looking for you' followed by a hearty laugh or 'I promise not to tell anyone you were here,' and he did it before they could utter a word. He was disarming and, quite simply, well-liked.

"At El Maestro we drank and laughed and danced until we couldn't move. The club opened at eleven each night of the week and closed at four in the morning. In other cities it would have been closed by the Nazis, but Berlin held on to the underground culture until the end simply because many of the government officials wanted a nightlife too.

"I was happy enough with Stephan, and I'd never even thought about an attraction to a woman until I met Emily. But the first time I shook her hand, a shock went through my entire body. She had a beautiful, innocent smile, with a spirit that could harm no one. I remember how soft her hand was, and how it fit perfectly into my own. When she let go I held it longer than normal, and I remember smiling awkwardly back at her, like she'd somehow passed a part of herself inside me. It wasn't something I could process then, and within seconds, Stephan had me out on the dance floor.

"When I came back to the table, she was sitting with her date, a young captain from the Spanish consulate who was buying glasses of Jamaican rum for everyone. Stephan was his usual charming self, laughing with the captain and flirting casually with all the women. Everyone loved Stephan. He was the type of man who would never lead, but who would always be close to the top, if you understand what I mean. He was a very good administrator, but he was not an ideologue—a manager but not a leader. I remember that he asked Emily to dance, and as they moved around the floor she was the one that I was watching move, not Stephan. She was thin and tall, and she had very long legs with brand new stockings. That was a big thing then, you know. It was not easy to get stockings. And the heels of her shoes were not so square as ours. Her hair was light brown, the length of her shoulders, and it was full of curls. I had never thought of British girls with curly hair, but Emily's was natural and her hair bounced when she danced with Stephan."

Bettina hadn't moved her position in a very long time and was lost in her past. Her shoulders were so low they almost fell on the table. Faure brought her another cup of hot water, and Bettina was meticulous in how she prepared her tea. She was thinking, and it occurred to me that she may never have told this story until now. It seemed she wanted someone to know, and telling a stranger made it easier. She had no need to feel shame because we had no history and more than likely, no future.

"I hope I'm not boring you." Boring? Compared to my usual interviews with PR hacks from fancy hotels, Bettina was a godsend. She smiled as I put my hand on top of hers.

"Bettina, you've lived a remarkable life. I'm grateful to be here for a small part of it." It sounded polite, but she knew I meant it.

"Remarkable, I don't know," she said. "I've missed out on so much."

"I'm not sure I understand."

"Friendships. Family. The war destroyed everything I'd ever known."

"But there was Emily. Please . . . tell me what happened next?"

"We met again two weeks later at the same club, but there was a group and it was hard to talk."

Bettina took a sip of tea, then carefully positioned the cup back in the saucer. Her mind was back in time.

"I'd been thinking of little besides Emily during our time apart, and as we were leaving that night, she helped me with my coat. It was then I suggested we meet for an afternoon get-together on Saturday. There was a small Greek bakery on Liepziger Strasse that served baklava and made thick espresso filled with sugar. It would be fun, I said.

"When she arrived that afternoon, she was wearing slacks, which was unusual, and a loose fitting cotton blouse. I was in a skirt and had chosen a tight fitting cashmere sweater that showed off my figure. It was something I'd worn often enough when courting Stephan five years earlier, but this occasion was different. I wasn't sure why, but I wanted Emily to be attracted to me. I was confused by my feelings, of course, because my attraction was so real, and yet it seemed so wrong. Emily had almost no makeup on, just enough to highlight her eyes a bit, but I'd spent an hour in front of the mirror. I felt silly, ashamed, really. But Emily was so lively that there was no room for shame. She was simply full of life and spirit and goodness, like no one I'd ever met before.

"We were quick friends with a mutual interest in girl things like jewelry and shopping, and we both liked hats, which is funny because they were not that popular at the time. She asked about Stephan and I asked about her Spanish captain. She said he was just a fling, typical of the diplomatic corps. But our conversation was much deeper than small talk because despite her outgoing personality, she was anything but shallow. Emily was an intellectual, and we found common ground in books, art, and politics. She'd read Rilke and seemed to understand him in a way that I, as a German, could not. I'd dabbled in Russian authors and found them depressing, but she could quote Dostoyevsky and somehow saw hope in his stories of despair. I found out she'd majored in literature at Oxford, but her interests went beyond books. It seemed she had a knowledge of everything, a memory like none I'd ever encountered, and I was soon attracted not only to her physically; I was enamored of her mind.

"As we were leaving the café, I tripped on the sidewalk near the gate and fell just a bit against her. It sounds almost contrived, really, anything but an accident. Maybe in my subconscious I had planned it because I wanted to feel her body against mine. She quickly asked if I was okay, which of course I was, and I remember looking into her eyes and seeing how genuine her concern for me was. I put my hand up to her face and we just looked at each other, perhaps for a moment too long because I could feel her need to pull away."

For the first time, I felt Bettina's exhaustion in telling her story. She took a very deep breath and looked at me with some distress.

"Bettina?" I said. "Perhaps you'd like to head back to your house now?"

She was tired, and the energy that had filled her at the start of the conversation was nearly gone. We walked slowly back, and when we arrived, Marriam was sitting on the porch steps waiting for us. Unlike the day before, she wasn't caustic, or even dramatic. Instead, she seemed happy to see that I was taking care of her grandmother.

"Thanks for taking her for a walk. It's good for her." Marriam said it like I was a caretaker, and as if Bettina wasn't able to comprehend her. But Bettina was too tired to respond and seemed grateful to be back home. Marriam helped her up the small flight of stairs and inside. As she was closing the door, Marriam asked when I was planning to come back. I simply said I'd be back the next day around two o'clock.

\\\\\

At the Hotel Ariosto, there was an email waiting for me from my editor at *La Fiesta!*, the Aero Peru in-flight magazine. They wanted a new spin on the Sacred Valley, something that downplayed Machu Picchu and got to the heart of the village of Ollantaytambo. With the tourist rush sweeping the entire area, there was big pressure on Machu Picchu—too many footprints in all the wrong places. They'd already had to rope off sections of the ruins to keep people from sitting on ledges or scratching their names on the rocks. And the grassy central plaza was no longer a meeting place where groups could sit beneath the giant tree as their guides told them lies about the origins of this sacred place. Machu Picchu was crowded.

There were fifteen new hotels under construction along the rail line between Aguas Calientes and Cuzco. I'd worked for the magazine before, and they knew I would deliver something worthwhile. Ollantaytambo was my favorite spot along the well-traveled tourist route. I loved the small alleys with irrigation channels running along six-hundred-year-old stone walkways. The people who lived there still had real lives as weavers and farmers, and except for a few hotel owners and restaurateurs, they didn't count on tourist dollars for survival.

Archeologists from Lima had only recently begun studying the giant pyramid at Ollantaytambo and, with the help of shaman from the area, they were beginning to understand the scope of this grand temple as more than an astronomical site. It was possible, they believed that Ollantay-tambo was the place of origin for the Inca ancestors, the heart of their creation myths. If that was the case, and it was certainly worth the speculation, then it really could rival Machu Picchu as a tourist destination. I needed the work, and I wrote back that I could begin the piece in less than a week.

\\\\

Julia arrived in the hotel bar at eight, sans Rocco. Much to his dismay, they'd parted ways at dawn after a second night of hedonism.

"We did it four times," she reported.

"That's more than I need to know." I handed Julia a pisco sour and left two hundred soles for the bartender. "What is it with you and these short-term guys anyway? Maybe you could find something more lasting with another woman?"

Julia punched me hard in the shoulder, and then gave me a look that suggested I'd spoken blasphemy to a Catholic schoolgirl nursed on Vatican II. I regretted it, if only because it felt like I was somehow belittling Bettina in my teasing, which was not my intention. It just came out.

"I drop a guy after a couple of dates and you question my sexuality?"

"I'm just saying maybe you should hang up the one-nighters. It must get rough on you, keeping 'em all straight."

"Or maybe I just happen to like it," she said. "Or maybe it's an escape. Or maybe it's not your business anyway."

We left the Ariosto for one of our usual haunts and spent the evening eating trout with sweet potato chips and talking about the Sacred Valley. For a small fee, Julia said she'd join me in Ollantaytambo. Because she spoke Quechua, she could translate. There was, she said, a co-op of weavers in the village of Chinchero who might also welcome some good print in *La Fiesta!* We ended the night early because Julia was tired.

"Who wouldn't be tired after having two hundred and fifty pounds of Rocco bouncing off you all night."

"Better than boobies!" Julia scrunched up her face and growled at me, then kissed both of my cheeks and was off, a creature of Lima's nightlife headed home for a rare night of sleeping alone.

\\\\

Marriam opened the door and ushered me in with little fanfare but a dramatic sweep of her hand. She was back to her original self.

"Bettina's upstairs," she said. "And you need to be brief today. She feels like shit but she won't tell you that. I was going to cancel you completely, but she insisted on seeing you. I'm not sure what the hell you two have going, but whatever it is, you better be good to my Grams!"

The tone of her threat had stiffened, out of love no doubt. Marriam meant business, and I was certain she'd try to punch me out if she had to. Still, I found myself admiring the way her upper body tensed when she threatened me. As she led me upstairs, I watched her bottom closely and gave a quick thought to planting a kiss on it. Her jeans were so tight they accented each cheek into separate but equal bubbles. Then, with my eyes clearly not on the short steps, I fell forward. My face landed within inches of her bare heels. I looked up in time to catch her shaking her head. I had become a serious underdog.

Bettina was sitting up against the backboard of her bed. She greeted me with a hand extended and asked me to pull a chair up next to her. Marriam excused herself and, when Bettina wasn't looking, she stuck her tongue out at me. Or maybe I simply dreamt that part up. I shook my head back to reality.

Someone, I assumed Marriam, had set a tray up near her bed with tea and Bettina's favorite cookies. There were two or three different types that I hadn't seen before, which made me feel special. The book she was reading was open on her nightstand.

"What are you reading now?" I asked.

"*The Zanzibar Chest*," she said. "It's a little known masterpiece, one you should read."

She went on to talk about the author, a Kenyan named Aidan Hartley, and how he'd managed to make the history of East Africa and Yemen so vivid for her.

"He was a war correspondent for the wire services. And yet with all the brutal things he's seen in Rwanda and Somalia he's somehow managed to love the places and the people. We are strange creatures, David. What human beings do to each other can be so heartless, and yet we find light and life and love where none should exist at all."

"Heartless, yes. Like Hitler," I said, hoping to talk about her life instead of the author's.

"Like Hitler yes, but the list is long. Idi Amin. Pol Pot. History is full of despots and Mr. Hartley writes about a few that most of us in the West have never heard of. Hitler just did it with his own cameras rolling and on the world stage. He believed the story he'd created for himself. Can you imagine the audacity of thinking there is a master race? Or that one man can be right about his choices for an entire world? We were fools. But we've covered that ground, haven't we?"

"We have, Bettina. I get the sense that you and Stephan were somehow trapped by it and had few options?"

"Oh, we had options, David, but we were cowards. Most people are. We become afraid of losing our status or our livelihood or our privileges, and we failed to protect those among us who were poor or vulnerable. It was shortsighted, of course. We could have spoken up. I'm part Jewish myself, and as soon as things got bad, neither Stephan nor I ever even mentioned it. I simply said I was part Flemish. My parents had died when I was fairly young, and whatever Jewish relatives I had had moved to Mexico when they saw the nightmare coming. I had no relatives left in Germany, except Stephan. Even my work had changed by the late thirties and I was spending more and more time translating for the government and less for business people."

Bettina shifted in her bed and reached for a cookie. I asked if I could help her with her tea but she shooed me away. I liked the way she had become comfortable with me, and I smiled at her as I fixed my own. When I looked around the room there was little to identify her with anyone or anything. Her possessions were simple, daily sorts of things—brushes, a hand mirror, makeup on a small silver platter on her dresser. To the right of her dresser, there was a pearl necklace hanging from the edges of an old photograph in a wooden frame. There were three people in the photo, two women and one man. It appeared as though it had been taken a long time ago. I had been stirring my tea for too long and she stopped me with her hand.

"The photo?" I asked.

"Stephan, Emily, and me. The Spanish captain took it as we stood in front of El Maestro one night. I'm the one on the right."

I got up to look closer. Stephan was rigid but smiling. He was handsome but short, just a few inches taller than Bettina. Bettina was stunning.

It was obvious where Marriam's looks came from because Bettina's hair was long and light, and even in black and white, her eyes were radiant. Emily was taller than Stephan by an inch or two. Her skirt was the long, tight-fitting kind that looks hard to walk in. It came to her ankles. She had on a short-sleeved blouse with silk-covered buttons and, around her neck, what appeared to be the same necklace that was hanging from the picture frame. I ran my hand along the pearls, knowing that Bettina had run her fingers along the same strand hundreds of times. It was hard to imagine what it had been like for them.

"They're hers, David. She gave them to me when she left Berlin in 1937." After a long pause during which I studied the photograph, Bettina asked me to come and sit near her. There was fatigue in her voice, and I knew that today would not be a long one. I carefully removed the pearls from the rim of the photograph and brought them to her. She closed the pearls in her hand, and held mine around hers. I sensed she was asking for more than comfort, it was as if she was asking for approval.

We looked at each other for a very long time. A tear rolled down her cheek and it seemed to fall forever. Somehow I knew that whatever she wanted to say would require me to ask.

"You were lovers, then?" There was no judgment in my voice. Bettina pushed the tear away and smiled at me. She took a long sip of her tea and as she set her cup down, I could see the same shaking I'd seen on my first visit.

"It wasn't acceptable, and I was married. But yes, we became lovers. Neither of us had ever been with a woman before, and it was awkward in so many ways. The only thing we had to guide us was our love. How we undressed each other, the ways we touched, our lips, all of it was so new. We were afraid of everything about it, really—the physical part between us, the emotions, and the fear of getting caught. There was really no place to be alone except at my apartment while Stephan was at work. We even started wearing the same perfume so the room would smell normal to Stephan. I knew I was betraying him, but nothing in my experience prepared me for what I felt with Emily. Even now I can't explain it."

Bettina looked at the pearls, running them through her fingers and remembering all she'd lost.

"I don't want to sound sad, David. It wasn't sad to be with her; it was the most beautiful part of my life. She was my joy. For almost a year, the three of us were inseparable. We would make dinners together and dance and entertain. Stephan might have known, perhaps he did. I've always wondered because there were so many times when our affections seemed obvious. When we were sitting beside each other, one of us might fix the other's hair. Or a hand on the shoulder would linger too long. Our feet under tables were almost always woven together. If he knew, he somehow accepted it. But it was never discussed.

"By the time Emily left, there were no choices for us. Americans, French, and the British were all forced to leave when the embassies were closing. Saying goodbye was the hardest thing I've ever done. It was also the end of whatever hope we had of being together. If she'd stayed, she would have been jailed or killed. And by then, there was no way for Stephan to leave, even though he, like so many, had become concerned about the course we were on. We were German, and there was nowhere for us to go."

I had stopped drinking tea and was leaning close to her with my elbows on my knees. My left hand was supporting my chin and my right thumb was moving back and forth across Bettina's forearm. Somehow the awkwardness of being in the bedroom of an elderly woman I'd only known for a few days didn't seem to matter.

"We spent the afternoon together making love," she said. "Neither of us was angry. There was nothing, really, that we could do. She kissed me so softly that last time, her lips barely touching mine. Then she removed her necklace and placed it around my neck. She wasn't crying. She was trying to be strong. But I'd had tears for weeks, and my eyes were full for both of us. My head fell into her neck and she just held me. We were near the door of the apartment and I knew she had to go. Her right hand rubbed my cheek a final time, and she whispered into my ear, 'I love you still . . . always.'"

"I never saw Emily again," said Bettina. "Years later, as the Russians were entering Berlin, Stephan and I managed to get out. If we'd stayed, we'd certainly have been killed. Stephan had relatives in Finland who harbored us for nearly a year; then we came here to Peru. After a few more years, once things settled down, I started working for the new German embassy. Stephan had not been a hateful person, David. He'd never killed anyone. But he never forgave himself for what happened in Germany. He was never able to separate himself from that time or from all the ways we'd failed. It helped to be here, to be so far away, almost as if those horrible things had never happened. We tried in so many ways. I became pregnant two times. I lost the first one to a miscarriage. My daughter Alexandra was born in 1949. Marriam is her youngest daughter."

Bettina asked me to fluff up her pillow and help raise her a bit in her bed. I was clumsy at it, but we laughed as I tried to pull up her tiny frame. We had a second cookie together because, as Bettina said, she was hardly watching her weight. She asked about my work and I told her I would be heading to Ollantaytambo in a day or two. It was her favorite spot in the Sacred Valley, and we both reminisced about what would soon be lost there. When it was time for me to leave, I gave Bettina a kiss on her forehead. I could feel her smiling, and I lingered a few seconds longer. As I pulled away, I laid the palm of my left hand against her cheek.

"Thank you, David. I wanted someone to know."

Marriam was watching a Peruvian soap opera in the den near the kitchen when I approached the doorway to say goodbye. She was painting her toes and the smell was unpleasant. She seemed relieved when I said I'd swing by the next day to say goodbye before I headed to the Andes. Her mother, she said, would be visiting in a few days.

When I returned to the Hotel Ariosto there were calls to return from back home. My father had been taken to the hospital for "tests" and his wife was already agonizing about the high cost of their deductible. They'd been living off his pension for a while now, and their health care needs gave them little room for error. If it was his spleen again she was going to tell the doctor to remove it "once and for all." She put Dad on the phone. He asked where I was and when the hell I'd be coming back. My older brother had purchased a new snowplow, and he sure could use my help, Dad said. Just as soon as the oak leaves dropped. Given that summer was just a few weeks away in Peru, I told him the chances of returning any time soon were unlikely.

Julia showed up and made faces at me while I worked my way through a very long goodbye. Dad had grown sentimental. I did my best to sound concerned, but it was hard to do while Julia flipped her eyelids back, rolled her lips up to her nose, and curled her tongue, but I managed to hide my distraction with a fit of coughing.

Julia couldn't go to dinner that night because an old friend from Cajamarca had shown up unexpectedly. "Old friend" was, I supposed, a euphemism, so her days without a playmate had totaled exactly zero, give or take a few hours. We had a quick beer on the patio and agreed to head to Ollantaytambo two days later. The old friend would be gone by then.

\|\|\|\|

When I went to Bettina's house the next day there was a padded envelope on the door. The handwriting was simple and blunt: *For David*.

I sat down on the porch and opened it. Inside, there was a handwritten note from Marriam and a small gift wrapped in faded white tissue.

Dear David,

I'm sorry to tell you this but Bettina passed away last night. Her death wasn't a surprise, of course, but that doesn't make it easier. Thank you for your last few days with her. You were kind, and you lifted her spirits. Before she died, Bettina asked me to give this to you. She had wrapped it herself and said you'd know why she wanted you to have it.

If you ever get to Vancouver, don't hesitate to call.

Marriam

There was nothing in Marriam's note about funeral arrangements, nor any invitation to be a part of personal things that now turned inward to family. When I opened the small package there was a second note from Bettina and the string of pearls that had once been Emily's. The note was almost illegible and it appeared as if Bettina had struggled to write it:

Dear David,

Each spring, on the anniversary of the day we arrived in Peru, Stephan and I would hang the old German flag for a few hours in the evening and listen to music from our youth. It was a ritual we performed to remember who we once were, a ritual to help us overcome the feeling of denial that happened so easily in a beautiful new country and a modest, peaceful city that had, in its ignorance, welcomed us. We needed to remember it all, especially our failures.

We did not do it with pride or to celebrate. We did it to feel the disgrace of being so self-absorbed in our youth that we offered no resistance to the tyranny that surrounded us. We did it so we would not forget the horrible things that happened as a result of our inaction and indifference.

We never asked for forgiveness from anyone, and we never forgave ourselves. I have lived every day wishing for others facing the consequences of despotism and cruelty to have the courage we never had. Once compromised by turning my back on the cries for help from others, my life was never again so precious.

You were the first to question our ceremony of shame, and I am grateful to you for letting me share with you that part of my life.

I never saw Emily again, and I suspect my letters to her during the war never made it out of Germany. Once we came here, it was never possible.

Thank you for listening. The pearls are now yours to watch over. Please keep them in a sacred place.

Affectionately,
Bettina Kohl

I carefully folded the note and put it in my shirt pocket. There was no right thing to do next, and I found myself counting the pearls like prayer beads. There were fifty-six of them. The clasp was loose and I knew I'd get it fixed. For the first time in many years, I could taste the salt of my own tears. It was silly in a way, I thought. I'd known Bettina for only a few days.

Though I considered knocking on the door, it was the wrong thing to do. If Marriam was still inside, she was grieving in her own way. Her intentions had been clear.

The bakery was just a block away, and I'd not yet been there. During our walk, Bettina had pointed out the one with the green and white striped awning. When I went inside, the owner pretended to ignore me, glancing occasionally as I looked over the glass case filled with pastries. On a hunch, I told him that I was a friend of Bettina's. He loosened up and said he'd been ordering her favorite cookies from Caraz for many years, and that any friend of hers was a friend of his. I ordered a small bag full and ate three on the walk back to the Hotel Ariosto.

HALF A REASON TO DIE

"**A HOTTER PLACE ON EARTH** is hard to find. No roads to speak of, houses built of dried mud, flash floods each spring, and the wells run dry by late July. The poverty is staggering, the women are abused, the children are malnourished."

The picture being painted could describe any number of developing nations—Congo, Sudan, Haiti, Bangladesh—but Major Grace Sommers was talking about Afghanistan.

I rewound the cassette tape and listened again. The unlabeled, bootleg copy of a private meeting between Major Sommers and her military lawyer had arrived by mail at my home address in a padded envelope sealed with duct tape. There was no return address, but the tape hadn't come to me by accident. Someone wanted her story told, and it was a good bet they were on her side. It was hard to believe what I was hearing, and harder still to know why the tape had come to me.

"That's the place," she said. "The place where everything that made sense started to unravel."

I could hear commotion in the room, shuffling papers, someone zipping a pack or briefcase, water pouring into a glass, then a stern male voice.

"They only care about one thing, Major Sommers. Were the Afghans alive at the time you found them?"

A female voice interrupted with a more sympathetic tone.

"It's your trial, Grace, and whatever the evidence, you're the only one who knows the truth. Just stay calm and tell us what happened."

There was a pause, and then someone pushed their metal chair back from the table. A moment later, I could hear a metal cell door roll closed. Then the tape went dead.

||||

The cassette machine in my car hadn't been used in ages and, when I pushed eject, it showed its opposition with a squeaky grind. Rather than ruin the only copy I had, I opted to enjoy the silence for the last part of my very long drive. I was traveling west out of Spring Green, Wisconsin, on Highway 14 en route to Viroqua. The flat two-lane stretch bends northwest near the BP station at Boaz, then rolls into Amish country filled with deep valleys of organic produce and hillsides populated by old growth hardwoods. It was just past two o'clock when I arrived at *The Infinite Brew*, a tiny coffee shop on Court Street.

"Dr. Sommers? Or do I call you Major?"

"You're the reporter?" She asked with condescension. "I expected someone older . . . and male."

I laughed. The past week had been one of those where I'd stared down the crow's feet around my eyes each morning while listening to the internal debate over the various reasons for and against Botox, for and against triathlon training, for and against my life-long need for the approval of others.

"I'm sorry, I wasn't trying to be funny," she said. "From your emails I imagined someone else."

"Not a problem. It's me. Female. I've been writing since the *Panther Review* in high school, and I've spent the last year trying to defy aging. Things happen to women as they approach forty."

"And what would that be?" Her tone was so critical it was hard to tell whether she was against my notion of aging or simply irritable.

"Babies," I said. I wanted to keep things light until we found a groove of some kind. "At least that's what my friends tell me. Even if you don't want one, you start realizing that the option won't be available much longer."

Most things don't go as planned, and the very last thing I'd imagined as an opening discussion with a disgraced and twice-convicted former Major from the Wisconsin Air National Guard was my own internal debate about motherhood.

"You mind if I grab a latte?" I said, changing the subject as quickly as possible. She looked at me curiously as I walked to the rear and ordered. I could still feel her looking at me as I tapped a wooden stir stick on the counter, then read the ingredients and calories on the cellophane-wrapped package of dark chocolate-covered vanilla wafers near the cash register. One hundred and twenty per wafer. Was it worth it? I wondered.

"You want anything?" I called out to her. "Brownie? Chocolate chip cookie?"

As she was shaking her head "no," I began sizing her up. Fifty, long gray hair pulled back in a ponytail, twenty pounds overweight, clothes casual but a bit upscale for a farm community. No wedding ring. It was tough to get an emotional read off her face. As the teenaged barista rang up my drink, I had her throw in the wafers with the rationale that dark chocolate is high in anti-oxidants. I'd read it somewhere. The major was taking a long sip from her drink as I returned to the table.

"Got what you wanted?" she asked. It was small talk, but not unfriendly.

"So, you were expecting someone older?"

"It's not a value judgment."

"And male?"

"I hadn't given it that much thought. I guess I'm just surprised. But then here we are."

"Well, a lot of magazine writers are a bit older," I said, "usually veterans who made it out of the newspaper business in time."

"How, exactly, did you come by the tape?" she asked.

"Let's just say we have a mutual friend." The major could tell I was avoiding the truth.

"Given that you're a reporter from a typical left-wing publication, and you have a recording that shouldn't exist in the first place, I'd hardly use the word 'friend.'"

"This may sound hard for you to believe, but the tape is safe with me." I let the "left wing" comment go.

"I would like to have it," she said. "And the copy it was made from. And the assurance that you're not planning to launch it on YouTube or some other privacy-depriving website."

"The assurance is not a problem. So far I'm the only one who's heard it besides my editor, and no one else ever will. As a matter of principle, I didn't duplicate the tape."

In the first five minutes of a meeting the major was reluctant to take, I'd failed to make her comfortable, failed to gain her confidence, failed to learn anything about her, and lost control of the interview before it even began.

"Why don't you grab your coffee and follow me," she said. "There's a place we can talk not far from here." When she got up to leave, I was struck by how tall she was. I imagined her in Afghanistan and how she must have stood out, not just as an American woman, but as an unusually tall American woman. She wasn't without feminine traits, but she was more of the classic tomboy, someone who could arm wrestle for a beer or lift her own bale of hay.

The old four-cylinder Corolla I was driving was no match for her F-150. She must have known I wouldn't make the last part of our drive and pulled into the visitor center at the Kickapoo Valley Preserve. I left my car in the parking lot and climbed into her truck.

"Eighty five hundred acres of paradise," she said.

"You live near here I take it?"

"Jug Creek Road. More like off the road, actually. Your car will be fine here."

"You mean nobody wants a '92 Corolla with 167,000 miles on it?

The major actually chuckled.

"Maybe I'll trade it in on something with royalties from the story."

"You're not afraid I'll send someone in to steal the cassette?"

"Are you thinking about it?"

"I am now." Her smile left me wondering whether she was kidding. With that, Grace turned to the east off Hwy. 131 onto Jug Creek Road. Except for a single lane bridge, the road was just wide enough for two passing vehicles, or one large tractor with a wagon full of hay. The road weaved dead center up a rugged valley passed a mix of organic alfalfa fields filled with cattle, and hillsides dense with virgin oaks, poplar, maple, and ash trees. About three-quarters of a mile in, Grace turned right past a crumbling wooden barn and onto an eroded two-track that wound its way halfway up the southern ridge.

"Your car might have made it," she said, as she shifted into a low gear, "or it might not."

"Why take the risk, right?" I sounded too cheerful, even for me. "Besides, it's good for me to see how you're living out here. You'd be a hard person to find."

Grace pulled to a stop in front of a small but charming log home. I'd not given much thought to where or how she might live before driving out, but she managed to exceed whatever expectations I didn't have. There was a shaded patch of lawn in front that descended into several terraced gardens filled with impatiens of all colors. The forest came within about thirty feet of the house. The ground cover included several kinds of woodland flowers, something we don't see any more near Chicago except in the manufactured wilderness patches in Lake Forest. I kneeled to smell a wild rose.

"They're native," she said. "But I admit to planting quite a few of them. The invasives are like the government," she said, "they've had their way with things for too long in places they don't belong."

"Invasives?"

"Invasive species. Garlic mustard. Spotted knappweed. Honeysuckle. Buckthorn. And now we've got the emerald ash borer from here to the

Mississippi. It doesn't take long before the invaders destroy indigenous species."

"You're talking about plants and trees?"

"At the moment, yes."

"Your home's beautiful." I wasn't being polite. Only an architect with respect for land could have built a retreat that blended so neatly into the hardwoods that it almost disappeared.

Grace invited me in and I was surprised that the living room had a vaulted ceiling, ten-foot windows, and a stunning view down the valley to the northwest. A tunnel of century old red oaks more than fifty feet high framed a path filled with bark chips and the occasional patch of Jacob's Ladder and Ginseng. The trail fanned wider in the distance to where an underground spring fed a small, algae-covered pond about a half acre in size. I'd never been to Afghanistan, but given what I knew of the place, it occurred to me that Grace Sommers had chosen to live as far from the war as she could find.

"You live here alone?" I asked.

"A friend shares it with me on weekends," she said, leaving the notion of 'friend' to my imagination. Same age, I thought, maybe a lover, definitely someone active with a passion for nature, but I had no idea whether the friend was male or female. It didn't matter, but I couldn't help being curious.

"The place fits me right now," she continued. "It takes about twenty minutes to get to work at the hospital in Viroqua, and out here, people are only as friendly as you need them to be."

The feeling of failure I'd had at the coffee shop was gone. Grace brought iced tea and we moved back to the front deck.

"You're off the grid here?"

"To a point, yes. We have solar hot water, enough wind power to make a difference, and the barn and greenhouse near the road are wired for emergency use but can get by on solar for a good seven or eight months of the year. You know about energy?"

"There's always a story breaking on something—wind, batteries, recaptured energy from the brakes on large trucks. I wouldn't call it a beat, exactly, but I keep my eye on it. The farmers in Germany are making almost as much money off solar power as they are off agriculture. And despite our heralded enlightenment, the US is way behind on monetizing alternatives."

Grace quit stirring her tea, and the silence was suddenly deafening. When she looked me in the eye, I could feel the huge gulf between us. It was more than distrust; we were very different people. She must have been afraid of the recording or she wouldn't have agreed to see me. Still, some part of her seemed to welcome an outsider, someone who didn't know her demons in a personal way. She held her gaze as if she was testing me. Was it something soldiers are taught to do when confronted by their captors? I wanted to tell Grace that I hadn't come to judge her, but I looked away instead.

"So we can keep talking like this, which I'd prefer, or you can tell me what you need," she said. "Afghanistan's a big subject and I'm not exactly an expert."

"You know the story I came for," I said. "I'm not here to talk about Taliban resurgence or the troop draw down."

"How do you talk about my story and not talk about the war?" As she raised her glass to her lips, her eyes seemed to burn a hole inside me. She wanted to divert me from my mission, but I would not let the controversy of war be her way out.

"Can we start with Belcharagh?" I asked. "Most of our readers know quite a bit about the war."

"People might think they do. But Afghanistan isn't Iraq or Syria. It's not Bosnia or Vietnam. It's not like other wars."

There was truth to what Grace was saying. History books are clear about Afghanistan. Ask the British. Ask an old Russian general. But I hadn't driven more than two hundred miles to listen to a former soldier use the war as a defense for her actions, or as something to hide behind. I wanted her story.

"Let's just start with Belcharagh," I said, bluntly. "Nothing else really matters."

\\\\

An entire surgical team arrived with the Wisconsin Air National Guard in January, 2004. Major Grace Sommers was one of four doctors. She'd returned to duty after losing a younger brother in the Pentagon attack on 9/11, but returning was something she later recalled as "a hasty and irrational decision." Grace had made the cutoff age by a couple of years, and her superiors saw her previous volunteer service on hotspot medical missions as a plus. She was no stranger to search and rescue, eating bad food, sleeping on a cot, or navigating diverse cultures. The emergency room at the Vernon County Hospital had also given Grace ample time to cut her teeth on accident victims, though the culprit was usually alcohol or meth, not landmines or IEDs. In the twelve weeks before she deployed, she'd had to triage seven teenagers after an ill-fated homecoming drive, she'd lost a bow hunter to a punctured esophagus, and she'd had to amputate Jacob Soder's left leg after he used it to un-jam the tight bearings on a horse drawn combine that was still attached to a skittish gelding.

Grace knew Afghanistan wouldn't be a picnic, but at least she wouldn't have spouses, siblings, and parents hanging on every word as their loved ones fought to stay alive in Viroqua's understaffed and underequipped ER. By the morning the earthquake hit northern Afghanistan, Grace had been on the base in Mazar-e-Sharif for almost nine months, long enough to live through "a winter so boring that it made a January in Wisconsin seem like paradise."

"We spent most of our time patching up insurgents," she said, "former Mujahideen who'd transferred their opposition from the Northern Alliance to the NATO-backed forces. A few Panjshiris. Most were probably Taliban at one time or another. It's hard to say. The locals joked that all a man had to do to survive when he saw trouble coming his way was to change the color of his turban. It was true then, it's true now. One of the mistakes the good guys make over and over is jumbling all the opposition together as Taliban when they're not. For a lot of people, especially in the north, they're just not *that* Muslim. Like the way I'm not *that* Christian. Until the Taliban extremists forced the issue in the 90s, a lot of Afghans were the type to celebrate Ramadan as long as it didn't interfere with something else. Just like I grew up going to the movies on Easter Sunday. Who the hell cares, especially when the main job is to put food on the table?"

"Extremists care."

"But that's my point. There aren't that many extremists. Politicians just say that to get elected. Mazer-e-Sharif is pretty quiet compared to Kandahar, or even Helmand Province, but the troubles in Helmand have more to do with fanaticism about finances than faith. They're producing more opium there than you get in all of northeast Burma or the Golden Triangle. It's not a bad way to make a living if you're Afghan."

"You're not opposed to opium production?" I asked the question with an incredulous tone and regretted it right away.

"Sure, as much as anyone else, but let's face it, the US government has a pretty long history of looking the other way when drugs are involved. You think Nancy Reagan got rid of drugs? Nope. Not a dent. It's big business, just like mining or oil, and somewhere along the line we've got our hand out like everyone else. For a farmer, it's supply and demand. Do you think we'd be growing organic tomatoes in Vernon County, Wisconsin, if there wasn't a demand at a premium price from affluent, white folks in Madison or Marin County? Unemployed coupon cutters might be dabbling in Afghan opium, maybe heroin, but I know they can't afford organic tomatoes. The question you should ask is why doesn't the US interrupt the opium supply chain? Why don't they stop the flow of weapons? Whether it's Bush, Obama, Ryan, or Trump, if they're letting it go, it's because some guy with power is making money off it. Ask the Saudis. Ask the French. Ask the Venezuelans.

As much as I wanted to put Major Sommers in a neat little box, I couldn't get a read on her politics. She was part lefty, part Libertarian, and yet cynically pragmatic like a cranky former Republican stewed in Ayn Rand.

"IEDs weren't much of a phenomenon in Afghanistan until after the surge in Iraq," she said. "During my time, I was treating more injuries from vehicle accidents and old Soviet landmines than from the war. That is, until the quake."

Bingo. Somewhere during the past couple of hours, she'd loosened up and was now anticipating a lot of my questions. I was taking notes furiously and only interrupted with the occasional hand motion suggesting she continue.

"Do you have any idea what a 7.6 is like?" she asked. I thought she would continue right away, but she really had directed the question at me, and paused to look me in the eyes. I noticed her left leg shaking, with the heel bouncing just above the surface of the wood deck.

"No." I put down my pen and pad. "I was in Santa Monica once when a four-point-something hit just a mile off the pier. It was three in the morning and I was asleep half-naked. When the bed started shaking I woke up, dove across the room and centered myself under the header of the bedroom door. But the quake was nothing, really, just enough to get the dogs barking."

She'd meant the question seriously, but she barely heard my answer.

"You okay?" I asked.

Her leg stopped abruptly and she looked at me quizzically. "Yeah, why?"

"So 7.6. No. I don't know what that's like. I've only seen pictures."

"Mazer's fairly flat," she said, "and our base had a lot of one-story, temporary buildings. Most of them were quick assembly structures made from a kit that uses molded Styrofoam logs covered in chicken wire and a quick dry plaster. Pretty ingenious, actually, because they're well insulated and weigh practically nothing if they collapse. When the quake hit, it kicked the shit out of all of us for about eighty seconds, but there were very few casualties on the base itself. Most of the heavy damage was done to the administrative offices. They were in the old commercial terminal, the same building the Soviets had used twenty-five years earlier when they took the same stupid pill we swallowed after 9/11. Anyway, the runway took some serious damage—large cracks in the asphalt, a few broken underground fuel lines. It took more than a week before supply planes could land so during the first couple of days, we were reduced to using helicopters. Most of us were pitching rubble by hand."

Her leg was shaking again, only this time she didn't try to stop it.

"The epicenter was much worse," she continued. "It was near a village about thirty kilometers up the dry riverbed from Maimana, a village that basically no longer exists."

"And you were called in for search and rescue?" I asked.

"Yes, and medical assist. The damage in Mazer-e-Sharif was manageable. Like I said, there weren't many serious casualties on the base, just structural damage on buildings that were worthless to begin with. The worst injury was a civilian mechanic from Richmond who got trapped under a hoist he was using to fix a jet engine. A couple of Tajik elders died in a six-story hotel that crumbled across the street from the Blue Mosque but that was off the base. The locals didn't see the quake coming any more than we did, but it wasn't their first rodeo either. They may not have the medical expertise we have but they know how to respond to crisis quickly and efficiently. Much better than we do. It comes from growing up with the uncertainty of conflict and loss."

"I can't imagine, really."

"What American can?" she asked. "We live a life of privilege and extraordinary ignorance. For most Americans, a crisis is not knowing how to pay off credit card debt."

"So you were called in. But not right away?"

"A couple of NGOs had offices in Maimana," she said. "They responded quickly, but it was almost two days before any word came back from Belcharagh."

"That's the village?" I asked.

"Yeah, about 1600 people," she said. "Most Afghan villages are inaccessible in the way we think of access, but that's because we're usually in a hurry. If you're using a camel, a mule, or walking, you can get pretty much anywhere. There is a road to Belcharagh, but about half of it involves driving either straight up or across the river, so it's not used during winter or the spring runoff when the water's high. At the time of the quake, the road was full of farmers headed to Maimana to sell their harvest. In less than a minute, they pretty much disappeared under landslides. By the time we flew in, I couldn't see a road anywhere."

"You came in why?" I asked. "At whose request?"

"If it had been up to me, we wouldn't have been there at all. Our mission as doctors was to provide medical treatment to American and NATO forces, not to rescue the enemy from a natural disaster."

"The enemy? I thought the north was friendly."

"Like I said, if you can figure out who's friendly and who's not, you'll end the war in a week. They all looked the same to me."

"You don't sound happy about the options you were given."

"We weren't given options. We were told to do the rescue. I followed my orders."

Grace took a deep breath as she rose from her chair. She hadn't asked for the rescue mission. She hadn't asked for my visit. Midday sun was warming the flowerpots on the railing of the deck. With her back to me, Grace busied herself by watering each pot in a slow, deliberate motion.

"So you were flown in at whose request?"

"One of the British NGOs worked out a deal with Afghan officials asking NATO forces to assist in emergency response. The humanitarians couldn't get through overland from Maimana, and whatever chance anyone there had for survival would be gone before they could reach it on foot. The river was running low enough to drive it, but huge parts of it had been diverted by the slides, or just buried under rock."

When Grace turned back toward me, she had a small, yellow flower pinched between the thumb and forefinger of her left hand. As if trying to connect with its beauty, its life force, she brushed each petal with her right forefinger. Yet her stern expression never changed. I made a note in the margin of my notebook: vulnerability, uniformity, order. There was no reason to smell the flower. Whatever answers Grace hoped for weren't there, and she pitched the flower over the deck. When she sat back down, she spread her legs and leaned forward with her forearms resting on her thighs. The feminine Grace was gone, replaced by a disciplined military officer.

"Our C.O. agreed to send our team in with the thinking that it would just be a couple of days and the goodwill gesture would outweigh the risks. A drive was impossible, but we covered the two hundred kilometers from Mazer in about ninety minutes. From the air, we scouted the damage at the school and the city offices. They were adjacent to each other."

"Boys? Girls? What kind of school?"

"Elementary school. Most kids don't get past sixth grade. The quake happened on a Saturday morning, so they were in school. I don't know the exact count, but at least seventeen or eighteen died when the building collapsed, including seven girls. Imagine, girls finally get the chance to go to school and then . . ."

Grace didn't finish her sentence. She paused for a moment, then excused herself and headed inside to make a call. I reviewed my notes, underlined a few remaining questions, sipped the last of my tea, and then decided to walk around. There was an apple tree just up the hill, and considering all the mildly obsessive landscaping around the house, I was surprised the tree was untended. The lower branches were dead and about half of the fall apples were rotting on the ground. A healthy perimeter of alfalfa was growing about twelve feet out from the trunk. The long blades were shaded, still damp from morning rain, and they didn't spring back into place when I walked around the tree. When I looked back, the trail of my footprints lacked intention. I picked an apple that was hanging low, took a bite and puckered up at the taste.

"Cooking apples," she said. "But I'm not much of a baker."

I turned, startled, and was trying to swallow but somehow managed to get out, "Well, who is?"

When Grace laughed, I realized for the first time how pretty she was. Her smile softened her, and I couldn't help thinking that life had taken things away from her, the things that had made her smile. Her innocence. Her hope. Even the kindness that happens in a place like Viroqua. I offered her a bite.

"Are you kidding me?" she said, her grin expanding. "No way I'm eating one of those."

She leaned over and picked up four fairly large apples, then handed me two.

"Whoever hits the pond first wins," she said.

"I'm not much of a thrower."

"That's two of us," she said. "I win, we're done talking. You win, I tell you the whole truth, and nothing but the truth."

Things had turned serious suddenly, and I didn't want to risk losing.

"Really, I can't throw," I said. I looked at the apples in my hands wondering how to get out of the contest when she made her first toss. It landed at least fifteen feet short of the pond.

"You're sure?" she asked. "You might win."

"I told you when I got here, you don't have to do this. Nobody's forcing you to talk to me."

Grace rolled up the sleeves of her cotton travel shirt. She had a tattoo I hadn't seen before, a small American flag on her right bicep. She wound up with a much bigger motion, drew backwards like a major league pitcher, and tossed her second apple. It was smaller, lighter, and it also fell short by several feet.

"I'll give you a free throw, just for fun." Grace winked at me, her spirit so playful I didn't want to disappoint her.

A large green apple dangled a bit beyond my reach, so I jumped and managed to grab it on the third try. I blew on it, polished it on my left sleeve, and then, sure that Grace was watching, I kissed the apple for luck. Grace had used the heel of her boot to draw a line across the wet alfalfa, so I decided to approach it with a few steps forward to give me momentum. When my throw landed with a splash, Grace smiled and patted my shoulder as if I'd just won a blue ribbon at a high school track meet. The contest was over, but it was too early to know who'd won.

"They played cricket in Mazer-e-Sharif," she said. "The British lost Afghanistan twice but they left behind roundabouts, paperwork in triplicate, soccer and cricket. You should read Kipling if you want to understand the place. It hasn't changed."

"How so?"

"It's a landlocked country. No harbor means no shipping, and not much trade. Plus, there's no rail system. So whatever comes in—anything that resembles the 21st century, that is—will be expensive. Out of their price range. Afghanistan was a crossroads at the time of the Silk Road, and most things that move from place to place today go the same way they did then. By mule or camel. It might not sound politically correct to you, but I'd call it primitive. Each valley is run like a different country, each with different leaders, sometimes a different language. Sometimes the people in the next valley are allies, sometimes they're not. It depends on what the issue is and who wants whatever they have. That's why it's so hard for a central government to really do much of what we consider governing. It's our problem, really, not theirs. I say let them have it however they want it."

"What about religion?" I asked.

"What about it?"

"Sharia can't be an easy way to live."

"Most Afghans never venture more than thirty or forty miles from their home," she said. "Most of them can't read. So it's hard to know how universal the Taliban's ideas really are. How much can be blamed on Islam? I don't know. I do know that patriarchy is alive and well, though it's hardly limited to Afghanistan. No woman has climbed higher than Secretary of State in the USA, and the three who have were working for men."

We'd made it back to the house, but Grace kept going, motioning me to the back of the house. The sun was sitting above the hills that run along the northwest end of the preserve.

"So you don't think we should be there?" I asked.

"I think we had every right to go in there and kick al-Qaeda's ass after 9/11. But Bush blew that. Even Obama couldn't get us out. And now we're doing the same lap dance that brought the Soviets to their knees. What, exactly, do we hope to accomplish there? We build a power grid, they blow it up. We build a bridge, they blow it up. We dangle foreign aid and promise infrastructure and security, but even we can't compete with corruption and opium profits."

The very last thing I'd wanted was a political discussion. I'd never studied Afghanistan, had no clue what I was talking about and didn't want to overstep my bounds as a journalist by offering a lame opinion I couldn't back up. Grace could tell I was out of my league before verbal combat began.

"I know you're here about the earthquake," she said. "But you can see that the war is part of the story, right? No war, no medical team. No medical team, no victims."

"I'm not sure I follow you. The victims of the earthquake would have been there whether you were in Mazer-e-Sharif or not."

"That's true. But if we hadn't been there, we wouldn't have gone to the rescue. Some Afghans would have died in the quake. Some would have become displaced. Some would have died later from cholera or hunger or dysentery. Even if the death toll had rivaled Haiti, no one would have read about it in the news."

"So you see yourself as a victim?" I asked.

"As much as they were, yes. Every soldier we send over there now is a victim if you ask me."

"Even if they're volunteering to go?"

"Of course. Some volunteer for patriotic reasons, especially after 9/11. But most soldiers need the paycheck."

More notes in the margin: Loss of faith in military and mission. Soldiers as victims.

"You can't put people in a war and expect them to make decisions everyone back home will agree with or understand one hundred percent of the time. It might be ideal, but it's not real," she said. "And if someone tells you it is, then they haven't been there. If a general says it's possible, it's because generals always have a scapegoat. They follow a rulebook that was written to favor the leaders. Look at Abu Ghraib. Karpinski takes the fall, Lynndie England goes to jail, and Donnie Rumsfeld hits the country club on the Maryland shore. How's that for patriarchy? What I'm saying is that if you're not there, how do you know what you'll do when a crisis hits? How does anyone know how she'll react under the pressure of war until she's there, until she's in a place with different attitudes, a different culture, a different God."

"So what happened in Belcharagh?"

The door was open. It was time for very direct questions. Grace motioned for me to sit with her on a bench carved from an oak trunk.

"Remember, it was the third day after the quake," she said. "It took two days for the NGOs to get word, then another to negotiate the deal, gear up, and fly in. We landed mid-afternoon. Anyone still alive in the fallen buildings was hanging by a thread. We were well equipped and immediately set up a temporary tent hospital on a dirt soccer field just a few feet from what had been the police station. We had two doctors, a young surgeon from a hospital in Green Bay and me. He and I had been in the same unit for a few months but rarely worked the same shift.

"Everyone was on edge because aftershocks were happening every couple of hours, and no one was sure what to expect. The last place anyone wanted to be was inside a poorly built structure of any kind. A second military helicopter arrived with a NGO team from Maimana and they began facilitating the basics: a food tent, latrines, and four-person tents for survivors. The villagers had heard the choppers and more than forty of the injured found a way to us within an hour. Most of them were mobile, but their injuries were severe—compound fractures, cuts down to the bone, dislocated limbs, internal bleeding, puncture wounds—just what you'd expect from a major earthquake. The nursing team started patching people up and got antibiotics flowing quickly. Men worked on men, women worked on women. There's always some good news, and in this case it was simple; the people who were showing up had injuries that were survivable. They'd managed to stop the bleeding on their own, and in some cases, had done a pretty good job with first aid. It was pretty easy to assume that anyone who was worse off was probably dead or dying.

"It was about an hour before sunset when we were finally able to start a recon of the village. Even the few buildings that looked intact weren't—everything was either rubble or on the verge of collapse. With the help of locals who weren't hurt and some who were simply ambulatory, we managed to find three survivors buried under crumbled homes and a handful of injured who wouldn't leave behind their dead relatives. One guy just sat in the rubble, staring at a row of tiny corpses, dead children he'd wrapped in bed linen. The three we got out were semiconscious, severely dehydrated, and two had wounds they weren't likely to recover from. We managed to get seven or eight people back to the makeshift hospital before dark and we performed two surgeries, both successful."

"Did most of the wounded survive?" I asked.

"Yes, actually. Only one died the first night, a little girl. I remember her because she was ethnic Hazara and everyone else was either Tajik or Uzbek. One of the police officers said her parents and siblings were already dead. Maybe he knew, maybe he didn't. It's hard to say if or how anyone actually knew anything."

"So you stopped searching at dark?"

"We didn't have a choice. There was no electricity, and other than the search lights on a couple of choppers, we were limited to whatever our generators could provide. We worked in what we called the hospital until after midnight, and by then it was quiet until sunrise."

"Where did you sleep?"

"Where did we sleep? Why does that matter?"

"I'm just trying to get a sense of what you were going through on a personal level. How you managed your own needs."

"I slept on the ground under the surgical tent. We had three nurses, and Dr. K. and I took turns monitoring the patients with whoever was awake. We tried to work it so everyone got at least three hours of sleep."

"Dr. K. was the other surgeon?"

"Karpfinger," said Grace. "We just called him Dr. K. Like I said, he'd been on the base for a while, but it was his first tour of duty, and his first time out of the States."

"That made it difficult for you?"

"That's a question?"

I nodded 'yes' while taking notes.

"No, there was nothing about Dr. K. that made anything difficult for me, or anyone else. We're trained to work as individuals and as part of a team. We're trained for emergency response, especially for those injured in battle. Dr. K. was consistent, calm, a good doctor. If he was freaked out by working in the dark with limited resources and no ability to speak the language to patients in a fucking cold tent in the middle of a war zone after a devastating earthquake, he wasn't showing it any more than the rest of us. Is that what you mean?"

"Yeah," I said. "I'll make a note that he wasn't freaked out." Her description had reset the bar in the tension between us. "I'm sorry. That wasn't fair of me. It had to be hell over there."

"We're military doctors. We're trained for the worst of the worst. Burns, open gut wounds, internal injuries, loss of limbs. It's never pretty."

"Couldn't his testimony have exonerated you?"

"He told the truth. Dr. K. didn't see what happened."

"But he was there."

"Yes. He was there the same way the Army boy's club was there when Pat Tillman was killed by friendly fire. But the difference is, we didn't cover it up like they did. Isn't that the right thing to do?" Grace was angry, but something had shifted, and the more we talked, the more she seemed to want her story told. War and patriarchy, yes. But there was also duty, loyalty, and honor.

"You want to keep going?" I asked.

"You want to give me the recording?"

To my dismay and immediate regret, I giggled. My own nerves were coming through, but it somehow made me human to her. I put my pen down and took a deep breath. Something on my face betrayed me. What next? I thought. How far did I want to take it?

"It's hard." Grace rose from her chair and stretched, then intersected her fingers and cracked her knuckles. "You're asking about the worst few days of my life. I'm sure you'd feel the same way if you'd been there."

"I don't know how I'd feel." I was intimidated by Grace towering over me, and my anxiety came through in questions that were suddenly sympathetic. "Like you said earlier, who does, right? Who knows what's possible in a war zone or after an earthquake? What I do know is that people should hear your side of the story, Grace."

"I told my story at the trial," she said. "I'm not sure why you think there's something else to say."

\|\|\|\|

After more than two years of legal wrangling and delays, the trial had taken place at Fort Hood, Texas. Testimony spanned four weeks with two military appointed attorneys doing little to defend Grace. Her team argued that her actions in the field were the result of battle fatigue induced by the stress of war and natural disaster. In other words, the defense rested on "temporary insanity." The political left saw Grace as the poster child for everything that was wrong with the Bush foreign policy. The right kept its mouth shut, not wanting to do anything to weaken what had already become a waning struggle against the Taliban and al-Qaeda. The media was limited to what the Army wanted them to know, which in a military trial isn't much. And late night comedians couldn't find anything funny about dead civilians in Afghanistan. Other than pundits battling it out on Fox and MSNBC, no one had much to go on. When the sentence came down, *The Washington Dispatch* labeled Dr. Grace Sommers the "Lieutenant Calley of our time." Victory, for Grace, meant agreeing not to dispute the so-called facts of the trial, a court martial conviction, a dishonorable discharge, a suspended sentence, no more time in the brig, and a three-year suspension of her license to practice medicine. Major Doctor Grace Sommers was free to go.

\\\\

What would have happened if it had been a man, I wondered. Was Grace really a victim too?

"There's always something else," I said.

"And you know this because?"

"I know this because I've got a family and a life of my own. I've got a serial adulterer for a mother, a father who hides his vodka inside a sealed garden hose, a brother who pretends to be straight whenever he visits home, and a sixty-eight-year-old uncle who still smokes pot every day."

Finally. Grace was laughing. Laughing hard.

"You want me to continue?" I had a smirk on my face and she could tell I was just getting going.

"Yes, please . . ."

"I had an abortion when I was twenty-seven, but won't tell a soul. My boyfriend is working through transgender issues and I love him either way. I slept with my cultural anthropology professor when I was a senior at Northwestern but still got a B- in his class, I'm afraid to go to a gynecologist—always—and I've lied about my age since I turned thirty. So yeah, I think there's something else. There's always something else."

Good old boys like to break out the whiskey to celebrate a bonding experience. For Grace and me, it was a move to the kitchen table and a very cold bottle of Pinot Grigio. I didn't know there was such a thing as a "good" Pinot Grigio, but Grace assured me (with a wink) that the eight dollar bottle of Mario Albinoni's she'd picked up at *Trader Joe's* in Madison was as good as they come. She unscrewed the top, filled two plastic tumblers half full, invited me to use my hand-held tape recorder for the first time, and took me back to Belcharagh.

\\\\

Grace was just getting going.

"On our second day we were underway before the sun came up," she said. "A child, he couldn't have been more than eight or nine, got past our Marine guards and came running into the surgical tent. He was shouting, speaking Farsi so fast that Walid had to slow him down."

"Who's Walid?"

"Our interpreter."

Grace took an unhealthy gulp of wine.

"I'd had my three hours sleep so a Marine guard, Walid, and I went with the boy to the east end of the village where the dirt road ended abruptly in a box canyon. It turned out that the boy's older brother—he called him Masood and said he took the name in honor of the dead freedom fighter—was standing on a rocky outcropping above the river, threatening to jump. The boy told us his brother had lost his young wife in the earthquake. Masood looked like anyone heartbroken by loss, and he kept repeating the same thing, over and over. 'He has no future,' said Walid. 'He says the only thing he has to live for is now gone.' I'd had some training in psychology, but the idea of talking down an illiterate Afghan teenager who'd lost his wife in the earthquake was beyond my skill set."

I could feel the wine, but still made a note that Grace had used the word "illiterate" in the pejorative. He may have been unable to read, but it was still an odd detail to throw in about a guy who was about to kill himself. It was also a good cue for me to slow down on the vino, so I asked Grace for a glass of water. As she filled it, she talked about how she and her partner had started out drinking water straight from the spring near the guesthouse. They'd never become sick, but they got cold feet when someone over near Lancaster sued the power plant for what they said were chemicals leaching into their well. Why take the risk? They'd installed an ozone filtration system about a year earlier. It was hard to know how much Atrazine was in the ground water, Grace said, and besides, the coffee tasted better since they'd switched over.

"So Masood was on the edge?" The diversions seemed to make Grace more comfortable with me, but I wanted to get back to her story.

"Not for long," she said, with unguarded sarcasm and a creepy grin. "Before we could do anything, he was just another dead Afghan slumped over the boulders along the dry riverbed below us."

Grace took a slow sip of wine and seemed to swirl it around in her mouth before swallowing.

"So you left him there, on the rocks?"

"We returned to the village. When you've got hundreds of dead bodies everywhere, what's another one? We went back to work on trying to save the living."

"And the boy?"

"Walid stayed with him for a while. I'm not sure what they talked about. Your tone makes it sound like I should have done something else," she said.

"Like you said, I wasn't there."

"There was no way to know how to help that boy, or his kid brother. What he saw was horrible; it had been a horrible few days, which in the life of most Afghans is like saying "situation normal, all fucked up." It wasn't the first time he'd seen death. It wasn't the first time he'd lost someone he loved. That he and his brother had survived the earthquake was already a miracle in a place that has no miracles."

Grace refilled her wine glass and topped off mine. I took a very light sip. If I'd learned anything over years of interviewing, it's that truth often shows up during silences. Grace ran her thumb over the embossed label on the bottle, pausing to rub each letter as if connecting with her thoughts. Her breathing was more labored and her leg had begun shaking again. She turned the bottle and became lost in the ingredients, the warnings to pregnant women, the percentage of alcohol by volume, until she found herself back in Belcharagh. Then she slowly peeled the moist label from the glass, and the layers she'd used to protect herself began to fall away.

"My radio went off," she said. "Dr. K. and the others were down river, at the school. They found survivors."

\|\|\|\|

By the time Grace and Walid arrived at the school, several local men, including the mayor, had already descended on the ruins of what had been a two-story building constructed against the stone wall of the canyon. They were helping four Marines pull away wood beams, strands of handmade rope, classroom debris, and huge slabs of cement wall. Just how makeshift the building had been was hard to determine, but it couldn't have held up long against the quake. Thirty-seven children had been in the building on Saturday morning. In addition to those known dead, six children and two teachers were still listed as missing at the time American forces arrived. When Grace had surveyed the school from the air a day earlier, she and the pilot had concluded that a survivor would be hard to find in the rubble. They were wrong.

"The Marines wanted to take charge, but under our rules of engagement, the mayor had authority. By the time I got there, he and the sergeant were squared off in a shouting match over how to proceed." Grace was fully engaged. Her leg was shaking again and I sensed she was reliving the rescue attempt as she spoke. "Their interpreter couldn't keep up, and each side seemed to think that saying things louder would somehow make it easier to understand. We could hear faint cries coming from under the rubble, and the fight was apparently about whether to try to move slabs and debris or find a way to tunnel to the victims. Dr. K. did what any good doctor would do, he ignored the argument and wormed his way into the maze. We were both trained in search and rescue, but neither of us could have imagined the chaos we were part of in Belcharagh. He was roped and had a helmet on, and as he squirmed his way in, I could see his feet just above the surface of the debris. I called in to him. He said there was at least one survivor, it sounded like a girl, but he couldn't see her and didn't know if she was alone. He could tell by the shafts of light streaming through that there was another possible way in just a few feet to his left. Since I outranked the sergeant, I told him to back off and let the mayor have his way. The mayor wasn't about to listen to a woman, and even though I'd sided with him, he seemed annoyed that the sergeant backed off at my command versus his.

"I had two small packs with me," she said. "The larger one wouldn't fit inside but I was able to re-position a small first aid hip pack across my chest. The sergeant helped me rig a harness and rope and I crawled into the opening Dr. K. had found. Have you ever been inside the rubble of a two story building?"

"You're kidding, right? I did some spelunking over near Platteville once, but earthquake rubble? Not many people have that experience."

"Exactly," Grace replied. "How many people have? How many people know what it's like? How many know the fear that comes from putting your life on the line? It's not a cave. It's a maze, an unstable maze that goes off in all directions like pick up sticks. And both Dr. K. and I had entered it a good twelve to fifteen feet above the ground. The quake had re-routed a lot of things, including a spring that had been diverted above the cliff. I could hear water coming inside and as I got lower, I could feel two things that didn't bode well for survivors: it was wet and cold."

"Could the two of you see each other?"

"I could see Dr. K.'s headlamp flashing here and there, and a few shafts of light from above helped to silhouette the obstacles and gave me a better sense of how to move through it. We could hear each other, and Dr. K. had managed to get to the girl. She was about fourteen, maybe fifteen. Her hip and thigh appeared fractured but Dr. K. couldn't see any compound fractures or external bleeding. Still, she screamed when he tried to move her. Walid shouted down that she wasn't screaming in pain; she was screaming because there were others still alive. She didn't want to leave them behind. She kept screaming about her brother."

"So you were climbing down head first?" I asked. "I'm just trying to get a picture of it."

"Yeah, down and sideways. But you're also trying to test your weight with every move so you don't cause more of a collapse."

"And what are the Marines doing at this point?"

"I have no idea, really. I sure as hell didn't want another body following me. I didn't want to put any more weight in there than needed to be there, and there was no reason to risk another life. The sergeant and I could hear each other, and I told him over and over to keep the area clear and wait for my instructions. If anyone was going to follow, I wanted Dr. K. on my tail. But he had a victim of his own."

"Did you ever manage to stand upright?"

"I did, yes. I was about twelve feet down when I found a fairly large opening. I maneuvered so I was hanging on the edge of a big slab of concrete. It was lodged in enough to hold my weight and I hung there for a moment until I was steady, then I let go. I dropped another two feet or so and sank immediately into several inches of mud. Freaked me out, to be honest with you, because I couldn't tell it was mud until I was in it. The spring had turned the whole damn ground into mud. I pulled off my headlamp and used it like a flashlight, spinning it around the opening. That's when I saw the other two."

"You're talking about the two who died?"

"Teacher and student. They were almost on top of each other. The teacher was about fifty or so, hard to say. He was definitely alive, but God knows why the earthquake hadn't killed him. The quake was only half a reason to die I guess, the four days that followed were the other half. But he was barely hanging on. He didn't speak, had a very slow pulse, and his legs were bent almost completely behind his back. It would have taken a pretty good sized crane to lift the slab off his midsection and that wasn't gonna happen."

"The boy?"

"I felt bad about the boy, really bad. The weird thing is that he was probably ambulatory. His legs didn't look broken, but his left arm was completely wedged under the teacher's back, which was under a concrete slab not to mention the several tons of rubble from above just waiting for a reason to dislodge and fall. If I could have freed him, he might have been able to walk. It's just a guess, but the teacher might have been holding him when the floors caved in, it might even have happened during an aftershock. The worst part, though, was the shaft of wood that had punctured all the way through his torso just above his right kidney. It was sticking out both sides of his body, and in his semi-standing position, it meant that for almost four days he'd have felt unbelievable pain every time he'd tried to lean in any direction.

"There wasn't much bleeding from the puncture; there almost never is unless you try to remove it. But these were big problems, and not surviv-able. First, the only way to move him was to spend a week moving rubble from above him by hand, and doing it at the risk of crushing him acci-dentally. Or we could have amputated his arm. Second, it appeared he had some really nasty internal wounds from the fall. His fever was spiking, he was hypothermic from the mud and cold nights, and both of them were dehydrated, delirious, and really, I can't say it any other way, they were barely alive."

"You said in your testimony that you knew they weren't going to make it."

"I did, yes. And anyone who doesn't believe that wasn't there. I don't even know what had kept them going. Hope? It had been nearly four days!"

"Neither could talk?"

"If they could, they didn't. Walid yelled down to them several times, but I never heard either of them try to speak. I could hear the girl speaking to them in Farsi, mostly in a whisper, but I have no idea what she was saying. I heard the word Allah more than once. It might have been a prayer."

"According to the trial transcripts, you tried to free the boy," I said. "But on the audio tape I was sent, you contradict that. Which story is true?"

"The simple answer is, if I could have freed him, I would have. You have to understand—the space I was in was too small to get another body in there. I could barely move myself. I'm a strong woman, but even if the sergeant had been in there, or Dr. K., we couldn't have freed the boy. There wasn't room for a wedge, not even a tire iron would have worked. In the trial, the prosecutor asked whether I'd done everything I could to get the boy out of the rubble. I said yes, which wasn't a lie."

"So the survivor, Dr. K.'s patient, she was the only witness?"

"Using the term loosely, I suppose. I could barely see her, and I couldn't see Dr. K. at all. Who knows what she saw. But think about what you're asking me. Think about what you or anyone else would have done."

"I also heard you say on tape that the teacher was as good as dead. That killing him was the right thing to do."

"It was the right thing to do. And I said that during what I thought was a private discussion with my legal counsel. I also said that as a doctor, the most merciful thing I could do was to kill him. To put him out of his misery."

"And in court?"

"In court was a different story. My lawyer convinced me that truth was my enemy. Was it? I didn't think so. But it's a given that if I'd told the truth, I wouldn't be sitting here with you now. I'd be in solitary confinement somewhere in Kansas."

"So what did happen, Grace? What's the truth?"

"Have you ever read C.S. Lewis?" she asked.

"No," I said. "I wasn't planning to."

"That's up to you," she said, "but there's an essay of his called "*Meditation in a Tool Shed*." And I think it's relevant if you want to understand. In the essay, Lewis is standing in a small, dark tool shed and there's a beam of light coming through the window. He says you can look at the beam one way and see the beam of light with particles and dust in it, but when you look along the beam of light, you start to see a different reality. When you look along it, you see through the cracks where the light comes through, and suddenly you're looking at trees and a horizon that stretches out into the distance. And you start to see that what's real from one perspective may not be real from another. Lewis argues that both views of the shaft of light are valid ways of looking at things, but that both reflect a different reality."

"And that applies how, exactly?" I asked.

"It applies because our realities are different. There's no way for you or anyone in a court martial here in America to see what I saw at that time. It's not possible. You weren't standing up to your ankles in mud underneath fifteen feet of earthquake rubble listening to the moans of a dying boy with a shaft of wood bulging through his stomach, or watching the heartbeat leave a man bent in half for three and a half days with his legs crushed under his own torso."

Grace pushed her chair back and went to the window, disappearing into the shadows of the living room. I felt a tear on my cheek and realized that she'd left me in Afghanistan. She'd left me in the mud. I was surrounded by the chaos. I could hear the gurgles of two contorted bodies, and I wondered when their souls had departed. I had the syringe of morphine in my hand. I found a vein and plunged the needle into the bend near the child's elbow, and squeezed the liquid in until the syringe was empty and the boy's tiny body sagged. The pressure of fighting to stay alive, fighting to do something that would end in failure, that pressure was released, and a peaceful expression came to the boy's face. When he was gone, I removed the shaft of wood from his torso and let his blood flow. I watched the teacher's eyes, searching for some acknowledgement of my actions, some kind of judgment one way or another. But it never came. I rolled up the sleeve on his right arm and pushed a second syringe into a tight vein in his wrist. The breathing I could barely hear was suddenly gone. I used my thumb to close his eyes, one at a time.

\\\\

Grace returned from the shadows. She could see my tears, but they only seemed to make her more defensive, as if she felt entitled to bear her guilt alone. She asked me if there was something else. Was there a reason for her to continue the telling? My welcome had run out, her tone was clipped, and whatever pleasantries we'd found during our hours together were gone.

"Do you think I need you to help me relive it?" she asked. "I see the boy in every boy I treat, in every child I see as I drive to and from work. I see his face in the Amish kids as they sling their books over their shoulder on the way to their schoolhouse. The old teacher is every man and every woman I encounter every day. When the earthquake hit, he did what a teacher does, Afghan or American. He tried to save a boy's life. He tried to cradle him and take the pressure off the terrible fall. I close the teacher's eyes every night before I close my own."

Grace began picking up glasses from the table. Mine was half full but she moved it to the sink. I turned off my recorder, put my pen deliberately in the sheath inside my case and organized the files of paper I had out, stacking them with more attention to detail than I usually give such things. I knew there was more, I wanted more, but Grace was volatile, and I was no match for the uncertainty I felt about another question, another answer. The Doctor in Grace had shown me all the humanity that drives people to healing, even the courage to risk her own life for others. But the Major in Grace had learned to live by order and organization, command, and rules of engagement. Everything was crisp and deliberate once again, even the way she re-corked the bottle of wine. She pressed her blouse with the palms of both hands, securing it neatly into the waist of her pants, and then wiped down the sink with a sponge until every last smudge was gone.

"Will that be all?" she asked, her posture perfect, but her right hand squeezing hard, then harder on the sponge. She was oblivious to the water dripping near her feet. I didn't feel a delay, but her sense of time was now different from mine and she barked, "I asked you, will that be all?"

I didn't answer, and we sat silently on the ride back to my car. The moon had disappeared and a light drizzle had begun to fall. I became distracted by the repetition of her wiper blades. When we pulled into the parking lot, Grace eased her truck behind the Corolla, shining her bright lights enough for me to find my way. Goodbye might have been easy at sunset, but now, in the darkness, it was awkward.

"Wait just a minute, if you will," I said.

I fumbled with my keys, retrieved them from a puddle near the left rear tire, then took forever to find the right one. I could feel her watching me as I tossed my bag into the back seat, then climbed into the front with my legs still hanging out the door. I had to start the car to eject the cassette, and I wondered if she knew what I was up to. The plastic case was cracked, but the compulsive in me had to insert it, and close it carefully. The rain had picked up and I could feel cool drops running down my back as I walked to the driver's side of her truck. She rolled the window down, but only half way. I passed the tape in to her and she grabbed it quickly as if it would stall some hunger she'd felt for years.

"Thanks, Grace. I'll be in touch." I said it just to say something, knowing that we'd never speak again. Knowing I could always find her on Jug Creek Road, or in the ER of the small town hospital. Knowing she wouldn't heal anytime soon, not in this lifetime. Not in this lifetime.

MOSQUITO LAKE

"**DEAD GIRL. 1991. FOUND HER** out by the river."

I'd only known Nadine for a couple of hours, but she had a knack for blunt answers.

"Naked too," she said. "No getting around it—the girl was molested."

By contrast, her husband Doc wouldn't have put it the same way. Doc liked knowing things the way a therapist does, but without the devotion to secrecy. It was a small town, and Doc had a reputation for bending the truth. I'd struck up a friendship with him a few years earlier while doing a documentary for a cable television channel. In a town with limited restaurant options, I'd learned not to turn down a dinner invitation. What began as a social get together, became an assignment when I asked a simple question intended as small talk: Had anyone ever been murdered in Haines, Alaska?

Doc began to answer with a fib, "not in anyone's recent memory." Then he smiled and said, "none that anyone's been caught for." Doc had a way of making history he didn't care for seem like it had never happened. But there was no getting around the way his wife Nadine blurted out the truth. Someone had been murdered, and it was recent enough that no one in town had forgotten about it.

"The killer's out there, Doc, you know that as well as anyone! Nadine suspected her husband of not saying what was really on his mind. Perhaps he was keeping a secret. "The girl had parents. She had plenty of friends, but there's plenty of creeps around here too. And, of course, there was the person who left her body in the tidal wash near the Chilkoot River. Same as the killer? Who knows."

"At least a thousand of the twenty five hundred people living in the borough were in Haines at the time," Doc replied. "We could all be suspects."

"The killer's still here most likely," Nadine said. "Probably someone I know. Maybe works here in town. Might be that widower that found her."

"So he left the body near the bridge?" I asked.

"Who said the killer was a he?" countered Doc. Doc did seem to know more than he was letting on. After all, he was the closest thing the village had to local law enforcement at the time. Before Doc could continue, Nadine put down her Chianti and punched out the details like it had happened yesterday.

"She was seventeen. A good kid. Good in gymnastics and had been training for the biathlon with her mom for more than a year. Olympic bound if you ask me. That girl could shoot the headlight out of a moving snow machine and she wasn't afraid to run the trails around here any time of year. A grizzly couldn't a caught that girl once she was up to speed."

"He asked about the killer," said Doc.

"I'm gettin' to that!" Doc was used to Nadine's raised voice, but it still rattled him. I watched him fuss with the frayed edge of the tablecloth, peeling away a loose thread.

"The girl was raped!" she said. "It ain't like she was killed by a woman. Doc knows that better than anyone."

"Why is that?" I asked.

"Because he was the first one there after that oddball found the body. A town this size doesn't have a full time medical examiner on the payroll. Just Doc."

"Damn it, Nadine. I really don't wanna remember the girl that way. Raped. I was her doctor for cryin' out loud. She was so pretty and full of hope. Heck, I still treat her brother—saw him yesterday." Doc had been mopping up tomato sauce with a piece of homemade bread for a while now, but his emotions were getting the better of him. I tried to keep my eyes on Nadine, but Doc was so nervous we both noticed him twist the corner of the tablecloth into a tight braid. His hands never stopped moving.

"It had to be difficult," I said. "We can talk about it another time if you'd like."

"No time like the present!" Nadine took another hearty sip of her wine and glared at Doc as if he was on trial. What did Doc know that he wasn't telling her? "You're the one who wanted to be a doctor, hon. Some things come with the territory."

Some things, sure, but Doc hadn't signed up for examining a seventeen-year-old murder victim, and the pain of the girl's death still haunted him.

\\\\

A late season salmon fisherman named Bob Priestly had found the naked body of seventeen-year-old Cassidy Sparks in an eddy near the mouth of the Chilkoot River. It was just under the bridge where the clear fresh snowmelt meets the muddy salt water of the Lynn Canal. Priestly couldn't see the girl's head, but her ankles were tied tight just above her hiking boots with what looked like thick white nylon rope—the kind that pretty much everyone in Haines would use for rafting, fishing, sailing, or tightening the tarp over their winter firewood. If it hadn't been for a strong October wind coming from the southwest, the body might have floated all the way to Juneau . . . or Japan. Instead, it was twirling slowly in the eddy, tangled with seaweed, face submerged in the brackish brown water.

Priestly was too upset to check on the body himself. He'd been a wreck after losing his sawing job when the lumber mill closed. And since his wife's death from breast cancer, Priestly had become so reclusive that no one but his Wheaten Terrier had heard him speak for months. The sight of a dead girl's blue body all bound up had startled him so badly that he actually ran to his Toyota pickup and drove the seven miles to Haines faster than he'd ever driven before. He parked at the Totem gas station, and then used the pay phone to make a collect call to the state trooper's office in Juneau. The supervisor, Officer Riley Carpenter, told Priestly to sit tight at the gas station and tell no one. On any other day, that would have been easy for Priestly. But the whole episode had made him feel like he was living outside his body. He couldn't control himself.

"Change for a dollar?" he asked.

Louella Houak, the forty-nine-year-old matriarch of Totem Gas, bit her lip and squinted her eyes as she opened the register. Priestly was not her favorite customer. In fact, no one wanted to serve Bob Priestly.

"Quarters and dimes, please."

As she was digging for change, Louella noticed that Priestly's hands were shaking.

"Whatever's for the machine," he said. "I just need a Coke, and I found a dead body over near the Chilkoot."

Louella had heard a lot of stories over the years. During the off-season, her station was the only one open between Haines and Mosquito Lake, the last stop before the Canadian border. Whether folks wanted gas or gossip, Louella was the only game in town. People used her station as the local hard drive of information, and on any given day, Louella had a conversation with a good twenty percent or more of the locals.

Her weight, adult onset diabetes, an alcoholic husband, and a bad case of gout were not enough to rattle Louella. Very little could. But two things had now come between her and the routine of a quiet late October afternoon, and she wasn't going to miss the opportunity for some excitement. First, everyone knew that Priestly hadn't uttered a single word in months so *something* had surely happened to rock his boat. Second, there'd never been a murder in Haines before—and she wasn't too sure there'd been one now. But if there was, she wanted to be on the scene.

"Dead body?" she said.

Priestly was pacing now, swigging on his cola, and afraid to make eye contact.

"Girl. Teenager. Her feet are tied, but I couldn't see her face because she was floating upside down. She's dead all right."

"But you're not sure?"

"Maybe I'm sure. Yeah, I'm sure. Nobody swims in the Chilkoot, Louella. Especially not this time a year."

"Then maybe we should go have a look," she said, "just in case. Coulda been a prank, this close to Halloween and all."

Priestly wasn't sure. "Troopers told me to stay put," he said. "Riley Carpenter said they are gonna send somebody over from Juneau right away on the ferry."

"But what if they could use our help," said Louella. "Maybe someone should be watching the body to make sure it doesn't float away. You know the currents around here."

"You got a point," said Priestly.

"The ferry's four hours, maybe four and a half with that wind," Louella informed him. "Either way, we ain't waitin' that long." As Louella grabbed her heavy jacket, she yelled out to Phil Lightfoot, her part-Tlingit half brother who'd been banging the head of a screwdriver on the carburetor of a snow machine.

"Get your coat on, Phil. You're comin' with me and Priestly up to the Chilkoot before it gets too dark to see."

"Huh?" Since his mining job as a blaster, Phil's hearing was shot. Louella tossed his old Harley jacket near his feet and motioned for him to come along. Phil threw his screwdriver into a bucket, grabbed his keys, and gave Louella the same "I hate my sibling" look he'd been perfecting for thirty-five years.

"Maybe we should call Doc?" said Priestly.

Priestly might have been an odd, old recluse, but Louella knew a good idea when she heard one. She phoned Doc at his office and got him just as he was closing up. There wasn't much reason for him to work past four this time of year, and when he heard the story (embellished just a bit by Louella who indicated the deceased might have her head stuffed in a crab pot), Doc phoned Nadine and let her know he'd be late for supper. No reason to rattle her yet, he thought.

In a town the size of Haines, it wasn't more than two minutes before Doc made the rendezvous at the Totem. Everyone was too independent to share a ride, so one Subaru and three American-made pickup trucks in various states of disrepair headed up to the mouth of the Chilkoot. Phil brought along his hunting dog, Moosekiller, a nine-year-old black Labrador with gray whiskers that blew back against his chin as he hung his head out the passenger window. Even though this was Priestly's find, Louella led the caravan.

More than ninety minutes had passed since Priestly discovered the body, time enough for the tide to leave the body further exposed against the bridge abutment. Moosekiller was the first to reach her. His barking was enough to capture the attention of two salmon fishermen about three hundred yards upstream. They saw the commotion, packed it in, and headed downstream to watch.

Six people and a dog had a good look at the backside of the body before Doc suggested the obvious.

"We can think this over as long as we want, but this girl is dead."

\\\\

By now it was clear that my innocent question about murder had put Doc in a strange mood with our flashback to 1991. He'd been lost in his thoughts while twirling a forkful of spaghetti on his spoon when Nadine interrupted him. Even though she hadn't been to the Chilkoot that day, she'd heard his story enough times to make it her own. While Doc had a knack for avoiding the truth, Nadine seemed less concerned and wasn't opposed to creating her own version. She had a wicked imagination that could feed off a handful of details.

"Cassidy's uncle," she said, "they call him Toad. That knucklehead has half a screw loose. I still think it coulda been him that did it with all his pot smoking and what not."

"This Toad is still around?" I asked.

"Toad used to drive the snowplow on the highway between here and the border. Still does, but we don't see him in town more than once or twice a year, usually only if he's binging over at Antlers Tap. He lives by himself up near the lake. Gets by like most folks that live subsistence."

"Half the valley lives subsistence," said Doc. "That doesn't mean he killed the girl."

Doc was right. I'd visited Haines dozens of times, enough to know that most folks in the borough lived off the land one way or another. It was practical to a point, and most year-round Alaskans considered it a source of pride. The area had enough moose and salmon to feed entire families, and the summer growing season was short but productive, with long hours of daylight. There were plenty of tomatoes and beans for canning. Except for wild blueberries, fruit was in short supply, but if someone could hit the fireweed blossoms at the right time, there'd be enough syrup to make the winter pancakes and oatmeal seem like meals made in heaven. The "Fireweed Syrup and Pancake Brunch" each February was still the largest fundraiser of the year for the Russian Orthodox chapel near the edge of the old Army fort.

"I'm not sure why you insist that Toad's the killer," said Doc. "What'd the man ever do to you?"

"To me? Nothing. But when he was a kid, he used to shoot his slingshot at bald eagles out on the river road. What kind of bonehead does that to the national bird?"

"Norma Schwartzman, for one," said Doc. "I hear she even eats them. And besides, it's not like we got an eagle shortage."

Doc was right again. Thousands of bald eagles feast in the open waters of a five-mile stretch of Chilkat River every autumn. Forget midair intercourse rituals or their skill in taking out unsuspecting chum salmon. To most of the locals (including Toad and Norma) they're mangy, lazy birds of prey with all the charm of turkey vultures gliding over the upper Mississippi River.

"What did eagles have to do with Cassidy's death?" I asked.

"Nothing," said Doc and Nadine in unison.

"I'm just sayin' that some folks are nuts enough to eat the damn birds is all." Nadine seemed dismayed that Doc talked right over her. She tensed up as if planning a quiet retaliation. When Doc patted her on the shoulder, she shrugged him off and crossed her arms defensively.

"There was nothing to link Toad to Cassidy's death in '91, and there's nothing to link him now," said Doc. "Cassidy was killed by a drifter."

As if on cue, Nadine spilled her half-filled glass. Blood red Chianti rolled over the pristine white tablecloth and squarely into Doc's lap. Doc didn't move, he just stared into the random flames lapping against logs in the woodstove. His mind was already back in 1991.

\\\\

By the time Alaska's finest had shown up, Doc and Phil had dragged the body up to the road. Using his power as an elected official, Doc had made the decision to move her when the receding tide exposed her bare blue bottom.

"Days are short, Riley. We had to get her out of there before dark."

"So you moved her from where, exactly?" Riley was so matter-of-fact about everything that Doc felt reassured.

"She was down by the abutment. Priestly found her." At the mention of his name, Bob Priestly took two steps forward from the darkness, lowering his head in fear as if the killer might rise up from the water's edge. Riley pointed his penlight into the distance but the light fell off short of the water.

"Tell him, Priestly. Tell him what you found."

Doc had known Priestly for decades. He'd cared for the man's wife when she was dying. The soothing quality of Doc's voice gave everyone a sense of security.

"Seaweed had her wrapped up good." Priestly removed his cap and ran his fingers through his thick hair. He was trying to recall the details. Then he wrapped his arms around his stiff neck and snapped his head left to right, twice.

"I couldn't see much of her. Enough to know it was a body floating out there."

But they could see everything now—her body naked except for an old pair of hiking boots and gray wool socks tight against her bloated calves. The headlights from Phil's truck cast a long beam of bright light across her body and the feet of the assembled crowd. Cassidy's cool blue eyes were stuck wide-open with ice already formed around her lashes and lips. Several of her fingers were frozen together, and her hair was stiff enough with ice to break right off with the touch of a hand.

"If I didn't know better, I'd think she'd been out cross-country skiing," said Phil. "Crusty hair and all."

"What girl skis in hiking boots you idiot!" Louella smacked him hard on the shoulder for disrespecting the dead.

"How long has she been lying here on the road?" Riley wrote everything down in a small ringed notebook. Though it limited his ability to ask questions, he had the odd but efficient habit of holding the penlight in his mouth as he took notes.

"Maybe thirty-five, forty minutes," said Louella.

Louella was holding the nylon rope that had bound Cassidy's legs and swirled it a bit too wide as she talked, the result, she would later tell Doc, of her "abundance of nerves that day." It would have been fine but she accidentally smacked "Officer Riley Carpenter" as he was writing. Riley glared at her, the penlight pointing straight at her shamed expression.

"I take full responsibility," she added. "It was me who told 'em to drag her up on the road. No way I was gonna let that beautiful girl float off into the darkness. Not this time of year."

Even though he took little pride in his official capacity, Doc glared at Louella, shaking his head at her zealous attempt to establish authority. Riley startled Priestly back from oblivion by asking him to hold the front end of a tape measure as the officer paced off the distance between

Cassidy's body and the exact spot where Priestly had first seen it. A penlight in the mouth didn't give Riley the confidence he needed to do his job at night and he made a mental note to put together a better kit for next time. But he did find the empty case for a belt-sized Leatherman tool lying on the rocks within a few feet of the bridge. Riley swung his head toward the case, made a note in his book, then knelt down and removed a tiny white thread tangled near the snap of the case.

"Could be from the rope he used," said Louella. She was leaning over Riley's shoulder and he didn't appreciate it. He took a deep breath and asked Doc to move folks back a few feet so he could do his job. Riley carefully placed the thread between pages of his notebook, then removed an evidence bag from his jacket pocket.

"Hold this open, will ya?" said Riley. Doc's hands were shaking as he held the bag open. Even burglary was rare in Haines, and Doc was having a hard time hiding his fear over a crime of this magnitude. The killer is out there, he thought, and they might have stumbled on hard evidence. Riley slid a fountain pen under the lid of the Leatherman case and put it into the bag.

Riley, Phil, Louella, and one of the fishermen, lifted Cassidy's stiff body onto the flatbed of Phil's truck. Priestly, so easily ignored, headed toward his truck. It may have been his discovery, but he was already retreating back into his misanthropic comfort zone. Moosekiller had left a hefty gift near the driver's door, but Priestly didn't realize it until he felt his right foot slide. He was wiping his heel on the gravel shoulder when Riley announced his plan.

"Doc, we'll need to use your observation room as a temporary morgue."

Doc wasn't thrilled about it, but he was the elected part-time coroner at a salary of nineteen hundred dollars a year under a state law passed for an occasion just like this one. The model of efficiency, Riley slid his penlight into a thin black pouch on his belt right next to his own versatile Leatherman tool. He methodically snapped the latch into place, then hiked up his belt.

"Body won't keep too well in the office," said Doc. "My garage is cold, and the bears can't get at her in there."

Much to Louella's chagrin, Cassidy's body spent the night in Doc Munger's garage. Phil Lightfoot went back to work on the broken carburetor at the Totem. The fishermen headed back to their comfortable log duplex on the ridge overlooking the Lynn Canal. Riley Carpenter headed off to break the news to Cassidy's mother, Margie Bjorkland. And Doc took a deep breath before heading inside to tell Nadine that they had a dead girl in the garage.

Preistly got in his truck, gave a parade wave to the first humans he'd spoken to in many a month, and headed off to the comfort of his woodstove and a bottle of peppermint schnapps. Only Louella saw him leave. She gave Bob Priestly a long, slow look in the eye and a definitive nod of her head, a show of respect he hadn't enjoyed in years.

"Thanks for makin' my day, Priestly," she whispered to herself. It had been an exciting six hours since Priestly came through her door, and now she headed home to her trailer on the north edge of town.

\\\\

The red wine had stained Doc's best pair of Carhartts but he didn't seem to care. His mind was clearly caught between past and present, and he'd snapped back to our dinner conversation when a strand of spaghetti caught in his throat.

"You always choke when you eat too fast, Hon," she said. And then, as if Doc wasn't in the room, "I swear he's like a little kid sometimes." Nadine seemed my perfect adolescent rival, but I bit my tongue.

"So. A drifter might have done it?" I asked.

"We get plenty of 'em," Doc said. He sat up straight and dabbed his napkin on the corner of his lip. "They come up the Alaskan Highway, some all the way from the Baja or Nogales. Even Florida. Some stay to work the mines near Whitehorse, a few come over here from Skagway after they realize there's nothing there for them but cruise ship fudgies and the greedy bastards that own the shops along the boardwalk. We had a Guatemalan here around that time—Miguel Chavez, or so he said. Illegal as they come."

"Riley Carpenter never, not once, ever said a thing about a drifter!" Nadine was back from the bathroom and reentered the conversation with the passion that comes along with a good buzz from cheap wine. "Especially not a Hispanic, so don't go blaming someone 'cause of the color of their skin."

I noticed that Doc's hands were back at it, tearing his napkin into tiny bits as he built a small pile near his fork.

"Miguel was a hard worker, Nadine, but you got to ask yourself, where did the man go? He up and left, middle of the night, never even picked up his last paycheck according to the folks at the Mountain Market."

"Lotta folks disappear," she said. "Lotta folks come up here to get away. Heck, I came up here to get away. If you ask me, it's none of my business why Miguel left the way he did. I think you know who did it, and we both know the killer's a goddamn local."

Nadine had had enough of long-stemmed glassware. The formalities associated with a dinner guest from the Lower 48 were finished. She unscrewed the lid from another bottle of Chianti and filled a juice glass to the rim. It was her way of letting Doc know that this conversation was a long way from over. Treading on the aggressive side of passive, Doc stood up and leaned over the round table to grab the bottle for himself. He filled my glass halfway before I waved him off. One of us would have to stay sober.

"Truth is, could have been a lot of folks did it," he said. "The question we couldn't figure at the time was why. Why kill Cassidy? That girl was as much an angel as we get around here."

Doc sat back down, took a long pull on the wine, and then stared out the window toward the Lynn Canal as if it helped him recall the details.

Nadine set a three-inch wedge of carrot cake in front of me. The white frosting was thicker than the cake, and a few carrot shavings protruded from the thin brown bottom.

"That's a lotta cake for one guy." I liked to think of myself as in good shape for a thirty-eight-year-old, but the truth was, I was just plain skinny. Still, I extended my belly beyond my belt, and rubbed it to indicate how stuffed I was.

"Alaska in the wintertime," she said. "Cooped up, dark outside, and you're either cold or wet or both. We gotta eat just out of boredom."

Nadine knew what she was talking about. At five foot four, she outweighed me by forty pounds. Her rounded shoulders rolled into her rounded stomach that flowed down toward her rounded bottom. She'd once been a state record holder in speed skating. But those days were gone. Nadine tried to hide her size under an oversized Old Navy sweatshirt that rested well below her waist. Plus-size didn't matter to Doc; he couldn't have cared less.

"Can't beat her carrot cake," shouted Doc from the kitchen.

I took a large bite and gave Nadine a wink of appreciation. Doc's piece was as big as mine, with a mug of coffee sitting beside it. Duct tape wrapped around on the handle suggested it was Doc's favorite mug—a tribute to the Chilkat River rafting company that had its logo across the middle.

"Could be a drifter," I said, leading the questioning. "Or the snowplow operator. Or Bob Priestly."

"Or her own father," said Nadine. "I wouldn't rule him out."

"Her father?" I asked.

"Nice enough fella if you ask me." Doc slid back into his chair and spooned an oversized bite of cake into his mouth.

"No one asked you," barked Nadine. "I don't mince my words and I'm telling you Rusty Sparks is a lame-ass bastard!"

The Chianti had mobilized Nadine's natural passions, and it was also making Doc bolder by the glass.

"The man's a river guide. Rusty was barely even in town back then and unless the cruise ships come to dock, he's barely in town now."

"My point exactly," she shot back. "What kind of man would father a child as beautiful as that girl Cassidy and then spend his time running away from his responsibility? And to leave her mother without a ring. What kind of man does that?"

Doc gave Nadine the sort of blank stare a spouse reserves for those few moments when they are truly surprised by an opinion they never knew existed. Then, slowly, as if milking the confidence he'd found in his last glass, Doc turned his attention back to me. I'd begun jotting down one of the few notes I made that night, but it was my way to avoid the conflict.

"Rusty wasn't even in town that whole month. He was rafting on the Bío Bío River down in Chile. I treated the man for a case of Giardia when he got back to Haines. It wasn't pretty, but it didn't kill him."

"I'm just sayin'," said Nadine, having little to add but the reminder that she was a woman of strong opinion.

"Did Rusty ever mention Cassidy having a boyfriend?" I asked.

Nadine retreated into her glass, stalking the conversation for her next move.

"Like I said, Rusty wasn't around much" said Doc. "He wasn't the fatherly type so it's not likely he'd have known. Her mom mighta—but if the girl had a beau it'd be damn hard to keep it quiet in this town. I'd say no."

"Was she a virgin?"

"You don't beat around the bush now, do ya?"

"Seems like an obvious question," I said. "You were her doctor."

"From the things she told me and the kind of prescriptions she wanted, I'd say no, she wasn't a virgin. But let's keep that little tidbit right here, off the record."

The more Nadine enjoyed her buzz, the more the newly confident Doc seemed to have a certain appeal to her that hadn't been so obvious when the evening began. Still, the contest wouldn't be won by anyone just yet, and Nadine couldn't resist a chance to have the last word.

"Yeah, well," she said, "that Priestly ain't no angel neither."

Doc shook his head remembering just how odd Bob Priestly was around Cassidy's dead body. Nothing seemed normal at the time.

\\\\\\

It was a good thing Cassidy couldn't see the scrunched-up face of Bob Priestly when he looked through Doc's garage window. It must have been 4:00 a.m., and with a fresh blanket of the season's first snow, the porch light bounced off the ground, casting long shadows against Priestly's face and orange hunting cap. He was as menacing a sight as Cassidy would have ever seen—except, perhaps, for the face of her killer. It had been just twenty-four hours since the surf sucked her screams out to sea, her voice barely audible to the beast who'd taken her against her will. The killer had been tormented by something old and demeaning, something so twisted up inside him that he couldn't feel the life force inside Cassidy Sparks, or anyone for that matter. He couldn't feel the innocence that lay beneath him. He couldn't feel the pain in his own hands as he muscled the life out of her body. When the cold wind blowing across the canal slapped his ruddy face back to reality, all he could feel was shame.

Priestly's fascination with the dead girl was another matter. Finding her body seemed to give him the recognition he'd never won in high school. Or maybe Cassidy just reminded him of the last person he'd seen dead, his wife Maureen, just after the cancer terminated her thirty-nine years in Haines. Whatever it was that caught his fancy, Priestly's voyeurism didn't last long. He'd managed to rile a sleepless Nadine enough to dash out the kitchen door and chase him all the way to the beach road. Dressed only in her cotton flowered robe and a pair of knee-high mukluks, Nadine meant business. As Priestly powered up his Toyota, Nadine swung the broom a final time, knocking his side view mirror clean off its bracket. Priestly drove away, his truck sliding around on the fresh snow, and from that time on, he never left Nadine's mind as a suspect.

Nadine knew she'd need proof of Priestly's obsessive behavior. There were a few footprints near the garage, but Nadine's mukluks made it look as if Bigfoot himself had been part of the chase. And by the time she could drag Doc back to the scene of Priestly's getaway truck, Cassidy's uncle Toad had come by with the snowplow. What was left of the side view mirror was mixed in with all the other debris that lined the highway.

Alaskan plowmen will do anything they can to stay awake while plowing in the middle of the night on a lonely state highway. Toad listened to cuts from his favorite Allman Brothers songs and blew a steady stream of pot smoke out the open window of his cab. During the half hour she tailed him with her headlights off, Toad never saw Louella Houak. She'd have followed him all the way to the border but, in truth, there was nothing suspicious about the way Toad was plowing the Haines Highway. She gave up her uneventful chase at the scenic overlook and headed back to Haines.

When Louella finally pulled off at the Totem, she had to honk her horn to get a moose to move away from the pumps. "Damn wildlife," she cussed under her breath. She shook the snow off when she got inside, turned the lights on, filled the coffee pot with fresh water, and opened for business a full hour early. As she opened the front door and flipped the welcome sign, a snow machine was approaching too fast for Louella's taste. Frenchy Jepson, nineteen years old and hot by anyone's standards, spun his ride around like a professional. He tossed Louella a copy of the *Haines Weekly*, gave her a smile too cute for scolding, then hit the gas hard with the thumb of his right hand. Louella flipped through the local rag looking for news of Cassidy's death, but no one had stopped the presses for the story. She turned on public radio but *Morning Edition* was waxing poetic about some private who'd saved the life of an orphaned Iraqi kid along the southern front with Kuwait. So much for yesterday's excitement, she thought. It would be up to Louella to convey the news to her customers—a job she pretended to hate. But the valley had no better messenger than Louella.

Riley Carpenter finished the Lumberjack Special at the Hotel Halsingland and was at Doc's door with Margie Bjorkland by 7:00 a.m. He positioned his hand behind Margie's lower back just in case she fell backwards. When they opened the garage door, the sight of poor Cassidy lying naked on a folding table next to a wall of power tools, crab pots, and old paint cans was just too much for any of them to handle.

Margie went to Cassidy straight away. She removed her coat and laid it across her daughter, then pushed the damaged hair away from her daughter's puffy face. She put her cheek up close to Cassidy's mouth as if to feel her breathing. Nothing. She put her ear to Cassidy's heart. Nothing. She looked around at Doc and Riley as her eyes filled with disbelief, then tears. Neither man could think of a word to say. Margie just stared at them as if trying to understand why they'd suddenly reached into her chest and ripped out her heart. When she looked back toward Cassidy, she let out a slow growl that within seconds became a howl loud enough to send shivers down Doc's spine.

"Jesus H. Christ," said Riley.

Doc went to her side. He hesitated for a moment, then reached his arms around Margie and pulled her into a full embrace. It was the most healing moment of his long career in medicine.

\\\\

Remembering it all had Doc bending his fork nearly in half. A tiny piece of cake frosting fell into his lap.

"Hardest damn thing I ever did." Doc's eyes welled up and he brushed the knuckle of his forefinger under his nose.

"I was in the kitchen, but I can still hear the howl," said Nadine. "It wasn't human, but then neither was what happened to that girl."

"Her mother was never the same after that," said Doc. "Who would be?"

There was a long silence while Doc licked the icing off his bent fork. Nadine twirled circles in the curdled cream on the surface of her coffee. I sat to the point of discomfort, wondering whether it was time to leave, then pushed my plate toward the center of the table.

"You don't want to finish your cake?" she asked.

"It's good, but I can't. I ate too much spaghetti."

"You want something else? We can wrap it up for you for breakfast if you'd like."

I shook my head, and when I slid my chair back from the table it gave a long squeak against the linoleum floor. Doc got up to toss more wood in the stove. I made a move to clear the dishes, but Nadine patted my hand and pushed me back in the chair. The dinner chat had been my idea, but I suddenly felt captive.

"Guests don't work in this house. Not unless you're plannin' to shovel the driveway." Doc and Nadine cackled. It was the kind of laugh that proved the old adage that comedy is subjective. I tapped my pencil, thinking over the next question.

"So Riley Carpenter never found the killer?" It sounded like a silly question, because if he had, I wouldn't be dredging it all up after twenty years.

"Maybe. Maybe not," said Nadine. "All depends on how you define killer."

"No arrests, I mean."

"No one charged," said Doc. "Not to this very day. But he had his theories. Everyone did."

The conundrum was enough for Doc to reach over the counter for his favorite bottle of single malt scotch. Winter in Alaska was enough of an excuse, but this was a special story, one that required a beverage as old as the crime. He twisted off the cap and savored the smell that filled his dimpled nostrils. Nadine wasn't one to miss the moment, and as soon as he'd broken a more-than-satisfied grin, she swirled the mouth of the bottle under her nose and inhaled deeply until her eyelids fluttered. In the midst of Doc's late evening rite of passage, I'd missed a small detail. Nadine had lined up three thick plastic tumblers molded in the shape of snifters. Doc filled each one about an inch and a half full as if to say, we're not going anywhere just yet.

"We took Cassidy's body to Juneau," said Doc. "Turned out the girl had been strangled barehanded. According to Riley, strangling someone's not an easy thing to do."

"And raped?"

"Well, maybe. Whoever it was used a condom so there was a theory the sex part may have been consensual."

"My ass!" said Nadine. "You aren't going to sit here near twenty years later and tell me that girl had consensual sex with her killer. Maybe he was a neat freak!" Her accent on the word "freak" made it clear she was talking about more than the man's tidiness. "For God's sake, Doc, you're saying it was consensual?"

"That wasn't what I said, Sweetie. It was a theory they had down in Juneau."

"You implied that Cassidy was putting out."

Doc took a deep breath and swallowed hard. Whatever leverage he'd gained with the chianti was dwindling with the scotch. He pinched the tails of his mustache with the thumb and forefinger of each hand. It was sticky from the carrot cake and he twisted the longest hairs into a neat strand.

"They came over with a whole team of forensic fellas from the state crime lab, but there wasn't a shred of evidence near the bridge to pin it on anyone. Whoever killed Cassidy Sparks had been careful to dump her body just before the tide was falling."

"So the killer wanted her washed out to sea?"

"Wouldn't be the first time someone used the ocean as a dump," said Nadine. "No telling where she would have wound up if it hadn't been for Priestly out fishin'."

"Dump sounds so, so crass, Nadine. What about grave? Or cemetery?" said Doc.

"Call it what you want, but we got enough crap washin' up on our beaches to supply the Goodwill Store down in Juneau." Nadine reached around toward the living room and pulled over a large wicker basket filled with crab pot floats of all sizes. She handed me one about the size of a baseball. "This is just a hobby for me, mind you. Everything washes up on that beach at some point. Found a human foot in a tennis shoe a couple a years back. Severed low at the ankle."

"That was different," said Doc. "They tied that to a serial killer down near Vancouver Island."

"Body part is a body part," said Nadine. "Point is, Cassidy's killer was hoping the tide would take her out to sea."

Doc's fidgeting had been replaced by his obsession with smelling the whiskey in his tumbler. I raised my glass as a courtesy, then took my first sip. It was well worth all those years spent in a wooden cask on the Scottish mainland. Still, the hint of peat moss seemed a long way from Haines.

"Anything odd about the mother?" I asked.

"Cheerful woman," said Nadine. "Before things went the way they did, she was just a single mom trying to make ends meet. Used to clerk at City Hall three mornings a week and would substitute teach around here and up at Klukwon Village."

"Rumor is she's living in Flagstaff now," said Doc. "Lotta folks winter down there."

"Any idea why the victim was bound up the way she was?" I asked. "What's the deal with the rope?"

"Riley said there was no way of knowing. The killer may or may not have known her. As for her being tied and naked, it could be that he raped her first. They never did find the rest of her clothes."

"Toilet?"

"Down the hall on your right," said Doc.

The hand towel that hung on the bathroom wall had a pattern of huge sunflowers. Lime was built up around the sink drain and faucet. Toothbrushes were lined upright in a purple plastic cup with caked Tom's of

Maine dribbled down the side. If Doc and Nadine's memories were as sloppy as their house and dining habits, a good defense attorney would minimize their testimony in a matter of minutes. When I got back to the table, Doc had flipped on the TV and was watching the Trailblazers beat the daylights out of the Bucks.

"Did Riley do any DNA tests? Under her fingernails, that sort of thing?"

"Pat Riley?" said Doc, just as Jabari slammed home his biggest basket of the night.

"Riley Carpenter," I said. The interview was deteriorating fast.

"You been watching too much television," said Nadine. "We're talking rural Alaska in 1991. Not much in the way of crime labs up here 'til recently."

"Nadine's right. Again." Doc flipped off the TV, then smiled at his wife as if petitioning for later. "The only thing still in an evidence drawer may be that thread of nylon rope and the Leatherman case. They didn't find semen, and there was no sign of a struggle on Cassidy's part."

"And no arrest warrants, right?"

"Riley didn't have enough to go after anyone in particular. Miguel was long gone, and it turned out Toad had an alibi."

"A shaky one if you ask me," interrupted Nadine.

"Nadine . . ."

"I'm just sayin' . . ."

"Toad's no angel, okay. But according to his cousin, Lupin, he was at her place puttin' up wallpaper the night Cassidy was killed."

"That wasn't all he was puttin' up if you ask me."

Any hope Doc had for spooning that night went out the window with the look he gave Nadine.

"They're cousins for Christ's sake!"

"The whole population of Mosquito Lake is related within one or two degrees," said Nadine. "You should know—you delivered more than half of them."

Fact may not equal truth, but stats are stats, Doc thought. It was rare that a man of any age accompanied a pregnant young woman from

Mosquito Lake into Doc's office for observation or delivery. He couldn't be sure of who was who or what was what up at the lake, and he usually had to sign the birth certificate of the single moms without knowing the other party behind the growing population of misfits.

Doc took a long, slow draw on his scotch and swirled it around his mouth. The logs Doc had put in the woodstove were smoldering, and Nadine began pushing them around with a copper poker.

"Were there tire tracks?" I asked. "Footprints?"

"Nada," said Nadine. "The tide comes damn near right up to the road on that stretch where the canal meets the Chilkoot."

"By the time Riley got there, it was mostly dark," said Doc. "Only tracks we saw were Priestly's and the two fishermen."

"What about his investigation? He must have spent more time here gathering information."

"Cassidy's bicycle was found outside the market, but most of the kids hang around there after school. According to Riley, her classmates didn't see anything unusual. She never showed up for her shooting lesson, but her teacher back then was a former Marine who runs the hotel by the harbor. He was at the hotel waiting for her until he went home for dinner with his wife, so he had an alibi."

It was my turn to stare into the plastic tumbler. I couldn't help imagining the brackish brown water at the mouth of the Chilkoot River lapping over Cassidy's dead body. It was a sad way to go. But Nadine wasn't much for silence.

"You gotta remember," she said, "people up here leave well enough alone. You might say hello at the market, but most folks hate the government, love their guns, and they're adamant about their privacy. Half of 'em came here to get away from something that didn't work out somewhere else. Every few months we lose someone to the weather or the waves, and it's a rare winter when the darkness doesn't get to somebody with a pistol too handy by their side. If you wanna get away with murder, this is as good a place as any you'll find."

The scotch was having an impact. Doc's eyes were getting heavy as he drifted back in time.

||||

Priestly watched them load Cassidy's body onto the Juneau ferry. The snow had turned to a steady rain and his glasses smeared when he rubbed the water off with his greasy hand. His vision wasn't that bad when he squinted, but all he would remember from that day was the out of focus image of Doc and Riley pushing a hand cart with a body-sized lump wrapped up in a sky blue tarp.

It was Louella who couldn't give up the search. There was a killer on the loose, and the odds were pretty good she knew the man. Everyone probably knew the man. The question was, who would want to kill Cassidy Sparks? Was it a crime of passion or a teen sex game gone awry? Did the killer know her so well she trusted him? Was he a nutcase waiting to kill again? Or was it that drifter, Miguel Chavez, the man who disappeared in the forty-eight hours before Priestly found the body? Everyone who came to Totem Gas that day had the same questions. Louella was more than curious—she was scared, and with Riley Carpenter headed back to Juneau, someone needed to find the man responsible for turning Haines, Alaska, upside down. The last school bus came to fill up at 2:45 p.m. and that was reason enough for her to turn things over to Phil. She had to kick Phil hard in the ankle to get him to roll out from under the forest green Subaru he'd been working on.

"You got the store," she said.

"What?"

"You got the store. I'm leaving early."

"Where you going?"

"Got here early, leaving early."

"What about the Subaru?"

Louella just rolled her eyes. She left the Totem and drove north to mile 29. The owners of Bart's Log Cabin Café had put plywood over the windows and shut things down until May, so there was no one around to see her park behind the building. Louella shoved a small flashlight into the front pocket of her camo-print hunting pants, pulled on a rubberized Helly Hansen slicker, and walked through the rain down the four-block footpath to Mosquito Lake.

"Thank Jehovah for rubber boots," she mumbled to no one in particular.

There wasn't any law against driving up to the lake, she thought. After all, it was a certified township and at least thirty-eight people occupied the eight houses and three trailers on the west side of the seventy-acre flowage above the dam. But Louella didn't want to be put in the position of answering questions on what was nothing more than a scouting mission.

It was near dusk and there were at least six inches of wet snow on the trail to the lake. Louella slipped more than once trying to cover her tracks until she finally gave up. It could be iced over and dark by the time she returned, she thought, so better to make this quick. Besides, she reminded herself, she wasn't doing anything wrong.

The trail broke into a clearing at the ball field, and Louella took a position behind the cedar dugout. She wasn't more than thirty yards away when she saw Toad exit the outhouse near the closest building. Barefoot in the snow for what he'd anticipated would be a quick trip, Toad pranced like a highly paid running back on the final ten yards toward the house. He was just about to the back porch door, pulling up the strap of his suspenders when his cousin Lupin, a stringy redhead about twenty-years-old, leaned out and tossed him a roll of toilet paper.

"Put this out there for later, will you?"

Just as Toad was about to complain, she lifted her skirt and flashed him along with a flirty giggle. Maybe Toad did have better things to do than kill Cassidy Sparks, thought Louella. He was so full of desire for Lupin that he tripped on his way up the porch steps just as she slammed the door in his face.

"Fuckin' A, Lupin, I'm gonna kill you." He said it in the nicest possible way, nice enough that Lupin smiled and stuck her tongue out at him from behind the locked door. The image of Toad standing barefoot in the snow, waving like a dopey kid and blowing kisses through the window was enough for Louella to write him off completely. Toad was a dork. When Lupin finally opened the door, he fell across the stoop as he chased her inside.

Two houses down from Toad's house, Willie Freeman was chopping wood. The pile was nearly waist-high so he'd been at it for some time, which also explained how he managed to stay warm in a soaking wet t-shirt. There was no sign of anyone else when Louella made a beeline for the smallest trailer on the lake owned by Laird Bristol. Louella had gone to school with Laird and never felt quite right about him. She hadn't talked to him since their ten-year class reunion when Laird went bragging on about his recipe for moose meat chili. She thought he was conceited and told him so even though he had won the blue ribbon for his chili at the Southeast Alaska State Fair. But there was no sign of Laird, and no tracks in the snow around his place. Laird's truck was gone.

"Went hunting a week ago, Louella."

"Oh my dickens, you scared the livin' shit out of me!" said Louella.

Willie's chubby biceps had stretched his old Harley Davidson tattoo to the point where it looked like a fat-wheel lowrider. Still, to Louella, there was something oddly sexy about the sweaty forty-five-year-old standing in the cold wearing nothing but a pair of faded jeans and a sleeveless t-shirt. The twinge she felt was just enough for her to shift her weight sideways, tilting her own burly hips in Willie's direction.

"Saw you lookin' around," he said. "Haven't seen you in these parts in a long time."

"How'd you know I was here?"

"You Indians ain't as light a foot as you think you are." Willie wasn't one for political correctness.

The air left Louella's tires quicker than a grizzly fart. She sized him up and decided not to give out much info. Then, as if on cue, a bald eagle flew low overhead on its way south. Willie wiped his sweaty brow and his mop of red hair twisted across his forehead. That's when it hit her that Willie was surely the father of Lupin, the young woman living with Toad. How many redheads could there be at Mosquito Lake?

"You that girl's father, the one that's shackin' up with Toad?"

"Not sure what business that is of yours, Louella."

"No law against askin' a question. She's a looker if you ask me."

"You here for somethin' in particular?"

"Laird owes the Totem some money is all. Thought I'd come pester him about it." It was as good a lie as any because everyone owed the Totem some money.

"I ain't seen him, but you know, it's a good time to get a moose. Could be he's all the way up to Whitehorse for all I know."

Hunting talk was like an aphrodisiac for Louella and she could feel her hips turn his way a second time as if they had a mind of their own.

"Phil got his limit last week," she said. "Saw a pregnant female, too, but he let her go."

Willie kicked up a bit of snow, then turned and started back. Though he'd probably fathered Lupin, Willie had no comfort zone for women as a general rule.

"If you talk to him, I wasn't here," she said. "No use makin' him panicky."

Louella knew when to fold 'em and she quickly made her way back the way she came. Maybe it was her eyes playing tricks on her, but just as she entered the clearing, Louella saw someone sitting behind the wheel of her truck. She tried running the last hundred yards, but there was no moving fast on the glazed over snow. The driver was gone by the time she arrived. Sure enough, there were tracks all around the parking spot. It was dark, she was almost thirty miles from Haines, and the drizzle was coating everything in a thin sheet of ice. So Louella did what anyone from southeast Alaska would do. She started walking.

||||

Reminiscing about Cassidy's murder and a strong cup of coffee were keeping Doc awake past his bedtime.

"I bet it was Priestly who did it," said Doc. "Louella never could leave well enough alone."

"Told you that guy was a creep," said Nadine. "Wasn't like he had an alibi either. And he's still an old nutcase today, if you ask me." No one had asked her, but that didn't stop Nadine from twirling her forefinger around her right ear as if to suggest Priestly had gone batty.

"Sounds like somebody was trying to scare her off," I said. "But Priestly sounds more broken than bad."

"Never found out who got the truck," said Nadine. "Coulda been a bored kid. Or Bart, maybe. She parked in the lot of his café you know."

Something didn't quite fit. Bart was known for boarding up the restaurant and heading to Costa Rica just as soon as the leaves turned color. But when I asked Nadine more about it, she just shrugged her shoulders.

"It was a long time ago," she said.

Doc was now staring hard at the fork he'd bent in half an hour earlier. Nadine was resting her chin in her hands, both elbows on the table, while blowing out slow, deep breaths between her puckered lips. All our snifters were empty, and I was quickly regretting that I'd abandoned of my cardinal rule—never drink with the interview subjects. Instead, I'd gone pound for pound with Doc and Nadine and I was feeling it.

"I gotta lie down," said Nadine. "Nine in the morning comes early when you only get a few hours of daylight."

Nadine surrendered. Doc watched her hips move as she tottered off to bed. Even in old age and under the influence, Doc was still a sucker for Nadine's short, solid frame and that exaggerated wiggle. Not tonight, he thought, but soon.

"Maybe I should be going," I said, breaking into Doc's fantasy.

"It wasn't Priestly," said Doc. "That man wouldn't harm a griz if the thing was bearing down on his carotid artery."

Grab your pen, I thought. Doc's ready to spill the beans. I pulled a fresh reporter's notebook out of the shell I had slung over the back of my chair and tried to kick-start the brain cells I hadn't killed.

"Was it Toad? Miguel? One of the fishermen?"

"We're off the record, right?"

I put my pad and pencil down on the table and brought my hands back to my lap. Off the record? How can a murder be off the record?

"Nadine doesn't know?"

"Some things she does, others not so much. I'm not real sure," he said, "but I think maybe my son killed the girl."

"David, right?"

"No, David belongs to Nadine and me. He lived down in Portland at the time. It's my other boy Dwight . . . Dwight is who Nadine doesn't know a thing about."

The very notion of Doc's bastard son had him back to twisting the corner of the tablecloth, but this time he was braiding it around his hand, undoing it, then twisting it tighter each time. The only thing harder than keeping a big secret is sharing it after years of silence. Whatever was on Doc's mind had been there a while.

"It was a different time back then," he said. "I fathered a child with a woman out at Mosquito Lake. I guess it was, you know, just sex."

Doc's humble rationalization assured me that he'd had exactly two lovers in his life, and one of them was sleeping it off in the next room.

"We met up at the fairgrounds. Her name was Daryl Lynn, the only Daryl Lynn I ever met. Even now I don't even know her last name. Taj Mahal was playing a concert at the fair, which was kind of a big deal for up here, and Daryl Lynn and I, well, both of us were dancing to the blues for the first time in our lives. We worked up quite a sweat, and you could say hormones got the best of us. It wasn't what I'd call real romantic or anything. We got into the back of my old pickup at a turnout halfway between here and Mosquito Lake. She had a boy nine months later, but by that time I was back doing undergrad at Washington State. Daryl Lynn probably could have found me, but she waited for a few months. Didn't ask for a thing. Starting with his first birthday, she'd send me a picture of him once a year. Dwight, as she called him, would've been twenty-one right about the time Cassidy was killed."

"He grew up at Mosquito Lake?"

"Yes, he lived there when he was young. This thing was hanging over my head for years, and I didn't handle it well. But when I got back from medical school and my residency, I went up to the lake to see Daryl Lynn. I guess I felt like I needed to do something, be a part of the kid's life somehow. I wasn't married to Nadine yet, and I wanted to be responsible. Guilt's a strange motivator, my friend. But the folks up there said she and Dwight had just moved on. Rumor was that they were living over near Anchorage with a guy that fished halibut."

"So Dwight was about eleven at the time?"

"He was, yep, and just a few months older than Cassidy. I checked the school records and they went to the same elementary school for several years.

"Anchorage is a two-day drive. What makes you think it was Dwight that killed Cassidy?"

"It had to do with the funeral," he said.

Doc had wrapped his left hand so tightly in the tablecloth that it was cutting off his circulation. He sat passively while I helped him untangle it. He looked at me helplessly, his face seemed years older than it had been when I'd arrived. My skills as a therapist would rival anyone's worst expectations, but somehow it made sense to hold both of his hands in mine to keep them still. We sat silently long enough that I began wishing I had my own bed just down the hall. It had become a long night, and Doc was lost again in his thoughts.

\|\|\|

Cassidy's body was under the probing hands of a medical examiner in Juneau for three days, but her corpse was finally returned in time for the funeral Margie Bjorkland had planned for her only daughter. There was a bit of an Indian summer going on when they rolled her coffin off the ferry in Haines. Most of the snow had melted, and a group of Cassidy's friends had pushed Margie to have the service outside on the parade grounds of old Fort Seward. Cassidy had been an outdoor girl and the few golden leaves left on the cottonwoods and patches of blue sky would have been just the sort of day she celebrated. Even the girl's dad, Rusty Sparks, showed up. It was the first time anyone could remember him wearing a jacket and tie. Rusty didn't say much, never even took off his Ray-Bans, but he was there. Rather than being angry for all the times he hadn't been, Margie slumped in under Rusty's burly left shoulder. Once he curled his arm around her, she didn't budge for the rest of the service.

Fourteen members of the Haines Borough Junior Achievers had put out more than two hundred folding chairs, but Mayor Karadis estimated that at least three hundred and eighty people showed up that day. Louella sat next to her half brother Phil. Moosekiller was there too, patiently letting Cassidy's youngest cousin climb all over his back. Priestly arrived early and sat alone in the back row, his view of the service obscured by the broad shoulders of Riley Carpenter.

Toad showed up with Lupin who, for a few moments, got more attention than Cassidy because of her flowing red hair and the abbreviated length of her black skirt. Doc and Nadine arrived too late for a seat, but from the uphill side they had a pretty good view of the podium. More than fifteen people attested to what a blessing Cassidy had been to those who knew her, with observances including "she could run like the wind," she was "a dead-eye of a shot, even better than her instructor," and "this beautiful girl was a lock for the Olympics." The Greek Orthodox priest who'd come up from Sitka did his best to help everyone cope with the grief they felt over the loss of a girl he'd never met.

"This lovely, innocent girl reminds us all of how fragile life can be," he said.

"Duh." Nadine whispered in Doc's ear.

Doc shushed her with his forefinger. He couldn't help thinking that Alaskans are constantly aware of how fragile life can be. In a land of blizzards and gales and grizzlies, a sudden end to human life was common-place. Cassidy just got it earlier and more violently than most.

Because it was a school day, only a handful of people made it over to the burial after the service. Doc and Nadine had no choice but to go. They were standing hand-in-hand, watching silently as the priest read one of the Gospels, when Nadine whispered to Doc that she sure didn't like seeing Margie all snuggled up with Rusty. It had been a long day of whispers and Doc absently blurted out "What the hell difference does it make?" loud enough for everyone to hear. Rusty shot a look at Doc and Nadine to respect the ceremony.

A gust of wind blew in from the Tsirku Glacier, and within seconds, huge wet flakes of snow began falling. Each was different from the other in shape and size, but they were equally irritating. The dirt around the side of Cassidy's grave looked like a mound of dimpled brown foam. A church secretary held a golf umbrella over Margie and Rusty, and the two grave-diggers began wiping down the top of the cedar wood casket.

As everyone scurried to take cover, Doc spotted Louella's short-bed pickup truck parked across the street at the RV park. It wouldn't have caught his eye except the windshield wipers were moving slowly back and forth, and he thought he saw a man inside the cab. He let go of Nadine's hand and told her he was going to the car to get their rain jackets.

Doc's pace quickened but it wasn't because of the weather. He was nervous as a kingfisher and fought the urge to look back at the truck. What kind of thief would want to drive the stolen rig back to Haines? he thought. When he opened the trunk of his car to pull out the rain jackets, Doc did the unthinkable. He stood bolt upright and stared straight at the man behind the wheel.

The photos Daryl Lynn had sent didn't lie. More than twenty years after a one-night stand at the Southeast Alaska State Fair, Doc knew he was staring straight into the eyes of a child he'd never known and barely considered.

"Hey," he shouted. "Hey, what are you doin' with Louella's truck?"

If the man behind the wheel recognized Doc, he showed no sign of it and quickly popped the gear into reverse. Suddenly desperate to meet his son face-to-face, Doc ran toward the truck. Nadine saw the commotion and came running, arriving just in time for a shower of roadside gravel as the driver sped toward the border.

"What was that about?" she asked.

"Thought for a minute it was Louella's truck."

"You been eating too much salt again?"

"Salt?"

"You're breathin' like you got high cholesterol or somethin'."

"I ran over to get the plate number," he said. "But maybe it wasn't her truck."

Questions raced through Doc's head. Why would Dwight show up at Cassidy's burial? And if Dwight knew Cassidy, why was he sitting in a truck half a football field away? Doc shivered at the thought of talking to Dwight, and at confronting a terrible suspicion that Dwight might have had something to do with Cassidy's murder. The snow had begun blowing, and Nadine startled him when she grabbed the jacket from his hands and stomped toward the passenger side of the car.

Doc looked back toward the graveyard. Only Rusty and Margie were still standing over the casket, her body still tucked into his. Doc wondered why there has to be an accident or death to make someone forgive, or to remember. He watched Margie throw a handful of dirt onto the casket lid as the workers lowered the body into the ground. When Doc looked back toward the RV park, he thought about what it was like for a boy to grow up without a father—or worse, with the wrong one.

||||

Doc's house was small, and we could hear Nadine snoring in the next room. He motioned me to keep quiet as he dimmed the light in the main room.

"Nadine never saw him?" I asked.

"Even if she had, she wouldn't have known who she was looking at. No one had seen Dwight around here in years."

"So what makes you think he was the killer? Maybe he was passing through."

"Maybe."

"You didn't report it to Riley?" I asked, knowing it was the stupidest question of the evening.

"What was I going to say? Hey Riley, there's this kid I saw on the day of the funeral in Luella' stolen truck, a kid that I mighta fathered a long time ago with a woman named Daryl Lynn, and he just might have been the one who killed Cassidy, but I got no idea why except an informed hunch?"

Doc's theory was believable and doubtful at the same time. I got up from the table and stretched. I put my hand on Doc's shoulder as I went toward the sink for some water. Touching him sympathetically seemed like the right thing to do, but Doc barely acknowledged it.

"I don't even know if the kid knew who I was," he said.

I set a full glass of water in front of Doc and took two big gulps myself. It was after midnight and I'd regained enough composure to start early on battling tomorrow's hangover. Doc stared into the glass of water, tapping the surface with his forefinger. I reached over and grabbed his hand.

"It's not like you could have done anything," I said.

"That's just it, I could have done a lot."

There were rumors after that, Doc said, especially gossip from Louella, but nothing solid enough to take to the authorities. Doc leaned back and stared up at the ceiling.

"Only rumors," he said.

||||

By late October in southeast Alaska, darkness sets in around three in the afternoon. It was in that moment of twilight that Dwight parked

Louella's truck back in the same spot at Bart's Log Cabin Café near the lake.

On the short trail to the shore of Mosquito Lake he looked for the last house to the south where the man lived who used to take him out canoe-ing—Laird Bristol. No one was around as he passed along the frontage to Laird's front porch. The canoe paddle was right where Dwight remem-bered it, just above the roof supports. They'd had a few good times, he thought, and quite a few more that weren't good at all. Dwight turned his head back toward the lake as two coots called out before making a soft landing.

As he pulled the old canoe off the wooden saw horses in the lean-to, Dwight sniffed the air, inhaling the odor of the slow-rotting trunks of old cedar near the dam. It was a smell he remembered from childhood, a smell he remembered with his face pressing against the damp soil. He could still feel the grit from Laird's trousers brushing against his naked bottom.

Dwight pushed the bow of the canoe into the water, cupped some water in his hand and took a sip. Once the canoe was resting halfway in, he laid the paddle across the stern and headed back to the shed. Within seconds, he found the two cement blocks. Heavy as they were, Dwight waded a few inches into the water and carefully set each block inside the canoe, exactly in the middle where the weight would be evenly distributed.

The sun was sliding below the horizon when Lupin left her kitchen to use the outhouse. She wasn't quite sure what she was looking at when she saw a man paddling out toward the center of the lake. It was odd to be paddling in twilight, she thought, and especially odd this time of year. Lupin called out to Toad from the yard, but he was in his own space, topping off a joint at the kitchen table, his Sony Walkman cranked as high as it would go.

"You gotta see this, Toad, there's somebody on the lake."

"What?" he said, removing his headset.

"Looks like someone paddling on the lake."

"You're seeing things," he said. "Help me out with this."

Lupin wasn't one to miss a good time with her lover, and she turned to go back inside. She smiled playfully as she let the screen door slam behind her. Dwight looked over as the sound of the door echoed across the water. When he got to the middle of the lake, Dwight back-paddled just enough to slow his forward motion, then he climbed into the middle of the canoe. He pulled a long strand of white nylon rope from his jacket and gave it a long toss away from the canoe. He counted each turn as he reeled it in on his elbow. Seventeen feet, he thought. Dwight tossed it again and when he rewound it a second time, he stopped at eight and a half turns, then used a Leatherman tool to cut the rope in half. He gripped the ends and pulled each strand against the other as if exact measurement meant something.

The cement blocks were leaning against each other, and Dwight laid them longwise on their side. He slid the rope through the hole in the blocks separately, then slowly, deliberately, tied each of his ankles to one of the blocks. He used a fisherman's knot he'd learned from Laird and tested each for knot strength until he was convinced there was no chance of the rope coming undone. Then, without a moment's hesitation, Dwight rolled the canoe to the side. There was barely a splash as his body sank to the bottom of Mosquito Lake.

When Laird arrived home the following morning, he was grateful for Toad and Willie's help unloading the moose meat he'd butchered. They put it into the underground freezer behind his lean-to. Willie was happy to help and knew there'd be at least a couple of flank steaks in it for him. But he nearly took Laird's head off for accusing him of leaving his canoe swamped over in the marsh on the east side of the lake. He couldn't convince Laird that he had nothing to do with the beached canoe. There's nothing worse than wrestling in wet snow so they let the matter drop.

The next day, Laird donned his rubber bibs and worked his way along the muddy shoreline. It took him more than an hour to get the canoe upright. The paddle was stuck floating inside, but there was no sign of any damage or foul play. Maybe a hunter took it, he thought, or some kids. By the time spring rolled around, Laird had forgotten about it.

||||

"What? What time is it?"

Doc was curled up on the sofa when I heard Nadine smack him a bit too hard on the back of his head.

"It's bedtime you old bean!"

I raised my head just slightly from the crook of my folded arms and looked across the table at the rooster clock on the mantle above the woodstove. It was after three in the morning, and somehow an army had found a way to use my mouth for boot camp. The tablecloth was a mess.

"Don't be letting some youngster keep you up all night," she said.

I shook my head. "I can let myself out," I mumbled.

It was too late for handshakes or long goodbyes. Doc grabbed Nadine's arm and pulled himself slowly off the sofa. I gathered my notes and jacket, and watched as he carefully checked each of his legs for balance. As Nadine shuffled down the hallway, Doc gave me a nod. I smiled back at him as the door closed behind me.

THE PLACE HE CALLED HEAVEN

IT WOULD BE HARD FOR me to call Ed a friend, but when no one else offered to give a eulogy, it fell to me. There were only five of us at the funeral, a small group considering who Ed was in life. I wasn't sure why I'd come, except that Ed had been hard to ignore. Still, here I was, rising from the stiff wooden pew in a small Baptist church to say a few words about a man I hardly knew. What I did know—church deacon, activist, one-time businessman, felon, divorcee—hardly spoke to the man's life. I said as much, leaving more questions to ponder than answers.

We had met under strange circumstances the previous spring, though I'd been aware of Ed well before that. Outside the clinic on Brady Street, Ed had spent five days a week parading the sidewalk for as long as anyone could remember. On the occasional Saturday, weather permitting, Ed was joined by a handful of fellow protesters who carried life-sized photographs of aborted fetuses and placards that suggested the world was black and white with no room for gray. At age sixty-four, Ed was the champion of the local antiabortion movement. His thick head of white hair suggested anything but surrender; it was deliberately trimmed in a conservative flat-top long out of style. Ed was a warrior. He'd logged enough hours harassing women and passersby that few people on the East side of Milwaukee had been spared.

The '73 Ford station wagon Ed drove to and from the clinic was part of local lore. A moving billboard plastered with anti-abortion bumper stickers, Ed had hand-painted Christian pro-life quotes on every available space. It wasn't hard to see where Ed stood on the issue, but just in case, he also drove up and down Wisconsin Avenue just after business hours spouting Bible verses through a huge loudspeaker positioned on the roof of his car. For good measure, the rack of a Texas Longhorn steer was mounted on the front grill, though no one seemed to know how antlers fit into Ed's message. When tourists would stare in amazement, it wouldn't take long before a local would stop and say, "It's just Ed," as if every city had one just like him.

The felony was big news back in 2013 when Ed had crossed the line. A fellow protester from Madison had been arrested for threatening to kill an abortion provider named Dr. Francis Beebe, and her clinic had been closed for security reasons. As many as fifty distraught yet determined women per week were showing up at the Brady Street Clinic, and Ed was there to greet them. He'd gone the extra mile to show support for his Madison brethren by filling a grocery cart with life-size baby dolls smothered in fake blood, then walking back and forth in front of the clinic door.

It was nasty business for any scared or conflicted young woman, and several turned back before entering. But one, twenty-one-year-old Alison Howard from nearby Waterford, challenged Ed to leave her and the other women alone. Witnesses said Alison made her request gracefully and from a careful distance, but with his adrenalin working at full tilt, Ed did the unthinkable—he threw a bloody doll at Alison with enough force to break her nose. To make matters worse for Ed, it had all been captured on a cell phone.

Within hours of Ed's arrest, more than five hundred people had gathered outside the county jail. Women of all ages in support of a woman's right to choose were there calling for the maximum penalty on Ed's felony assault charge. Anything less than twenty-five years, they said, would be a travesty of justice. A local Unitarian minister spoke out loudly in favor of individual choice and tried to inspire a pro-choice chant, but few, if any, of the women listened to him. When Alison's attorney arrived, news cameras swarmed around her as she read a brief statement. Her client, a young woman from rural Wisconsin, requested privacy. Plastic surgeons said her face would be close to normal in a matter of weeks, but the emotional scars were of grave concern. How could anyone ever be the same after such a brutal, unprovoked attack? She and her client would let the judicial system play out the charges against her attacker.

A roughly equal number of overtly Christian protesters were also there in support of Ed. Led by a mega-church Evangelical named Chase Westerly and a priest named Father Robb, they each tried to turn the media's attention to what they called the bigger issue—the violent slaughter of the unborn. A Jesuit by training, Father Robb encouraged his followers to kneel silently in prayer and to avoid physical or verbal confrontation of any kind. By contrast, Westerly's career was on the rise and he knew exactly when the cameras were rolling. He was a fiery speaker who confronted a woman carrying a "pro-choice" sign by calling her a thoughtless killer and screaming to his followers that pro-choice meant pro-murder. The police were on Westerly before he could raise the decibel level, and the event was soon diluted into a gathering of warring tribes battling within a police-imposed boundary defined by a brick sidewalk. Because it was a school night, everyone went their own way shortly after nine.

Meanwhile, Ed sat things out in his tiny cell, staring blankly at the decade's worth of graffiti that decorated his new surroundings. From a short distance, it didn't look all that different from the side panels on Ed's station wagon. On closer inspection, Ed wasn't prepared for the myriad ways in which fuck, asshole, bitch, bastard, prick, dick, pussy, tit, whore, shit, and hell could be used to turn a phrase. He was shocked into shame by the jailhouse sentiment of those who came before him. After a sleepless night, Ed entered the courtroom dressed in an orange jumpsuit and cuffs, his head hanging low. The courtroom was packed with the usual suspects and the overflow carried onto the courthouse steps. But to everyone's surprise, there would be no trial. Ed used his arraignment to plead guilty. It would mean a quick end to the self-serving forum longed for by those who'd brought their passion to what they hoped would be the great debate.

The judge, who had political ambitions in a state that was leaning conservative, went easy on Ed. She had been around long enough to know that most controversial decisions blow over by election time. Her record on what she considered "real" crime was solid enough. She'd also been a vocal supporter of handgun legislation, and she'd nailed men on domestic violence charges with a gusto the bench hadn't seen in years. In other words, Judge Debra Tepper was hard to classify, and giving one to the antiabortion crowd could work in her favor and she knew it.

After six months in the county jail, Ed was back on Brady Street claiming to be a changed man. At a press conference, Ed's attorney told reporters, "Abortion is killing, no doubt about it. But Ed had no right to hurt that woman. God will punish her for her decisions; it's not up to Ed." Ed then spoke up to say that God had spoken to him personally and told him it was no use getting arrested if America's judicial system wasn't going to support the rights and personal freedoms of the unborn. Apparently, Ed didn't see his sentence as light, and he hadn't lost his conviction.

From now on, Ed said, he would carry simple signs for a simple message: "*Abortion Kills!*" or "*Be Pro-Life not Pro-Abortion!*" He'd speak only when spoken to, and he'd maximize the power of the silent vigil. He'd avoid visitors to the clinic by at least fifty feet. "The letter of the law," is the phrase Ed used with reporters when describing his personal behavior. There would be no more personal attacks on anyone.

Ed was flying under the radar when I sought him out for an article I was writing for a site called WireSource.net. There was a new Supreme Court nominee and the abortion issue had heated up again. The "right to life movement" wasn't my first choice of topics, but I'd never shied away from religion and politics. As a twenty-eight-year-old, single, mildly depressed, overqualified female freelance journalist who was new to town, I had plenty of firsthand knowledge about bad decisions. And besides, I needed the work.

The streets were filled with a few inches of fast-melting March slush when I parked across from the clinic. I put two quarters in the meter and started across the street. Ed had spotted me, and he had that careful look as if trying to decide whether I was a clinic patient or an employee. Just as I gave him a friendly wave, a driver went out of her way to hit a puddle near Ed, splashing him from head to toe. I trotted a step faster toward him, offering to help. But Ed quickly waved me off, brushing the muddy water from his old nylon jacket.

"I'm used to it," he said. When Ed spoke, he had a habit of drawing out one or more of his words. It wasn't a speech impediment. It was more like a man prone to slowing himself down so he could think about what he was saying.

"I'm so sorry. Is there anything I can do?"

"Really, it's normal," he said, bluntly. This was, of course, the beginning of my story, the very reason I'd come to see Ed. That is, to find out what made him tick. If getting a face full of spring snowmelt from an angry motorist was normal, what else did Ed have in store for me?

"What do you mean by 'it's normal,'" I asked. I was offering Ed my small pack of tissues, but he wouldn't take it. He wiped his hands on his jeans and ran his left hand across his forehead, pushing his flattop back into place.

"What I mean is this is what happens to me. Every day, it's something. My colleagues and I just never know what it will be until it happens. But we are not treated like other human beings."

I held up a reporter's notebook.

"Do you mind? I'd like to take notes."

"You are the writer lady, correct?"

"Yes, sorry. I'm Kate. Kate Bruce."

"So you have two first names?"

"I've never really thought of it, but yes, I guess I do."

I gestured to Ed that we consider moving to a nearby bus stop bench.

"Wanna sit?" I asked.

He tucked his sign under his arm and we walked to the corner. I noticed that in addition to his wet jacket and pants, his clothes were a long way from new. The cuffs were frayed and his fake leather shoes had salt rings up to the laces. When we approached the bench, Ed removed his soggy handkerchief and wiped off the seat, then motioned me to the spot he'd cleared.

"I don't use a tape recorder," I said, "just a notepad."

"Whatever works. I'll talk as slooooow as you'd like." The word thing wasn't just a quirk, it was also Ed's dopey way of trying to be cute. It struck me that as much time as he spent berating the women who entered the clinic, he might not know how to have a normal conversation with one.

"Okay, let's get started."

"Do you mind if I touch your hair?" Ed asked. I'd worn it down that day and was suddenly dreading my mistake. "Never wear your hair down if you want to be taken seriously," was something an old journalism professor of mine had said a hundred times.

"Yes, Ed. I *do* mind if you touch my hair. Let's stick with the interview."

"My wife, when I met her, had beautiful hair like yours," he said. "I'm sorry for asking." Ed's tone had shifted, reflecting both sadness and shame. I wasn't quite sure what I felt, but I responded in the worst way I could have, grabbing a handful of my own long hair and holding it out for Ed to feel.

"It's fine, you can touch it." I couldn't believe the words were coming out of my mouth as I was saying it, but Ed seemed so innocent. He reached out toward my hair, then pulled back just before touching it.

"Maybe I can just answer your questions," he said. "Maybe that's best." Ed sat back on the bench, crossing his arms and looking, finally, serious. The posture was defensive and I realized that he was bouncing back and forth between being closed and withdrawn and being outgoing and assertive. Whatever damage had been done to Ed had happened long ago.

"Take that one there." Ed pointed to a girl, about nineteen, entering the clinic. "She's going to kill her baby, and really, there's nothing I can do about it. Most of them have it in their heart what they want to do before they get here."

"Not everyone comes here to abort a fetus, Ed. The vast majority come for counseling or reproductive health reasons."

"But most come to kill their babies. It's in their heart."

"You've said that twice now—what do you mean it's in their heart?"

"Killing. God made us that way. We're either killers or we're not."

"So you think that girl's a killer?"

"Stone cold. Might as well be Charlie Manson if you ask me."

"I am asking you, Ed. What makes that girl a killer, in your opinion?"

"Look. She had her choices. Got knocked up. Might not know who the father is. No responsibility for her actions. Nowadays they make abortion just as easy as intercourse."

"Neither choice is easy for a lot of people, Ed." It wasn't a question, and I'd promised myself I'd stick to questions. But the pain in the young woman's face had been obvious.

"Maybe true." Ed leaned back and pushed both hands through his thick flattop. He took a deep breath as if thinking things through deeper than he'd done before. "Maybe there are degrees of killers. For some, it weighs on their conscience more than others. Doesn't make it any more right, though. Once you walk through that door, wrong is wrong."

"Do you have any sympathy for that woman, Ed?"

"Honestly? No."

"Because?"

"Because somewhere along the line, she let the devil inside her, Kate. Easy or not, she made a choice to have sex, probably with someone she's not married to, and last time I heard, not many folks are out there having sex without knowing that it can make a baby."

"Rape? Incest?"

"Yep, I've heard that argument and it's a good one. But it's still wrong. There's a human life in there, Kate. Just as real as you or me. The way we're made, see, we're made to give that life in the womb a chance. Some folks get the idea that they don't owe that life anything, that it's just a part of them so they have a right to decide. But it's not. No matter where it came from, that's a little person in there. That baby could be the next Einstein or Martin Luther King."

A middle-aged woman was standing near the far end of the bench, out of sight of Ed. It must have been her regular stop because she was using her hands to pantomime "yap yap yap" toward me, the assumption being that Ed had somehow trapped me in his lair. The bus was arriving and she couldn't resist commenting.

"Ed, why don't you leave the poor girl alone!" she said. "We've all heard what you have to say."

Without missing a beat or turning around, Ed replied, "And we've all heard you, Mrs. Fraser. Last I looked, we still have a First Amendment."

"You're the felon, Ed, not me." Her words were stinging, a touché of sorts, and the bus door closed before Ed could reply. His guilty plea was so public that many of his opponents, including the clinic neighbors he'd harassed for years, felt vindicated. This was Ed's life now. He stood up and motioned me to follow him as we walked back toward the clinic.

"I'm not allowed within fifty feet of the door," he said. "Restraining order. But Kate, it's not like I'd ever hurt anyone intentionally. I really didn't mean to hurt that girl last year."

"You don't have to defend yourself to me, Ed. That's not what I'm here for."

"What are you here for, then? Most of the papers, they really didn't come to listen to my side, they just made me out as a monster."

"Do you see yourself that way, Ed?"

"As a monster? No. I mean I hope not. But I did what I did and there's no way to take it back. What else am I supposed to do now?" Somehow the idea of Ed asking me what to do felt like we'd crossed a line. My mind was racing, and I needed to regain my footing.

"I'm not sure what your time's like, Ed. But if it's alright, let's pick up tomorrow, but not right here by the clinic."

"There's a diner on Prospect near the theater, do you know that place?"

"I do, yeah. Sally's."

"Right. I could meet you there tomorrow, but it would have to be early. Is seven okay?"

"It is. Coffee at seven. Sally's."

"I'll have about an hour, but I gotta be back here when the door opens."

Ed's demeanor shifted to one of determination. He picked up his sign and started pacing the sidewalk with the kind of comfort that comes from familiarity. I watched him from my car for a few minutes and was surprised by the paradox. He was affable and friendly to people walking by and said hello as if greeting a neighbor. At the same time, the sign he was carrying suggested there was mass murder going on just a few feet away and that he was the only one who seemed to understand or care. When someone would open the door to enter or leave, he'd yell from a distance, calling out "murderer" as if he expected the police to show up and make an arrest.

On the way back to my flat, Billy called. We hadn't spoken since I'd left in late summer, but he was back from a trip to Patagonia and having his every-once-in-a-while need for connection. There were so many things about him that I missed, but not seeing or talking to him had given me the strength I'd been looking for. It went out the window when I heard his voice.

"It's amazing, Kate, glaciers everywhere. You have to go there with me."

Drizzle was pelting my windshield and I tried to focus on the rhythm of the wipers. Anything to avoid another seduction, I thought. I counted each swipe.

"Kate?"

"Billy, this is a new life for me, you know that."

"I know you have to do whatever you're doing. But nothing's permanent. You can take the girl out of Alaska but you can't take Alaska out of . . ."

I stopped him so cold it surprised both of us.

"We're done, Billy. It's not that I don't want to go to Patagonia or see friends in Alaska. But there's no 'we' anymore. You have to move on."

The silence was long enough for me to think he'd lost his signal.

"You there?"

"Yeah. But I'm not sure how you can just stop. We have something really worthwhile."

"Worthwhile? Interesting choice of words. Worthwhile to you, maybe. As long as you can come and go and I'm there whenever you decide to be around. So yeah, worthwhile to you."

"I've been around long enough to know the truth when I see it, Kate. It was good for both of us. We have something special. I can see it in your eyes every time I look at you."

My eyes were tearing up and I had to pull the car over. All the training I'd had for my work, the balance, the fairness, the objectivity, seeing the world through someone else's eyes, it all went out the window when Billy called. I'd just spent an hour with an unblinking moralist who had no doubts about right and wrong. As simple as Ed made things sound, the very nature of a relationship changed everything. Being two is complicated.

Before I could fixate on all the options Billy wanted me to consider, or be persuaded by the boyish, charming ways he'd navigated all my desires and my fears for nearly a decade, I heard myself speak.

"Billy, I love you. Maybe too much. But what we want, the way we want to live our lives, it's not the same thing. You know that. I loved the idea of us, but the reality isn't the same. What I need is a lover who will build a home with me, maybe build a family."

"Well the home's pretty empty right now, babe. I look out and I see the snowy peaks, I see the trail where we like to bike. But your things are gone, you're gone."

"When I say the word family, you talk about other things. Experiences. Places. Adventures. When I say home, you talk about a house."

I rolled the window down so I could breathe. Billy's silence said everything I needed to hear.

"Look, I've gotta get inside to a meeting. I really can't have this discussion right now," I said.

"You still renting from your mom?" asked Billy. "Tell her I said hello."

I was swallowing my tears, hoping he couldn't hear me. I took a deep breath and tried to feel my feet, anything to ground me.

"Tell her I'll send her some of that sweet Fireweed syrup when it comes in next spring."

The idea of Billy standing in front of the window of a place we'd built together was killing me. The house was the only thing that was ours. I could remember the first time we'd stood on the lot, looking out at the Lynn Canal, watching the ferries come and go from Juneau and Skagway. Living there was a dream we shared, two people together with the same vision right down to the sun-filled summers and the long winter nights by an old woodstove. We'd pooled enough money for hardwood floors and we had enough windows and skylights that we'd always have the sense that we were inside nature instead of a house. But I also remembered how many days and nights I was alone there while Billy was off on some great adventure. The loft we'd built for our bed was the warmest, safest place I'd ever been when he was there, and the loneliest place on Earth when he was gone.

Now, sitting on the side of a road in downtown Milwaukee, rain freezing to my windshield, I felt as far away as I could be. It wasn't a safe place, but living together hadn't been safe either. I lost myself there. Every part of me was tearing against itself. I wanted to fall right back into Billy and the dream, but I knew it was just that. When we hung up, I wondered how long it would be before our next call. The part of me that wanted to dial him back lost out to the part that wanted to move on. I started the car and drove back to the apartment.

\\\\

Sally's wasn't the classic greasy spoon from college days with a screaming ex-con fry cook strung out on speed. It was, instead, the kind of place that borrowed on quaint Midwest tradition, with pies in a spinning glass cabinet, florescent lights, and fake brass railings separating long rows of booths. I sat near a window so it would be easier for Ed to find me. The waitress brought me an egg-colored ceramic mug of coffee and a glass of water with two small ice cubes. Crossword puzzles were a hand-me-down from my mom, and I was filling in the one on the paper placemat when Ed surprised me.

"What's a four letter word for potato?"

"Hey Ed, have a seat."

The waitress was close behind Ed, aware of who he was and clearly trying to make sure he wasn't going to be a bother to the customers or to me. She backed off with my greeting, but only a little.

"Spud," he said, answering his own question. Then he ordered a coffee from the waitress, who looked displeased that she had to serve him.

"Will you two be having anything else?"

"You have egg beaters?" he asked.

"We do."

"I'll take two egg beaters scrambled and whole wheat toast."

"Nothing else for me, thanks." I caught the waitress's eye as she was writing, and thought I witnessed a pleading moment, as if she was begging me to get out while I could. She walked away, still writing.

"So you like crosswords," he said.

"Just killing time." It wasn't my best choice of words but I rebounded quickly. "You did something different?" I said. Ed had spruced up for our rendezvous. There was some kind of gel holding his flattop steady.

"Oh, you know, a good shave comes and goes with my moods, I guess. But cleanliness is next to Godliness."

I wondered whether Ed was trying to impress me. Not the reporter me, but the woman me. I kept my mouth shut and took a long sip of coffee using both hands on the mug to hide my expression. His leg wasn't touching mine beneath the table, but I could feel it shaking up and down, nervously.

"Why do you do what you do, Ed?"

"What do you mean?" His leg stopped abruptly.

"I mean, what drives you? It takes a lot of courage for any person to stand up for their beliefs. And a lot of perseverance to do it all day, every day, especially without compensation."

"I do it because it's what I believe in."

"I think it's more than that. You're committed to it, but it's more than that. Aren't you a bit obsessed?"

Ed didn't know what to make of my question. Perhaps it was more than conviction, but if it was, he didn't want to let on. I was searching for something deeper. I wondered what emotional damage played into Ed's choices.

"You married?" asked Ed. His leg was shaking again.

"Spoken for," I said. "A man from Alaska. He's a whitewater river guide."

"A river guide. That's a profession?"

"Some would say it's not," I said, smiling. "But he finds a way to make ends meet. And he gets to live in nature more than the rest of us."

"And you're here? Why are you here?"

"I thought I was the one asking questions."

"If you're here and he's there, then maybe you're hiding the truth about being 'spoken for.'"

"Now Ed, that's quite an accusation."

"I don't mean lying in the big scheme of things. I mean, maybe there's more to your story."

"Isn't there more to everyone's story?" I asked. "And since you brought it up, do you see degrees to lying? I mean, is lying black and white in the way you see abortion, or are there acceptable reasons for a lie?"

"God knows either way," said Ed. "I guess some people need to lie to convince themselves they're safer, or maybe to hide something they're afraid of. But God knows the answers, not me."

"What about the people who don't believe in God? A lot of them still don't believe in lying."

"Morals came from somewhere, Kate. I believe they came from God, not the Greeks. If someone doesn't believe in God, that doesn't always make her bad. It just means they're not going to be saved. I might feel sorry for her, but it's God's will that matters, not mine."

"And you—are you married?"

"I was. I told you about her hair, remember?"

"I do, yes. I'm sorry for your loss."

"She's not dead, Kate. Just remarried. We were divorced about fifteen years ago."

"You and half of all Americans." I said it to provide some comfort, but Ed clearly had a different view.

"One half too many, I'd say. What my wife wanted, I didn't. But in this state, there's nothing I could do about it. In my mind, we were married for life."

"So have you been with other woman since your divorce?"

"I don't covet other women, no. I have men and women friends at church, and I talk to Reverend Marena from time to time about things church-related. But in my mind, I'm still married."

"Why did she want out, Ed, if you don't mind my asking."

The timing of my question wasn't as good as I'd have liked because the waitress showed up right then with Ed's toast and Egg Beaters. She put it down in front of him with a rude thud.

"Anything else I can get the two of you?" She asked as a professional courtesy, while wanting to turn away as quickly as possible.

Ed shook his head. I didn't want to dignify her behavior with eye contact and she huffed off.

"Has anyone else ever interviewed you before, Ed?"

"You're the first." He took a large bite and chewed with his mouth open. "I figured you wanted to talk to me 'cause of the felony. And as I said, I didn't mean to hurt that woman."

"I already interviewed the woman who runs the clinic," I said. "And two women who made very different choices about their pregnancies.

One kept her child; the other visited the clinic last week. It's a better story if I know what you think too. With each person, I'm trying to put a face on the issue by finding out who someone is, and why they think the way they do."

"The abortion ones—They're killers, end of story." Most people would stop eating while making such a statement, but not Ed. It was rote to him and he kept talking with his mouth half full.

"You've said that."

"I've said it 'cause it's true. And I'll keep saying it."

"Can we talk about your wife again?"

"Only if we can talk about your Mister River Guide." He said it with some disdain and a bit of a dare.

"My significant other has a name. It's Billy. And yes, we had been living together, but not married, before I came here. Why is that important to you?"

"Because it tells me what kind of person you are, what kind of choices you make. You're a liberal."

"I'm a journalist."

"Biased like the rest of them."

"You asked me about Billy and I told you the truth. Whether I live with him or am married has no bearing on how I write my story."

Ed stopped eating and looked at me directly. I could feel the assault of his eyes and the tone of his voice as if I was the one walking into the clinic.

"You're a liberal and that means you're pro-abortion."

The risk of losing Ed and the interview had happened so suddenly, and getting defensive was only going to make it worse. I'd made a mistake by answering his question instead of deflecting it, but being honest had somehow seemed like an advantage.

"Your wife, Ed. Why did she want a divorce?"

Ed pushed away his plate. As he'd done a day earlier, he ran both hands through his thick hair. When he took a deep breath, he seemed to get smaller and smaller in the booth, losing confidence as his diaphragm deflated and the air rushed back through his mouth. His answer was direct but the manner of his expression was timid.

"It was simple, really. I wanted children, she didn't. God put us here to multiply, Kate. My wife didn't feel the same way about things."

"That had to be very difficult for you."

He answered with a frown, as if words had become too much of a burden. His leg was shaking again and I realized that it wasn't because of his proximity to me. If he had any attraction at all for me when he sat down, it was innocent enough. What seemed more real was Ed's very human need to connect with someone. I wondered when the last time was that Ed sat down to a meal with another person, anyone at all. He had no wife, no children, and from what I could gather, no close friends.

"Are you and your wife still in contact?"

"Because we didn't have children, once we broke things up it was easy for her to move on. She left town, and last I heard, got remarried as I said. Apparently he had some kids from his first marriage. So go figure."

"I'm sorry. Maybe you should move on too? It may sound trite but life is short."

"Like I said, in my mind, we're married for life."

"But Ed . . ."

"When I met her, I was twenty-three and just out of the Army. I took two jobs to support us while she went to technical school. We were in love, and by the time we were twenty-eight, we had a house of our own. It had three pretty good-sized bedrooms with plenty of room for a family. For the first few years, I just figured she wasn't ready, so I mentored kids from the local school and volunteered as a Big Brother. I put aside money for our own kids and did what I could to support the local groups with checks here and there—a new basketball hoop, uniforms for the band, and a nativity scene for the county courthouse back when it was still legal to celebrate Christmas. By the time we were in our mid-thirties, it was pretty clear she didn't want children. I thought she was self-centered then, and I still do now."

Ed took a long sip of his coffee and I could see a small tear well up in the corner of his eye. Whoever she was, she'd changed the course of Ed's life. Now, in his early sixties, the few things he had left in his life defined him. Whether he really felt as strongly about his clinic protests as others believed he did just didn't matter. The mission kept his mind off all the things his life had never become.

The waitress brought us a bill. We reached for it at the same time and began a friendly tug-of-war, then laughed out loud when it ripped in half. Ed won the battle, and I left the tip, making sure it was about the same amount so I wouldn't have any ethical issues with him paying. He had to get to the clinic to get started with his day and suggested that we could meet up again if there was something else I wanted to know. Otherwise, he said, he was happy to have met me. We exchanged phone numbers and he offered me a ride, but I declined by saying that I had a bit more writing to do and would sit for a while longer.

The parking lot was adjacent to the restaurant, and I smiled as I watched Ed pull out. It looked as if the antlers on the bumper were pulling his vehicle from behind. Just before he turned into the street, he looked back toward me with his microphone in hand. He smiled and raised his eyebrows like a precocious child with a new toy, then said, "See you later, Kate," through the loudspeaker on top of his car. I felt myself blush as I turned back to my notebook.

\\\\

The article appeared two weeks later. In some ways, it was more of the same, except that it gave a fair voice to Ed. The women I profiled who had chosen abortion had fairly predictable circumstances. Too young, no partner. Too old, no finances. Too many mouths to feed. They were unplanned, accidental pregnancies terminated by likeable, socially conscious women who weighed the options and decided their circumstances dictated continuing their life on the course intended. They said they believed it was better for all involved to terminate the pregnancy before conception would lead to a fully developed fetus and, eventually, a child. Because these women seemed intelligent, reasonable, and thoughtful, many readers no doubt felt sympathy for their circumstances and choices. Other women saw themselves in the same situation, having either been there or, perhaps, knowing that they'd just missed being there by the luck of the draw.

Two men emailed me complaining that I was a typical female writer who'd once again ignored the impact of abortion on the male partners. One suggested that I stake out the waiting room for a day and write about the horrible burden that supportive men have to endure. I suspect his notion that I couldn't comprehend all they were going through was true enough since I couldn't find a way to see their odyssey with the same complexity as a woman's. I might have been more delicate in my response, but I'd lived in Alaska long enough that suggesting he shove his keyboard up his ass just popped out.

In contrast, a longtime friend from Vermont called to thank me for the article, reminding me of my own abortion during our sophomore year in Burlington. Though I'd not intended the article to reflect a point of view, she'd clearly read it as at least vaguely apologetic based on her perception of my own guilt. She also criticized Billy, but given the way she'd flirted with me over the years, I didn't let the conversation linger. Another friend, who'd had three visits to a clinic, thanked me for "standing fast" on the issue of a woman's right to choose. I imagined her with a glass of Chablis and a cigarette in her hand as she laughingly asked me about "that crazy Ed guy" and "what kind of wacko" he must have been. "Thank God," she said, "those people give me the creeps." She'd used abortion as contraception for years, but she still saw Ed as "kind of wacko."

It hadn't been my intention to criticize Ed in any way. In fact, I'd tried to show him as a real human being, albeit an unusual one. But the photo editor had included not only the mug shot of Ed, but also an archival photo of the shopping cart full of bloody dolls from the day of his arrest.

Pictures have a language of their own and the images of Ed were less than flattering.

\\\\

The test, for me, came at Ed's funeral. Somehow I'd imagined that his entire flock would show up, maybe even carrying signs of support for their fallen comrade. The hundreds of followers who joined him for the occasional Saturday protests along Lake Drive would be there. The conservative politicians who campaigned pro-life and attended evangelical churches for Sunday morning photo ops would be there. The bishops and ministers who used the newspapers and talk radio to argue their positions would be there. After all, Ed was the most famous antiabortion protester in Wisconsin. He might not have been a leader in the classic sense, but he'd taken the fall time and again as the movement's man on the street.

I felt conflicted about attending, but Ed had touched me. He was both honest and a bit naive, which for a man of his age was unusual. But it was more than that. Ed was passionate and committed, and while I didn't personally agree with him, I don't think Ed meant to hurt anyone. He might not have understood the women entering the clinic on Brady Street, but it was a two-way street. Many of those same women didn't understand Ed, and for thousands of reasons, most weren't inclined to. There may not be a worse day in a woman's life than the day she enters an abortion clinic. Nobody wants an abortion, but that didn't stop Ed from name calling and deriding each woman every time one entered the clinic.

Imagine making the hardest decision you've ever faced, then carrying it out in secret without the knowledge or support of almost everyone you care about. You call in sick to work for a day. You decide not to tell your boyfriend or husband, either because of fear of rejection or, worse, a fear they'll challenge your decision. You beg a close girlfriend to come along with you because you know you'll break down if you see your partner in the waiting room after the procedure is done. And, more than anything, you hope you won't have to talk about it. It's easy to support the right to choose—you can do that. But the ethics are complicated, and an unwanted pregnancy brings them to the surface. Add in the terrible reality that the clock is ticking. You're running out of time. You make your choice, hope you can live with it, and on the way inside, you run into Ed. There he is, the crazy guy from the television and newspapers and this time, he's not yelling at someone else, he's yelling at you. Today, you are the one Ed's calling a killer.

I wondered how Ed could be so judgmental. Why was it even his business? What would Christ have thought of Ed and the way he spewed his violent rhetoric toward the women entering the clinic? What was it, I wondered, that made Ed give up everything in his life to stand vigil on a dingy street corner in a city that thought of him as a nuisance, or at best, a joke?

\\\\

The casket was open in front of the altar, and Ed looked surprisingly good. His cheeks were flush with rouge, his hair the perfect flattop, and he was wearing a pressed suit that looked like it had cost at least two hundred dollars. His lips were pressed slightly upward into a somewhat wry smile. Perhaps because there were so few of us, Reverend Marena asked us to rise and stand with her in front of the casket instead of sitting spread out in the pews. She spoke kindly of Ed, remembering him as a man who gave so much of himself without asking anything in return. She talked about how Ed had first given up his career as a roofing contractor, and then his life savings for his cause. When he died, he was living alone in a single room at a boarding house on the near west side. Outside of his fabled station wagon, Ed had left behind virtually nothing of value. The world wouldn't remember Ed for long, she said, but many would remember the cause he stood for and the commitment he'd made. As a deacon, Ed had given more hours to the church than anyone in recent memory.

The five of us in attendance were asked whether we wanted to say anything. His landlady commented that he always paid his rent on time and shoveled the sidewalks "all the way to the corner every time it snowed." Two old gentlemen mumbled that they really didn't want to say much, but one gave a thumbs up. A grayish, heavyset woman about Ed's age just shook her head. When the reverend looked at me, I felt too conflicted to refuse. I couldn't say no because I kept seeing Ed's smiling face on our last encounter, wishing me goodbye through his loudspeaker. What came out was not noteworthy; in fact, it was so grimly simple and unknowing of who Ed might have been that I could feel him laughing at me from the place he called heaven.

"He was a man of commitment," I said. "In the end, I guess, that means something."

There wasn't much reason for a wake or meal after the service, and the minister said as much. The burial was open to the public, but none of us made a move to follow the coffin as it was wheeled toward the front door. I didn't want to look too conspicuous by running out quickly, which meant walking the long aisle with the heavyset woman in tow. We tried a bit of small talk before she asked me how I knew Ed.

"I can't really say I knew him."

"Doesn't look like you're alone," she said with a laugh. "That was the smallest funeral I've ever been to."

"Were you his friend for a long time?"

"Not exactly. More that I was his friend a long time ago. Former sister-in-law would be more accurate."

"He told me he was still married . . . in his mind, that is."

"From the day she died, he was never the same."

"His wife died?"

I played back the conversation Ed and I had about lying. Whatever the truth was, Ed had chosen to keep it between him and his God.

"It wasn't that simple," she said. "Her name was Angela. She was my younger sister and we were close. They were about as happy as any couple I'd ever seen, but they had trouble getting pregnant. It took years, but when Angie finally did, she was about five months along when she was diagnosed with cervical cancer."

"And Ed wanted to keep the baby?"

"No. The doctors said there was no chance for Angie to live without starting treatment, which meant aborting the pregnancy. Ed was adamant that he wanted her to start the chemo. To him, it was most important to save Angie's life.

"So the abortion was his choice?"

"Inasmuch as you can call it a choice. They buried their unborn in April. Gave it a name and a tombstone, which may have been a comfort, but it was too weird for me. Even with the treatment, my sister was dead by late September, and Ed was never the same."

"Who would be?"

"In a way," she said, "the cancer killed all three of them."

We were in the lobby near the front door and there was commotion over how to get the coffin down the front steps with the minister and a maintenance person working together to get it onto the ramp. My head was suddenly spinning, trying to make sense of Ed's life and the sadness he was forced to bear.

There was a long pause as we watched the doors close behind Ed's coffin. I said a quick goodbye, but as I was walking away, she called after me. I watched her navigate her obesity as she walked slowly down the steps. The world moved at her speed.

"You are the lady that wrote the article, right?"

"I am."

"Probably seems odd, but he asked me to tell you something before he died. He called me after you interviewed him, said you were kind to him, listening to him in a way that other people hadn't."

"Half my job is to listen, the other half is to write. He seemed like a man who hadn't had a lot of friendly ears."

"I didn't know what he meant at the time, but he wanted you to forgive him for lying to you. There were just some things too secret, too painful to confess out loud."

"We face them when we can," I said, "or we die with them. I'm not the one to judge him."

"He was such a lovely man back then," she said, "a little odd even then, but lovely. And now here he is with just five people at his funeral."

Her bus was approaching and she flagged the driver with her cane, then moved considerably faster than I'd imagined she could to get to it in time.

The minister was loading the coffin into the hearse and I watched for a while from a few feet away. The spring flowers were in full bloom and I thought how beautiful it was outside compared to the day I'd first met Ed. Before they closed the back door, I twisted off a few strands of lilac from a bush near the roadside. I took a deep whiff, pulled a rubber band from my hair, and wrapped them together at the stem. I laid the small bouquet on top of Ed's coffin and heard myself say "goodbye."

88 CHUNKS

"THAT GUY DEAD YET?"

The disembodied voice startled me. I had my feet tucked under the thin blanket that was covering Uncle Marty's torso, and when I jerked back in my chair, I accidentally disconnected his catheter.

"Shit, shit, shit." I pinched off the end and was reconnecting it when the voice came again.

"I'm not pushing it, mind you, but the guy's wheezing kept me up all night. It's not easy listening to that crap."

When I pulled back the flimsy curtain, the ugliest kid I'd ever seen was grinning at me. His smile was wide but creepy, his teeth bucked forward, the left one chipped in half. He was hairy like a Bernese mountain dog, but long and lean like a Dachshund. His feet hung over the foot of the bed and his hospital gown barely made it below his privates. There was a hideous quality to his toenails—they'd been growing so long they were tucking back around toward the bottom of his feet.

"Does he look like he's dead to you?" I asked.

"Matter of fact . . ."

Before he could finish his sentence, I pulled the privacy curtain back—his cue to stop talking. The problem was, Uncle Marty did look dead. He'd been in a coma for more than a month, but his physical condition had improved enough for him to be transferred out of the ICU and into a shared room the insurance company thought it could afford. I was checking Marty's catheter again when the new roommate decided to play "Here's Johnny." He stuck his burly head into Marty's room with the curtain wrapped tight around all but his face. Then the grin, again.

"Can't you show some respect?"

"It's not like he can hear us," he said. "The guy's coma-toast."

"Coma*tose*."

"Like I said, he can't hear us. You could fart in the old boy's face and not get a reaction. Want me to let one go?"

"No, actually. I want you to leave us alone. You're disgusting."

The curtain dropped and I could hear the bed squeak just a bit when he sat back down. I picked up the book I'd been reading and tried to get comfortable in the chair. *The Love Poems of Rumi*. It was the only thing I'd found at my sister Holly's house besides the latest copy of *US Weekly* and a year old issue of *People*. She kept the small volume of poetry atop the crocheted liner on the back of her toilet. With Holly's turnstile approach to boyfriends, I wondered how many had been impressed.

"You some kind of fairy or something?" It was now clear the curtain wouldn't stop the interruptions.

"What are you talking about?"

"Dude . . . *The Love Poems of Rumi*? You trying to bang a nurse or something?"

"What would you know about it?" I refused to give the guy an inch. "If you've been spying on Uncle Marty when there's no family member here then I can ask to have you transferred."

"You won't find love by reading the musings of a nine hundred year old Sufi is all I'm saying."

"So you're an expert on love . . . or Sufism?"

"Love, actually."

"I'm guessing you spend a lot of time in truck stop parking lots?"

"Here's the deal. I know that most women aren't as concerned with romantic literacy as they are with financial literacy. Yours or mine. You can talk equality all you want, but financial security rules."

That was it. I stood up and ripped back the curtain.

"What are you here for, anyway?"

"Who's asking?"

"Don't be a jerk. What are you here for?"

"Well, let's see. I've got an IV in this arm for antibiotics in case the little critters in my GI tract get too hungry, a chest tube pumping in Malto Meal just in case I get hungry, an oxygen tube in my nose and, oh yeah, I've got late stage Non-hodgkins lymphoma, which explains the bags under my eyes and the sepia-toned skin. The great personality comes from the pain injection I got about an hour ago when you were sleeping one off with your Uncle Marty."

"Why do you have so much hair, then? What about the chemo?"

"What chemo? When I said late stage I guess I forgot to mention that I ignored the symptoms long enough that those treatment options were no longer available."

"So you're here to die?"

"No, that's hospice. I'm here because some dickweed from Medical U is coming to take my temperature tomorrow morning on the assumption that I've qualified for some super-secret government program where they send unrepentant walking dead guys like me into the stratosphere to see if the ozone layer really is deteriorating."

"Sounds like your kind of program."

"Sounds like your kind of program." With a sneer and a mocking tone, he repeated me word for word.

I'd had enough, and rather than try to beat the crap out of a dying *twentysomething*, I decided to go buy the day old tabouli platter from the over-priced cafeteria. As I was leaving the room, I stopped to take a serious look at Uncle Marty. Absolutely nothing about him had changed during the past month except the depth of his face. He wore the same empty expression, but his cheeks were sinking lower and lower to the point where I could see the outline of his false teeth. I thought for a moment that he looked dangerous, dangerous like the trapped Malcolm McDowell with his eyelids pulled back in *A Clockwork Orange* or Anthony

Hopkins pressing his face against the cell bars while making slurping sounds in *Silence of the Lambs*. He had that uncertain quality, as if he might leap up and grab me after playing dead, hour after hour. For a reason I can't explain, I reached down and lifted Uncle Marty's top lip and, sure enough, his dentures were still in place. As if releasing a rubber band, I let go, but his lip was soft and flabby and it returned slowly to the stationary position he'd held onto for weeks.

\\\\\

Holly was in the cafeteria with her two toddlers and her latest Dutch au pair, a skinny nineteen-year-old named Flea. Flea, whose nickname may have been fun in Holland, had flown in from suburban Amsterdam, then spent a few weeks in Buffalo on her junior-year-abroad program. The USA was still an infatuation for her so she opted for a part-time, off-the-immigration-grid gig juggling my sister's preschool kids for ten bucks an hour in cash. Flea's English was as flawless as her skin, her teeth, her hair, her smile, and her bottom. The lazy eye, however, was a bit of a distraction if only because I couldn't figure out which one to look into when we were talking, a task made slightly easier by having virtually nothing to say to each other.

"You gonna eat that?" asked Holly. To her dismay, I'd taken the last piece of chilled rhubarb pie. I looked down at the stiff crust and compacted shreds of dried-out rhubarb and decided the pie had seen its better days. In a rare act of appeasement, I turned the plate over to Holly.

"No, that's okay."

"No really, take it."

"I don't want to take the last piece. Really, it's yours."

"I insist."

"I can't, really."

"It's yours. Really. It's speaking to you . . . listen." I put the plate up to her ear, gritted my teeth in a sinister smile and gave her my best ventriloquist voice a la Vincent Price whispering in *The Fly*. "Eat me . . . eeeeeat me . . . eeeeeeeat me."

The sad thing about Holly is that she can be so oblivious that she takes the fun out of being a jerk. She thought I was being cute. She thought I actually cared. And then she took my pie.

"Did you see Marty's new roommate?" I asked.

"Oh no, someone new? That means the ZZ Top look-alike has sailed on."

"You mean passed on."

"Passed on, whatever. Died. Croaked."

"Kicked the bucket. Bought the farm. Hit the high road to Heaven City."

Holly looked at me quizzically. I'd hit one too many clichés, and she'd lost track of our discussion.

"The guy's unusual, to say the least," I said.

"How so?"

"For starters, he's hairy. Like that Griffin Dunne character in *American Werewolf in London*. You remember that film?"

"No. It's from like a century ago. Like all your favorite movies. But I do know what a werewolf is."

Things moved at an awkward pace with Holly, so I changed the subject. "How's the pie?"

"I knew you'd hold it against me for eating your pie."

Nothing could transform a generation of discord. I refused her offer for a bite and pushed my chair back to get some space. The cafeteria was nearly empty, and with little more than a sudden burst of energy and slippery linoleum to go on, Flea was sliding the toddlers between tables on cafeteria trays. Everything was going fine until Sydney, the youngest, hit her head on the metal bars used to support the soda dispensers. She let out a garbled yelp just before the blood began flowing. Flea, the suddenly not-quite-perfect au pair, gasped, then screamed for help as Holly leaped into action. It was enough to make Sydney wail, a sound not unheard of in hospitals, though it was rare enough in the cafeteria to grab the attention of the kitchen help. A stoned high school kid on his first part-time, after-school job was carrying a metal tray of replacement peas for the cafeteria line and managed to send them flying. Holly practically threw two-year-old John Ryan into my arms with an exclamation that went something like "watch him or I'll kill you!" before grabbing Sydney in her arms and rushing down the hall toward the E.R. Proximity can play tricks on people in crisis, and as much as it may have played into Holly's hands in saving poor Sydney the agony of scar tissue on the forehead, Flea seemed pleased at the notion of staying behind and finishing up Holly's half-eaten pie.

"She left her pie" was all Flea needed to say as I handed her a clean fork.

"There's nothing I'd rather do right now than leave John Ryan in your capable hands," I said, "but one of us has to stay here and wait for an update from nurse Florence Nightingale. So with your permission, the two of us, J.R. and me that is, are going to head up to Uncle Marty's room to finish watch duty before dear Aunt Mimi shows up from her appointment at Supercuts. Does that work for you, Flea?"

Flea nodded yes, and while I couldn't exactly say who she was looking at, I took the absence of others in the area as a pretty good sign she was acknowledging me.

\\\\

"You ever see a guy in a coma?" My nephew, John Ryan, was riding on my back as we entered Uncle Marty's room. J.R. wouldn't have known Marty from any other patient. For that matter, he was just learning the difference between Marty and the obese pet bunny he had caged up in the pen at home. Both were barely breathing. Both had stopped hopping long ago. And neither had much to offer a two-year-old preoccupied with motion.

I sat down on the hard-backed chair with the faux leather, turquoise colored padding and put J.R. on my lap. We made funny faces at each other, then practiced parade waves trying to get Marty's attention. With nothing offered in return, J.R. lost interest quickly. I was bouncing him on my leg and filling his tiny hand with chopped ice from Marty's plastic cup when Furboy opened the curtain again.

"I'm baaaack." he said, imitating the prescient child from *Poltergeist*.

"I don't caaaare," I replied. But clearly, whatever I thought would in no way dissuade Mr. Ugly.

"Did you bring me anything?" He flashed a well-timed grin that was mildly endearing.

"Their deep fryer was on the fritz," I said, quietly congratulating myself for the cunning though not-too-subtle insult. Still, it was enough to send Hairball back to his side of the curtain. A full minute of prolonged silence was deafening, and J.R. let it be known by smacking me hard on the shoulder. Had I really hurt the roommate's feelings?

"What are you in for again?" I asked through the curtain.

"I'm dying, remember."

"Oh yeah, I forgot."

"That's okay. You and everyone else."

Crap. The Son of Wolf Man had done the impossible. He'd found a way to shame me into caring, however brief the feeling. I'd have to repair my damaged armor later.

"No folks? No girlfriend?"

"Do I look like I have a girlfriend to you Mr. Wizard?"

"It would take a rare woman, but there's always Tumblr."

Comforted by our dialogue, J.R. took the cue to doze off. I laid him down in the bed just under Uncle Marty's right arm. His body hadn't moved in a month so the odds were pretty good he wouldn't accidentally toss the little nipper out of bed. The posed encounter of nephew and uncle was mildly cute (albeit a bit sick) and I snapped a quick photo with my phone. Then I pulled back the curtain. My new best friend Lassie was lying on his back, legs up and crossed, and clipping his fingernails.

"You should think about giving your toenails a ride with that thing too," I said.

"Aren't we a regular Jimmy Kimmel. Did it ever occur to you that I might like my toenails just the way they are?"

"No. But thanks for planting that seed." I took a long sip from the 24-ounce melted Slurpee I'd brought back from the cafeteria. "I'm sorry to hear you're alone in here, really. That has to suck."

"Look, I'm not exactly charming," he said. "And I've burned a few bridges along the way."

"That's hard to believe."

"Funny."

"Everyone's burned a few bridges. Even Uncle Marty here. You may have noticed that the only people dropping by are relatives still young enough to covet a miniscule inheritance."

"What kind of bridges did old Marty burn?"

We'd dialed down the animus meter a bit. The question was enough of an icebreaker that I pulled up a chair. I took another sip of Slurpee, pulled a Twix out of my shirt pocket and began unwrapping it. I offered up half, and when Godzilla grabbed his portion, I wondered how anyone could have that much hair on his knuckles.

"Thanks."

"No problem. My sister ate my pie. Well, her and the Little Dutch Girl nanny that is."

"You lost me."

"Whatever. Let's go with Uncle Marty. Old Uncle Marty. Part-time realtor, full-time alcoholic. The big family secret is that Marty knocked up a displaced South Korean woman during the winter of '54. There's no proof, of course, but Auntie Mimi makes a point of letting everyone know about it whenever Marty passes out at a family dinner party. It goes something like this: Marty shows up all fat and happy around 4 o'clock. He slaps a few backs, then goes straight for the Jim Beam. Marty likes nuts with his booze so no matter who's hosting, there's always a can of Planters Dry Roasted on the coffee table. Mimi always wears a hat and spends most of her time modeling it for attention. Sometimes she poses for the rest of us, sometimes she just looks at herself in the hallway mirror. Mimi isn't that particular as long as someone is commenting on how beautiful the hat looks. It never does, of course, but Holly and her former husband Joe have always made a point of telling her how beautiful it looks while giving equal attention to her pair of matching shoes. It wouldn't be all that odd except Mimi still makes two or three visits a week to the her favorite beauty parlor in Yonkers. The big question is, why curl the hair and then wear a hat?"

"This is going somewhere, right?" he asked. "Otherwise you might win my lame-ass-story-of-the-day award."

"You have a name?"

"Barry." When he extended his hand, the IV tube came with it.

"Forrest." It wasn't my name but Furball would never know.

"You do what, exactly? I mean, when you're not living out in the woods?"

"Look, I don't want to get too familiar if that's okay. I'd rather talk about Uncle Marty than me."

"I've got nothing but time, but let's get to the good stuff quick or I'm calling a nurse for more pain meds."

"Marty got busted for window-peeping back when the family lived in Omaha. He'd been out gambling horses at the Aksarben Race Track, lost his ass on a horse named Noodle Soup that pulled up lame, and he drank whatever he could still afford on the drive home. He parked his car in a neighbor's driveway, and the cops busted him standing in front of the picture window with his pants down."

"What makes you think he was peeping?"

"That's just it. Marty claimed up and down that he thought he was at his own house. When his key didn't work in the lock, he'd tried to wake up Mimi. When she didn't show, he had to take a leak. It's possible, I guess. If he'd been four houses further north at his own place, it would have been a disorderly conduct charge for public urination. Instead, he's registered on the Nebraska sexual predator list."

"That's not exactly what I'd call burning bridges, Forrest."

"Well, there was the time he got whacked by the IRS for tax fraud, he lost a few pals there. Then he embezzled more than twenty-eight thousand bucks from Mimi's mother on an art deal. She wasn't the only one."

"Now we're talking. An art deal?"

"Deal. Scam. Whatever you want to call it. He was double-selling Rauschenbergs and Jasper Johns out of a small gallery owned by an old buddy of his down in Noho. There was always one real piece of art and he'd give the buyer a look-see; then he'd move it around on loan to institutions, banks, and insurance companies based on some pre-existing albeit non-existent contracts. At any given time, either of the two or three owners could go see it if they wanted to because it was always hanging behind some receptionist's head."

"I'm feelin' better about old Uncle Marty right now," said Barry.

"Like I said, he wasn't exactly a great role model."

"You're the nephew?"

"The only one. Holly's the only niece. Though, as I mentioned, there might be someone in South Korea with his DNA. Otherwise, we're his closest relatives." I took another gulp. "So tell me about you. What charm school did you go to?"

Before Barry could open up, Dr. B.L. Makepeace came in followed by a team of residents with clipboards.

"Hello Horton," said Dr. Makepeace. "How are we feeling today?" Horton? Hmm. So Barry was really Horton.

"We?" said Horton.

"The proverbial 'we,'" said Dr. Makepeace. He glanced around at the team of young physicians and gave them a wink. It was his way of notifying everyone that he had things completely under control.

"You could say I'm one day closer to the death trap," said Horton. "You?"

"I'm fine, thanks for asking. But it's you we're here to check up on."

"I'm flattered."

Rather than check the beeping monitor a foot away, Dr. Makepeace checked Horton's pulse the old-fashioned way. Then he listened in on Horton's heart with a cold stethoscope. When he was sure of Horton's heart rate, he grabbed a clipboard from a very tall resident and made a note.

"Your mother says you lost a good fifty pounds before you came in." Horton glanced around the room to be sure Dr. Makepeace was talking to him.

"Speaking of mom, how is she anyway?"

Dr. Makepeace avoided the question.

"Again, you lost some weight?"

"Yeah, I was on the Subway diet," Horton shot back. "I'm working toward my own advertising contract since Jared Fogle took the plea bargain."

"Your mother also said you were sleeping more than ten hours a day."

"And exactly how would she know this?"

"You know mothers."

"I know clinical depression. And a little hamburger helper called Prozac. Did Mom mention that too? It goes really well with a chilled bottle of Don Julio."

"Look, we're going to start your surgery at 6:00 a.m. Why don't you get some sleep."

"Make up your mind, Doc. Sleep. Don't sleep. Too much sleep. Let's just hope your game of surgical Russian Roulette puts Horton's lights out for good."

Dr. Makepeace stopped the friendly chatter after Horton accused him of dropping his psych rotation after three weeks. He turned back toward his entourage and off they went. During the three minutes and twenty-six seconds the surgical team and residents had been in the room, not a single member had made eye contact with Barry a.k.a. Horton. The intern furthest in back had been texting, two others with pent up sexual energy had managed to rub hands, bottoms, and that sweet spot on the lower back, and the two closest to Dr. B.L. Makepeace had, wisely, kept their eyes glued on their mentor.

The visit had drained Horton of any further desire to be a thorn in my side.

"Why don't you close the curtain and go back to old Uncle Marty the art thief. Isn't it about time to roll him over or something?"

"Why'd you lie about your name?"

"Why'd you lie about yours?"

"Who says I did?"

"I went through your wallet earlier." I felt my back pocket and my wallet was right where it had been since I walked in from work. Horton smiled at my paranoia.

"You do that to people a lot, don't you?" he asked.

"Lie about my name? No, you're the first. Given your sparkling personality, I didn't want you to know who I was."

"If you were really somebody important, you wouldn't be here," said Horton. "You'd send someone in your place, then pay a two-minute courtesy call once a week. Nobody cares what your real name is Forrest. Including me."

"I'm sorry about the doctor."

"What's your day job, anyway?"

"Part-time bartender, part-time journalist," I said. "With maybe a bit more time at the bar of late."

"And you're also a part-time consulting physician?"

"Enough of a consultant to know that you and the sterling medical team are out of sync."

"Look, I'm so outta here. The last thing that bone-knob medic is going to experience is the feeling of success. I have every intention of dying on the surgical slab."

"How'd you get like this, Horton? Really, something must have happened to you."

"Life happened. Why do you care?"

"I don't care all that much, frankly. We just met. But if what you say is true, then I'm the last person you're gonna have a real conversation with before checking out. That makes me like your priest or something."

"You have a pretty high opinion of yourself."

"High or low, I'm the one sitting here listening. So what happened?"

Horton slithered out of bed and dragged his IV with him on his way to the bathroom. He gave me a long stare as he backed in, then closed the door. I looked back at J.R. who was fast asleep under Uncle Marty's forearm. I pulled the blanket up and tucked it tight around him, then laid Marty's arm around J.R. as if his grand nephew was being hugged. J.R. snuggled in closer and, for a moment, there was an uptick in the heart monitor over Marty's bed. His pulse went up, spiked at normal for about five seconds, then returned to the slow pace he'd been keeping for weeks. J.R. smiled, and I might have been seeing things but it sure looked like old Uncle Marty put up an affectionate grin as well.

The toilet flushed. Horton pushed the door open with his IV stand, then shuffled in his thin slippers along the cold tile floor. Late afternoon sunlight cast a shadow through the blinds. When Horton sat down, horizontal lines crossed his face.

"You wouldn't believe me if I told you," he said.

"Try me."

"Because?"

"Because J.R.'s sleeping, Marty's in a coma, I'm forced to sit here until Holly or Auntie Mimi shows up, and you're stuck in here waiting for a miracle. What difference does it make whether I believe you? None.

Nothing is about belief, Horton. Only religion is about belief, and even then most people have their doubts because nothing's verifiable. Still, they want to feel comfortable. So if you ask me, it's about connecting to things like your past, or whatever gives your life some meaning."

Horton smiled. We'd never be friends. We'd never bond over boilermakers or bachelor parties or college football games. But somehow, we'd found a connection. I put my feet up on his bed. Horton leaned back on a pillow and pulled the thin blanket over his feet.

\\\\

"At age nine, I was giving piano recitals all over the place," he said. "Edinburgh. Washington DC. Singapore. Capetown. I was the hottest musical prodigy on the planet and spoiled shitless. As long as I performed up to parental expectations, I could have anything I wanted. I could watch TV late at night. Eat as much pizza or mac and cheese as room service could deliver. I could have anything except 'normal.' I spent six hours a day rolling my fingers across 88 chunks of ebony and ivory topped off by two performances a week with me in a custom-made tuxedo and shiny black shoes. You have any idea what that's like?"

"You want me to answer that?"

Horton nodded yes.

"No, I have no idea what that's like. I grew up in North Platte, Nebraska watching *The Simpsons* and chasing cheerleaders around haystacks. Outside of a couple of third place ribbons in the two-mile relay my sophomore year, I was good at pretty much nothing."

"Well, Forrest, consider yourself lucky that you have nothing to be proud of. I was front page news in Green Bay, Wisconsin by age four. By age six I had my own booth at the Wisconsin State Fair. Every kid in town could get a creampuff, ride the Tilt-a-Whirl, or listen to me play Chopin. One summer I played *Piano Sonata Number 2* backwards just to freak people out, but no one even knew. Or maybe no one cared. Most people thought I was some kind of circus act, so we moved to the big city. By age eight, I was sitting on a phone book on Jay Leno's couch chatting it up after a solo performance of Rachmaninoff's *Prelude in C-Sharp Minor*. And the thing is, Leno had no clue what to do with me. I wasn't cute. I was just some strangely tall, hairy kid who had no life experience outside of classical music. I had no sense of humor, and I talked like a New York City grownup. I only knew grownups. By age ten, I'd spent so much time with fawning adults that I didn't know what a video game was. Or snow boarding. Or summer camp. I was six feet tall in third grade but had never bounced a basketball. You get that, right? The only coach my parents would let near me was some piano nerd who could barely understand what I was doing. They said I had natural talent, but there was nothing natural about it. You wanna talk about connecting? About meaning? I was on the road year-round, and other than a freak for a mother who doubled as a math tutor, I had no one real in my life. My life sucked."

"I'd like to say you've come a long way but . . . .."

"That's funny, Forrest."

"Sorry, it's just that we're in a hospital, and sarcasm is contagious."

"Maybe you should wear a mask."

"I do feel bad for you, actually. It's not in my nature to feel bad for someone else, but there's something oddly likeable about you."

"And what would that be?"

"I haven't put my finger on it yet. But it's kinda like the story of my friend Jack who's spending his life in prison for murder. We've been pen pals for years. I tell people that if you can get past the fact that he killed a few people, he's really not a bad guy."

For the first time, Horton actually laughed, hard. And when he tilted his head back, he managed to stretch his oxygen tube to the point where it popped right out of his nose. His laugh became a roar at that point, and I couldn't help but join him. We were loud enough to alert the nurse's station, and within seconds, a linebacker in a pink-flowered smock was standing in the doorway looking at us with muted exasperation as if we were the last people anyone would expect on the death floor of a New York City hospital.

She leaned on the doorframe and crossed her arms in a show of strength. "You mind telling me what's so funny?"

That, of course, was all we needed to laugh even harder. She stormed away without any effort to assist Horton with his oxygen tube. Once we were both breathing normally again, I poured us each a glass of water.

"Your life could have been worse," I said.

"Worse than what?"

"I just mean that a lot of life sucks, prodigy or no prodigy."

"Whatever self-loathing I might bring to the table, Forrest, I never felt like a victim. It wasn't like someone was beating me up every day. I had food, shelter—what's the rub, right? But wherever I was, I didn't belong. To kids my age, I was an alien."

"And . . ."

"Well, what are aliens doing here, right? They're nothing like us. They don't look like us. They don't act like us. They show up on Earth with some agenda people don't understand, put on a big show, blow up a few skyscrapers, and spend their whole time on terra firma trying to figure out how to get back home. Their arrival here was nothing but a freak accident. Do aliens make friends, socialize, share their troubles, ask for advice, come by for dinner? No."

"But you're not really an alien, Horton. You're just . . . special."

"Well, by the time I reached puberty, being special sucked. The thing is, an eight-year-old prodigy is, by definition, a kid endowed with exceptional abilities. You're in the papers, on television, the Internet. You can still find my performances on YouTube. But by age sixteen, you're no longer young, and the special thing has worn off. Now you're part of a club. There were a couple hundred of us who had real chops, and we were all tweeners. No one thinks you're cute anymore and you're too professional to be a contestant on *America's Got Talent*. So you compete with each other. The judges are just like you only they're fifteen years older and burned out."

"And you didn't like winning?"

"I didn't care. So I played everything just like I was supposed to up to a point. Then I added in my own little signature. Maybe a riff played backward. Or I'd drop the bass notes and just play with my right hand. Or I'd go off the head and start improvising. I was like Keith Jarrett playing Schumann or Brahms, which isn't exactly what the judges have in mind."

"But that sounds like something judges would appreciate."

"Maybe if they'd had the same skills I had. Or if they'd had the courage to take the same liberties back when they were competing. There were rules, Forrest. And by sixteen, I'd broken so many that the only invitations I was getting were to stay away."

"Which is what you wanted, right?"

"Me? Yes. My parents? No. So we made a deal. You've heard of the Global Grand Piano Competition, right?"

"I can't say I have, no."

"Well, there's 'Eastman,' and the 'World' in Cincinnati, and 'Piano Arts' in Pasadena, all kinds of competitions. Every city's got one. But the big daddy is the Global Grand in South Ossetia."

I demonstrated my ignorance with a blank expression.

"Eastern Europe. So the deal I made was that if I won the Global Grand, my folks would stop forcing me to play. I could go cold turkey if I wanted to. My life and my choices would be my own."

"Judging by the way you keep your fingernails, you must have lost."

"Some old habits die hard, Forrest," he said, looking at his neatly trimmed nails. "Or maybe not. I flew in to Tskhinvali on May 17, 2003. Security was tight because America was in the middle of a little conflict with Iraq at the time, but I'd had my visa in place before the fighting broke out, and there was no reason to fear South Ossetia, right?"

As I was nodding "yes," J.R. began squirming under Uncle Marty's arm. I stood up to roll him over just as the linebacker nurse peeked back in the door.

"They like that you know," she said, referring to Uncle Marty.

"I'm not sure he knows his grand nephew from a fuzzy blanket," I said.

"Bless him, your Uncle knows. And the comatose like prayer too."

"Well as soon as my sister gets here I'll pass that along." The linebacker spun an about face and headed down the hall. I motioned at Horton to continue.

"When I got to the hotel I saw all the usual faces—kids from India, Brazil, France, and Denmark, and most of the teenagers I'd competed with from America were there with their parents. The previous year's winner was there to judge, which is how they throw a ringer into things. She was a 14-year-old from the Uighur province in China who didn't speak a bit of English. So who would know what she really thought, right? But it didn't matter, because I never made it on stage."

Suddenly, Holly and her entourage pushed through the door like a tempest. J.R. woke up and started crying when Sydney, her head lightly bandaged, pulled him by his ear. J.R. crawled over Uncle Marty's torso to get away. As Flea struggled to wrestle him back, Sydney started pulling the string on a 'Get Well' balloon and quickly turned it into a punching bag. Whatever had happened to her head, the wound hadn't slowed her down.

"Welcome to my life, Jeffrey," said Holly. Uh oh. The cat was out of the bag. I looked over at Horton. In an effort to avoid the chaos, he'd shut down and pulled his blanket above his torso. But he did manage a grin at the mention of my real name.

"Where's Mimi, anyway?" Holly asked.

"You're asking me? How the hell would I know?"

"Well considering I was in the emergency room with my badly disfigured daughter, I just thought maybe you had your eye on the ball up here. She had two stitches. It's much worse than it looks. They put a little butterfly bandage on to keep her from scarring, but no one could guarantee it.

And they wouldn't let me see a plastic surgeon." I'd played Holly's game for years but wasn't in the mood to pour on the phony sympathy.

"Let's stay focused on Marty. Does it look like there's a ball to watch?"

Annoyed by the latest distraction, the linebacker was back. She clapped her hands hard to get everyone's attention.

"This is NOT a gymnasium! Who's in charge here?" Both Flea and I pointed at Holly and, in a show of mock support, Horton gave a head bob in her direction.

"Get those kids down, and either they sit still or you'll all have to leave. This is a hospital!"

Holly was never one to give in to authority figures and she showed it with a fierce display of body language. She pulled J.R. hard into her arms and took Sydney by the wrist, then stormed out the door. Flea gave me a confused look, then took off after them. With her hands on her hips, the linebacker tilted her head my direction.

"I'll be leaving too," I said. "Just let me say goodbye to Horton."

When she was gone, Horton leaned on his left arm with his hand under his chin.

"You never played in South Ossetia. Why not?"

"Poison," he said. "I drank a cup full of toilet cleaner I'd found in the linen closet at the hotel."

The thought of drinking toilet cleaner made me grimace.

"It didn't taste as bad as you might think."

"But it didn't work, obviously. You're still here."

"It pretty much killed my liver. And my career as a pianist. It just didn't kill me."

"Something tells me you're not going to say why you did it?"

"Something tells me you don't need an explanation."

"Did you ever get to be normal? Did you get to do what you wanted with your life?"

"I did manage a couple years of college that seemed pretty normal," he said. "I studied astronomy at NYU. Lost my virginity to an overweight cello player from Martinique. Played a lot of street chess in Washington Square Park. But I think I always knew I wouldn't be around long enough to graduate, so I dropped out after two years."

"Any friends?"

"I can't say friends became a strength of mine, Jeffrey."

Horton's surgery was now less than twelve hours away. Another nurse came in and politely asked Horton to roll over for an injection. She recoiled just a bit when she saw his hairy back, but still managed to fill his left buttock with a full syringe of sedative.

When she was gone, he rolled back and looked at me. The fire he'd shown earlier was gone. His eyes weren't blank, just resigned. I knew I had to leave, and there was a good chance I wouldn't see him again. I went toward his bedside and extended my hand.

"Friends?" I said. Horton took my hand and nodded in an approving way, but he couldn't quite bring himself to smile.

As I moved toward the door, he flipped his bedside remote. I looked back to say goodbye, but Horton wasn't much for exits. He never took his eyes off the television.

DEATH ON A HARVEST MOON

THE LETTER ARRIVED IN THE black plastic tray in my office just like all the others Jack had sent, a small white envelope with *Wisconsin Correctional Institute* stamped in red over the return address. I looked forward to hearing from Jack, but after thirty-six years behind bars, his correspondence lacked a sense of urgency. Once he'd realized I wasn't his get-out-of-jail-free-card, our game changed. He resorted to writing out of boredom, and the real insights into Jack's life that I was looking for became a rarity. I tossed Jack's letter in my computer case with every intention of reading it when I got home. Then, I thought, I'd file the letter alongside the fifty-seven others I'd received since 1985.

\\\\\

Any number of small things in a day can be considered coincidence, and when I was driving home it didn't seem remarkable to watch the sun setting behind Ed Schuett's silo west of Highway C. It was beautiful, to be sure, but not uncommon for late August. High-topped storm clouds fanned out north and south over a ten-mile stretch. Long straight rays of pink climbed up to rein them in, and as the last bits of hard sunlight cast north, they turned the low ceiling into a menacing gray. The single sheet of rain in the southeast reflected enough light to make it worth a photograph. I stopped and took a photo just because it's what I do, but also knowing it had no more value than the thousands of other sunsets I'd filed away over the years.

After filling the tank and hitting a produce stand for fresh tomatoes, I made it home in time to listen to the Milwaukee Brewers melt down against the Cubs . . . again. The fifth inning hadn't been good to them all year, especially during away games. Local news was buzzing about Aaron Rodgers and the offensive line, President Obama was pushing his climate initiative in Paris, talk radio hacks from Breitbart were urging everyone to strap on a side arm, Russia was supporting the Assad team in Syria, ISIS was flaunting its latest beheading, and a nearly 70-year-old white female politician with a mediocre track record was battling wits against a nearly 70-year-old white billionaire with bad orange hair and a penchant for Tic Tacs. Such events have a way of running together, but that wasn't true for Jack's letter on this particular day. It stood out, and the last few paragraphs changed my night:

> What makes a home has nothing to do with the size of a bed or a private bathroom. And for me, living in semi-solitude, it has nothing to do with a life partner, a vegetable garden, or a pet collie. I have a few books on loan from the prison library, and the warden let me bring them along when he moved my cell for the first time, but there was nothing else to carry forward. Just the stories inside those pages and the places they could send my overworked imagination.
>
> Thirty-six years is a long time. When they came for me, I stood in the doorway and stared back inside long enough to make the guard impatient. I made some last mental notes. The pale green walls hadn't seen a fresh coat of paint since I'd arrived. The marks I'd made on the wall during my

first year were still near the head of the bed: 247
days were accounted for with a vertical scratch
before I gave up. The cell bars were polished, but
I'd always left a few patches of rust near the top
and bottom as my own small act of defiance. The
springs sagged in the middle of the bed where I'd
curled up night after night, using my body heat to
try to stay warm. There was a toilet with no seat,
and a sink with one cold water faucet. There were
two overhead lights without a switch.

   You asked me once what prison smells like and I
couldn't find the words. But I can tell you now.
Prison smells like death. When I looked back at my
little box, that's what came over me. I was only
moving to a building across the yard, but it felt
like I was headed to a new place in hell.

The letter seemed heavier when I put it down on the end table. I poured
a glass of cheap Bordeaux from Trader Joe's and sat facing west to watch
the advancing storm. Lightning was tearing across the sky, rain was pelting the skylight, and I thought back to my first meeting with Jack in late
1984. He'd just completed his master's degree in prison and the achievement had made local headlines. I went to see him knowing that whatever
I wrote about him wasn't likely to evoke the sort of sympathy enjoyed by
killer Robert Stroud after his kindly portrayal by Burt Lancaster in *The
Birdman of Alcatraz*. As an inmate with a late-in-life penchant for feeding
canaries, Stroud was anything but kindly. His years in solitary confinement were the result of violence against other inmates and his brutal
murder of a guard at Leavenworth. But with the empathetic portrayal by
Lancaster, Stroud was all but forgiven.

Jack didn't have a screenwriter manipulating public sentiment, and
there was little beyond his academic achievements and heinous crime to

bring him notoriety. Jack had been convicted for the violent murder of three people on a summer evening in 1979, yet when I first met him five years after his cell door closed for the first time, prison officials regarded him as a quiet, polite, and unassuming detainee.

Some details stay with us, and my first encounter with Jack is among them. Wet snow and sleet had pounded my windshield for the better part of an hour before I'd arrived in the city of Waupun. Putting the parking lot four blocks to the south of the prison was a pretty good indication of the way officials felt about visitors. By the time I made it to the warden's office, I was soaked. After another hour of waiting on a hard-backed metal chair, my clothes were still soggy, and my good will had evaporated.

"You can come in now." The deep-voiced receptionist was a lifer, an inmate who'd shown such peaceful tendencies and general good nature that he'd landed the best job in the joint. After binging on tequila and painkillers, he'd slit the throat of his sleeping lover seventeen years earlier. Now he was the warden's office boy.

"Welcome, welcome, come on in," said Warden Mac Weaver with an outstretched hand. "Morris, get us some coffee, will you?"

The governor had hailed Weaver's appointment as an example of his own progressive stand on racial diversity. But the truth was that Weaver, a forty-five year old with broad shoulders and a trim waistline, had a master's degree in criminal justice and he'd worked his way up through the system just like any other good administrator.

As we shook hands, Weaver stared at me long enough to be impolite. Or perhaps it was a tactic.

"Have we met before?" he asked.

"Not that I can recall," I said. "Did you happen to go to Madison?"

"Loyola undergrad," he said. "Masters from Northwestern. I'm an Illinois kid."

Prison wardens are rarely fans of the media, so chit chat had its limits.

"Coincidence then."

"You've got that Peter Fonda thing going," he said.

"I've heard that, yes." I didn't want to get too friendly.

"You're here to see Jack Degatano?" he said.

"I am, yes."

"Not unexpected, I guess, on a slow news day."

"What makes you think it's a slow news day?"

He laughed my question off like a seasoned bureaucrat, slapped me on the back, and directed me to the chair across from his desk. There was a casual sitting area near the door, but Weaver wanted the power that came from sitting behind his desk.

"Degatano's a unique case," he said.

"How so?"

"Not many inmates get their bachelor's degree here, let alone a masters in sociology."

"Unique because of his academic accomplishments?"

"Yes, but it's more complicated than that. Degatano's a loner. Some guys come in here and look for alliances. Some do their time bodybuilding, beefing up. A few look for ways to serve the powers that be on the inside. Degatano keeps to himself. He spends his time doing three things: reading, writing, and meeting with the prison pastor. If it weren't for work assignments, I'm not sure he'd interact with anyone else."

Morris interrupted when he brought in two Styrofoam cups of coffee on a small plastic tray.

"Will there be anything else?" Morris averted his head as he waited to be dismissed. Just in case I hadn't noticed who was in charge, Weaver gave Morris a casual wave of his right hand.

"Sugar? Creamer? All we have is the powder, mind you." Weaver sprinkled some in his cup, then added, "State cutbacks. Now that's what you guys should cover if you ask me."

"Black's fine." The first sip confirmed my suspicion. It was the worst coffee I'd tasted in years. I set the cup on the corner of the warden's desk, just out of arm's reach. "You describe Degatano as if there's something wrong with him making the choices he's made. But it sounds like he's doing something positive in here. Am I missing something?"

Weaver pulled a jar of honey out from his top desk drawer, then dipped a plastic spoon deep inside. Slowly, for effect, he twirled the spoon around a few times, wiped the bottom of the jar lid clean, then let the honey dribble into his coffee. It was part ritual, and again, part tactical.

"Am I missing something, Warden Weaver?" Asking a second time made a point of its own.

"Positive? Hmm. Positive. I suppose that depends on how you define positive."

"For a man whose first shot at parole is when he's eighty-five years old, academic achievement appears to be a good use of his time here," I said.

"Yes, he'll be an old man, won't he? If he's even alive by then. Looks like you've done your homework."

"With no capital punishment, three consecutive life terms seemed to seal the deal. I'd say he's here for life."

"Do you have questions for me, or are you just looking to meet with Degatano?"

"Nothing too heady," I said. "But I'm sure people will want to know how the Department of Corrections views his . . . accomplishment. Conservatives are hailing it as a sign that incarceration is working. What do you think?"

"I think that when a man kills three people, it doesn't matter how he does his time in prison. We shouldn't be giving him any accolades. Fair enough?"

"Fair enough," I wrote it down for effect. "But does an inmate graduating from a prison academic program show that rehabilitation programs are working? Or is Degatano simply an exception?"

"That's for others to judge. I'm sure the Governor doesn't want me making the case one way or the other."

"But you must have an opinion. Certainly you've helped in some way, by providing access to research, perhaps? Extra hours allowed in the prison library?"

Weaver leaned forward and put his chin in his hands. His tone changed with his body language, the chumminess vanished.

"Off the record?

"Sure. Off the record."

"There was a riot here four years ago," he said. "Degatano was studying in the library at the time and things spilled over from the yard. Inmates affiliated with the Ninth Street Kings took over the infirmary and the library. They held twelve people hostage for almost two days. I'm sure you remember it. A visiting nurse from Green Bay was raped, nearly lost her life. What you may not know is that Degatano was also one of the hostages. He took a knife blade in his left side just above his hip. Word is that he was trying to protect the nurse, but that's not official. You'll see him walking with a limp though. He got it pretty good, lost a lot of blood."

Weaver paused and stirred the honey into his coffee.

"Now what do I think? I think the prison has an obligation to make sure whoever's in here is safe. Degatano belongs in here because of his crime, but I am sorry he was injured because that shouldn't happen. Not to him, not to the nurse, not to anyone. That's why my predecessor is gone. That's why I'm here now. But I'm not here to tell you whether Degatano or anyone else deserves the right to use a library or a chance to earn some kind of college degree. Maybe I'll run the department some day, and if I do, I'll let you know. But for now, the question of rehabilitation is above my pay grade."

Weaver got up and grabbed his sports coat off the hook in the corner of the office. He pulled on his right sleeve, then motioned me with his right hand unfolded toward the door. With Weaver as my guide, we left his office and spent the next twenty minutes passing through three heavily guarded gates before arriving in a small waiting area deep inside the prison. It was my first time in a penitentiary and the impression was complete—no one was likely to escape without help from the outside. Including me.

Jack was about thirty at the time, and I'd imagined him to be a frail, repentant young grad student who'd carved out a monk's existence, oblivious to the concerns of the outside world. There was an air of confidence about Jack, but he was far from frail, and any sign of repentance went away when he began our interview by telling me that he was innocent of the murders.

"All inmates say they're innocent," I replied. "But your thesis is based on detailed oral histories of inmates who admit their guilt."

Jack didn't miss a beat.

"Exactly," he said. "It's something I know better than the guys on the outside, the guys doing their research from an armchair at a university. You spend some time here, even a few days, and you can tell who's innocent and who's not."

"And are there many who are innocent?"

"Very few. But I am. If I were guilty, I wouldn't be able to sleep at night. My own father was murdered for Christ sake. My brother. Three people were bludgeoned to death. You think I could do that?"

Jack had a lot of energy and we were in a small room. He stood up abruptly, turned the chair around, leaned his arms on the top of the chair back, and continued. "I regained consciousness six days after my alleged crime. Six days. First thing I remember? My hands were cuffed, each one separately to the side of a hospital bed with two cops positioned outside my door. I overdosed, went into a coma. I should be dead."

At least he was consistent, I thought. From everything I'd read he'd been apprehended on the morning after the murders. Acting on a tip, two undercover officers found him passed out on the couch at his father's house. He'd suffered an overdose on cheap acid, and there was a shoebox full of pills and about $300.00 in cash on the floor next to him. According to police reports, he was covered in blood and there were small wounds on his right hand that police said happened during the murders. It was just a few years after Charles Manson and his "family" had killed the actress Sharon Tate, and whether Jack or someone else wrote it, "helter skelter" was spelled out in blood on the living room wall.

"You were a dealer?" I asked.

"Petty stuff. Mostly dime bags of pot to college kids in Oshkosh and Stevens Point. To this day I don't know where the pills came from."

"But you had hallucinogens in your system."

"Exactly. I'm not disputing that. My girlfriend and I dropped acid a few times over the Labor Day weekend. And dust, once. It was fun, but not something I was planning to make a part of everyday life. I used speed occasionally, but I didn't deal pills."

"Let's talk about your new degree."

"You're tired of the innocent thing, right?"

"I'm just not the guy to prove it for you, okay?"

"So who is? Dan Rather? Don't you think that if I could prove it from behind bars that I would have done it by now?"

"What I think is that you're not going anywhere any time soon. I have a story due at six tonight, and either you want to participate in it or you don't. Beyond that, we can stay pen pals for as long as you'd like. If I turn up things from time to time, I'll share them with you."

"And you'll review the trial testimony?"

"I'll write today's story and see where things go."

"Just follow the evidence, that's all I ask."

I'd said enough and looked at him across the top rim of my glasses.

"What do you want to know about my academic achievement?" He gave me a warm smile and a friendly handshake. Jack may have been a murderer, but he was also surprisingly charming. In that moment, we began a very strange relationship.

\\\\

During the years since that first visit, Jack and I had written occasionally but I'd only visited twice, and both times I was asking for his help on stories unrelated to his crime. When it came to the inner workings of the penal system, Jack was an expert. Though the public rarely heard much about him, he'd become something of a celebrity in academic circles. He did something few inmates had done before—he got ahead by using the prison as a research facility.

Suddenly, a bolt of lightning hit close enough to split a silver oak on my neighbor's lawn. The thunder followed so quickly it caught me off guard. The kitchen lights flickered, came on full for a second, then everything went dark. I kept a headlamp in the kitchen for occasions just like this. Power failures have such an unnerving quality to them that it's hard to believe my great grandparents lived their entire lives without electricity. As I groped my way along the hallway, a second bolt of lightning threw shadows around the room. There was nothing to be nervous about, but I could feel myself crumple Jack's letter in my hand. I found the headlamp hanging where I'd left it near an old wall phone. I pulled the strap around my head and sat on the edge of a kitchen stool. Another bolt danced sideways along the horizon as if it pulled by a violent, unseen partner. I adjusted the small lamp for reading, then continued with Jack's letter. Something had shifted with his move to the new cellblock, and I had a feeling it would involve me. I just didn't know how.

I arrived in my new cell with an armful of
bedding and a shoebox of fresh toiletries-a gift
from the pastor I visited with twice each week. I'd
love to say you would have noticed the difference
in my surroundings, but it required a penchant for
subtle observation that my regular visitors just
don't have. The walls were a darker shade of green.

I made the bed and tested it for firmness, relieved that it was no worse than the one I'd left behind. The ring of rust near the bottom of the egg white toilet was at least 2 inches lower than my previous commode, and the cell door didn't squeak on the rail when the guard pushed it closed. When dinner was called at six, I opted to pass--it's one of the few decisions we can make on our own. And that's when it happened. I was lying on my mattress and getting acquainted with the late August shadows on the cell walls. I noticed that they had hard edges, no doubt from a light source that was direct, not diffused.

I got up and pressed my face into the bars and looked in both directions. To my right, there was a large window cut into the wall about fifteen feet out from the cell block. I hadn't seen direct natural light inside my cell since I'd been incarcerated, but what made it so amazing, what let me feel life and even hope, was that the sun was setting outside the window. I couldn't see the sun directly, but I could see bits of pink sky and golden light moving across the leaves at the top of a giant oak just beyond the prison wall.

I laughed to myself at first, strangely giddy, and then I lost my breath and the tears came. It was my first sunset in so many years. What would I see next . . . a full moon? A sky filled with stars that goes on forever? I found myself believing in the outside world again . . . and that's enough to keep me going . . .

I went back to the den, grabbed the camera I'd used earlier, and flipped through the viewer. The screen cast a glow so I turned off my headlamp. I'd photographed four sunsets on the drive home, all about the same. The tops of the clouds in the east went to more than twenty thousand feet, the upper half reflecting back the orange light from the west. Two nights earlier, Jack had been peeking through cell bars at a sliver of pink horizon. It was enough to keep him going, he said. The question I asked myself was why, after all our correspondence, did it take his letter for me to imagine the limits imposed by a small cell with no view of the outside world?

\\\\

The clock was flashing 11:45 p.m. when I woke up, a signal that the electricity had been repaired. The storm had moved across Lake Michigan by now, and if my math was correct, Muskegon was taking the same beating we'd had six hours earlier. As much as I had on my plate for the day, I opted to cancel things and head to the prison. It had been at least eight years since I'd seen Jack in person. It was a Saturday and there was a pretty good chance I could get in as a visitor.

When I approached the walk-up gate, there was a framed 8x10 of the current warden, a speckled fifty-something with a double chin. A brass-engraved plate on the bottom of the cheap frame said Clifford Zale. When the guard asked my relation to the inmate, I said "friend."

"Does he know you're coming?"

"No," I said. "But I'm on his approved list. And it's visiting day, right?"

The guard was a veteran at most everything in the joint, including abusing the job security he enjoyed as a member of one of the few state employee unions supported by the Republican governor. He turned his back, pulled his belt up over his size forty-six waist, and handed a clipboard with my request over to a supervisor who sat behind a charcoal gray metal desk as old as the prison. When the supervisor looked back my way, he simply motioned for me to sit. I slid into a line of plastic chairs filled with wives, girlfriends, children, and parents of any number of the one thousand two hundred and forty-six inmates currently housed in maximum security.

The file I had with me included a manila envelope filled with letters Jack had sent me over the years. Until yesterday, he'd kept his feelings close to the vest. When I glanced through the pile, there was nothing emotional on the pages, just insights and observations:

Anyone who romanticizes prison life has no real experience with the misery of confinement. Prison is a very odd and depressing place.

By personal observation, Two Broke Girls is the highest rated network program in the joint. You can hear a pin drop when it's on. It's a great time to get my thinking done.

The advantage of being convicted of three counts of pre-meditated murder is that I've been deemed too dangerous to share my cell with newcomers. Did I mention that this place is over-crowded? What's going on out there in the world anyway?

I learned to keep to myself early on. Why I didn't get the usual beatings or raped is a mystery, but maybe it has something to do with MY mystery. Everyone's afraid of me before I even meet them.

New gal moved in down the hall. He/she is using the handles of a jump rope to curl his/her hair and pencil shavings to darken his/her eyes. He/she cut his/her t-shirt into a midriff. I just hope he/she doesn't try to get lucky within earshot because I enjoy the quiet when I can get it.

Day 9,855. I'm halfway to parole (assuming I get parole). I wonder who will be governor in 2046?

Occasionally, Jack would ask me questions in his letters, but I usually figured they were less curiosity about the outside world and more his way of getting me to write back. Receiving a letter had to be among the highlights of an inmate's week and one of the only ways to break routine. Sometimes Jack tried to be funny, others he seemed genuinely interested in my answer. Too often, his questions were dated by cultural and social references that quickly drifted from the public's consciousness:

> Is there any truth to the rumor that Farrah
> Fawcett dumped Ryan O'Neil again so she could
> pursue a relationship with me? If so, please give
> her my address and number.
>
> The library is closed for repairs . . . again. I
> think it's a ploy by the new warden who seems out
> to get me. Is there any chance you could send me a
> copy of the original blueprints for Kings College
> in Oxford?
>
> Reagan lied on camera (and I wasn't surprised),
> but what's the deal with Clinton and Lewinksy? "It
> depends on what the meaning of is, is . . ." Yeah,
> right.
>
> What is going on with WMD in Iraq? All I know for
> sure is that you won't find them here.
>
> What I'm reading about organic farming suggests
> that while the produce may be better for you (I'll
> never know), it's clearly unaffordable for the
> masses. How does this play with your journalist
> crowd?
>
> The only reason we avoided violence at the 2004
> Olympics in Athens is because the bad guys were

bought off by the office of the VP. Why don't
you put on your I-TEAM hat and prove it for the
American public once and for all? Follow the money!

I'm appealing to the governor for a pardon and
won't get many chances. Is there any way you can
write a letter on my behalf? Who knows when we'll
get another lame duck liberal. After all these
years, it goes without saying that I'm counting on
you.

By the time Jack pulled off the pardon hearing in 2009, he'd put together support from more than forty academics and former prison employees who saw him as a benefit to society. My letter was not among them, but Jack seemed unfazed by my reluctance to assist him. In the years since his pardon was denied, he'd published less and less. His letters arrived less frequently and when they did, they were brief and matter-of-fact. What hope was left to keep Jack going, I wondered?

"You'll have to leave your briefcase in a locker." The guard was back to escort me.

"No pen and paper?" I asked. "I've been through three metal detectors already."

"Not if you want to go inside," he said. "It's up to you."

I put everything into the small locker, grabbed the thin plastic key and went inside a visiting room that was crammed full. Fifteen inmates were already there visiting their wives, girlfriends, and kids. When Jack walked in, I didn't recognize him at first, but he came straight toward me with a big grin and a bear hug.

"No touching!" snapped a guard. Jack shot him a scornful glance as we sat down across from each other on two pale orange plastic chairs.

"Been a while," he said.

"I've got some quarters. You want a soda, some candy maybe?"

Jack seemed pleased by the offer and I bought us each a Coke and a Milky Way. As he was unwrapping his, he asked me just what the candy bar had in common with the galaxy of the same name?

'Not much," I said. "But then who would have thought the word Google would become synonymous with Internet search engines?"

"The Internet's a luxury I've not had the pleasure of trying," he said. "But the library does provide two twenty-year-old HPs and the occasional use of a dot matrix printer. What's it like?"

"Google? Well, there are two answers to that question. In terms of information access, it changes the game. You want to know about the assassination of Haile Selassie? Presto. You want to read an article on the latest techniques to combat ovarian cancer? Find a new online dating site? Or scour data on Einstein's wave particle duality? Done. In seconds. But there's also the other Google."

"Meaning . . .?"

"Meaning privacy is out the window, Jack. They know how old you are. They know what you like to wear, eat, drink, watch on TV, where you live, where you travel, pretty much everything. It's a marketer's dream come true that makes the user the product. But how long 'til the government decides it wants a piece of that action?"

"What else is out there?" asked Jack. "I'm still limited to fifty-year-old hard covers of Tom Sawyer with missing pages and pencil doodles filling every blank space possible."

We went back and forth for fifteen minutes while I filled him in on video streaming, high-speed trains, self-driving cars, smart fabrics, GPS, medical imaging, presidential tweets, and the two hundred free apps I had downloaded into my mobile phone. When he slurped the last drop of soda, I could feel him looking at me over the top of the can.

"You didn't come for any old visit, did you?"

"It was something you said in your letter, Jack. You said prison smelled like death."

"You're here. You can't smell it?"

"I smell disinfectant. Body odor. Cheap perfume and hairspray. The guard smelled like laundry detergent when I came in. But no, I don't smell death."

Jack didn't say much. He seemed to pull away, leaning back, crossing his arms and taking in the other visitors. Suddenly, the other parts of the room were more interesting to him than I was.

"I haven't been up to the visiting room in a while," he said. "Since I stopped publishing, not as many shrinks come by to see me."

"You don't want to talk about it, that's okay. I've never pressured you to talk about anything."

"So what do you want now?"

"You wrote to me for a reason," I said. "Could have been anyone, but you chose me. Your first sunset in thirty-five years? I've seen so many that I take them for granted, but for you, it's like landing on a new planet. A moon in the night sky, stars . . . come on, Jack. You were sharing with me. You were telling me like you'd tell a friend. Or a close family member. And there's nothing wrong with that. It's why I drove up to see you."

If body language doesn't lie, then Jack was more uncomfortable than I'd ever seen him. Only gravity kept him from launching skyward.

"I'll stand with my last question. What do you want now?"

"Nothing, Jack. Absolutely nothing."

We sat in silence too long for comfort. If it weren't for the novelty of sitting in the visitor center, I'm sure he'd have gone back to his cell. He did take a deep breath when we were interrupted by two seven-year-olds playing a game that someone else thought was funny. They were asking each inmate "what are you in for?" and then moving on to the next. When they got to Jack, he said, "I'm just in here visiting my friend," and he pointed to me. It broke the ice and we laughed.

"You've always wanted to know if I really did the crime," he said. "You didn't believe me from day one."

"If admitting guilt hadn't been such a big part of your thesis, no one would be surprised by your claims. But it's hard to imagine that you didn't commit the murders. And it's not like some cold case detective is coming forward with DNA evidence that proves you're innocent."

"What if they did?" he asked. "What if there was someone else that night? What if the real killer is still out there and they've got the wrong guy locked up? You don't think I've considered it? I wasn't even conscious that night. I have no recollection of anything."

"But you've seen the crime scene photos. You've seen the physical evidence. There were cuts on your hands. Your clothes were full of the victim's blood."

"Why didn't I kill my girlfriend then? Why overdose? There was $35,000.00 in cash in my parent's house and it's gone. My brother's dead. But I'm in here."

"Thirty five thousand dollars? Why don't I know about this?"

"It's a pretty big incentive," said Jack.

"Who else knew about the money?"

"Until that night, it was just my brother and me, and we weren't supposed to know. Our father had it stashed in a box in the crawlspace above the coat closet. There was always money in there, from the time we were little kids. I told my lawyer at the time, but he thought I was making it up. All I know is the police never found it, and according to the district attorney, it never existed."

"How did your dad come by that kind of money?"

"You'd have to ask him," said Jack. Then he laughed. "But how stupid is that? The money doesn't exist, right? And he's not talkin'. So you figure it out."

"Anyone else ever know about it?"

"Maybe my mom, but she died before I hit kindergarten."

"No business associates of your father? An uncle?"

"Not that I know of."

"How did you know it was there?"

"When we were kids, we'd play hide and seek when the cousins were over. I found it when I was eight. My brother and I would climb up there and look at it when my dad was away."

"Drugs?"

"Hard to say. He was pretty straight laced at home, never even drank alcohol. But it wasn't like I really knew him."

"You create more questions than answers, Jack."

"I've got thirty-six years in prison for something I didn't do."

"What about your girlfriend? What happened to her?"

"Married. Moved to Washington State is the last I heard. Under the circumstances, we haven't kept in touch." Jack smiled.

"Anything else I should know about her?"

"How much homework are you up for?"

"Try me."

"She delivered a son eight months after I was arrested. It's a pretty good bet I'm the kid's father."

It was a nice bombshell. There was some guy in his late-30s living in Seattle with DNA courtesy of a convicted mass murderer. It occurred to me that with time on his hands, creating any story was possible for Jack, but it'd be easy to check out.

"Your father's money. It doesn't make much sense."

"There wasn't much about him that did. When we were really young, he was gone all the time. I remember a lot of excitement when he'd come home. He'd always bring us something, a fountain pen, a lapel pin, those little matchbox cars, little things."

"So he traveled for work?"

"That's what we were told."

"What languages did he speak?"

"A little Spanish. I don't know, maybe something else. He was twice my mom's age when I was born, which may not seem like a big deal except that she was a high school junior at the time. What guy wants to be a forty-year-old single father? After she was gone, the guy was practically a recluse."

Around the time I'd first interviewed Jack, I'd read all the local papers for the few weeks following the murders. *The Fondulac Freeman* reported that his father, Al Degatano, had been working as a graphic artist in a print shop at the time of his death. When I talked to Al's boss, all I could find out was that he showed up on time, knew how to do an ad layout, and didn't go out of his way to make friends. Jack's brother Jason was a welding apprentice at a machine shop in Omro and was still living at home when the murders occurred.

"Anyone have anything against your brother?" I asked.

"According to the police, no one but me. I know where you're goin', and they ruled out your idea because the woman I supposedly killed was my girlfriend's mother. Jason barely knew her."

"But Jason knew about the money?"

"He did. But he was clean. A bit shy maybe, but real clean. He looked up to me during high school. After I moved out, he pretty much kept to himself."

The flashing light indicating the end of visiting hours had been going for a while, and families were starting to file out. The two kids who'd come by earlier gave us a thumbs up as they pushed each other toward the door. What's it like to visit your dad in prison once a month, I wondered?

"Let's wrap it up girls!" The guard was working on his comedy chops. "No hand holding on the way out."

"Hard to imagine who's got it worse," said Jack. "Him or me."

||||

It wasn't until I made it through the last metal door that I realized how much my body had responded to being inside again. Every muscle was tight, and it felt like I'd had a giant blood pressure cuff around my torso for hours with Jack squeezing it tighter and tighter at each new revelation. I sucked in the fresh air. The space inside my car had gotten smaller, and I opened all four windows before heading south on Hwy. 26.

In less than a day, I'd gone from the occasional pen pal of a highly educated murderer to a full-fledged confidant with a growing doubt about the legal system. Was it possible that 19-year-old Jack Degatano had been framed?

\\\\

Maybe it was denial. Maybe it was work and my mid-life commitment to a few hours of personal time. Either way, two weeks passed during which I repeatedly pushed thoughts about Jack out of my mind. By the time his next letter arrived, I found his story impossible to ignore. I became suspicious when I looked at the envelope. The same red stamp was over the return address, but the seal was covered by tape. Someone was reading Jack's mail, I thought. I didn't delay this time, I opened it at my desk. There were the usual pleasantries, but he came to the point quicker this time:

> . . . maybe it's just me getting older. Maybe the cooks started adding more pepper to their overcooked red beans. I don't know, but it seems I can't sleep through the night in my new box. I've never been one for nightmares, but since the move, that's all I get. No sweet dreams to carry me away from this place. Can you imagine waking up from a nightmare to this? Leaving the wildness of your unconscious for the silhouette of vertical steel bars blocking your path to freedom? When the walls close in, I slap myself to see what "awake" is because I'm not sure whether the real nightmare is from my unconscious mind or part of my consciousness.

There's nothing unusual about an inmate having nightmares or wondering aloud about freedom. And Jack knew that most of his mail was read by someone before it left the prison. He'd been manipulating people long enough that I assumed he was being chummy to coerce me into another visit. What he didn't know was that I was using my own sleepless nights to canvass birth records from Brown County, circa 1954. Jack Nathan Degatano had been born to Patricia Lynn and Albert Matthew Degatano Jr. on June 17 at 5:25 a.m. There was no birth record at all for Jason. But what made things even more complicated was that Patricia Lynn had also been born to one Albert Matthew Degatano, Jr. just sixteen years earlier.

\\\\

"So you knew?" I asked. It was mid-morning at the visitor's center and Jack had already pressured me with a highly charged plea for caffeine and sugar. I slipped him a second can of Coke and some mint-flavored M&Ms.

"So you knew?" I repeated the question with more authority.

Jack's posture changed. He crossed his arms and brought his left leg up across his right.

"Can I assume that no answer is an answer?" He hadn't seen me this assertive before, and his defensive posture belied the discomfort he felt talking about his mother's origins.

"My mother's mother was killed by a drunk driver in 1943," Jack said. "By the time Tricia was 16, it had been just her and my dad for nearly a decade. It was a different time."

"Different as in 'sleep with your daughter' different?"

"Look, I didn't find out until I was eighteen. That's when his sister, my aunt Cheryl, figured I had a right to know the truth. Of course I was pissed off, but that doesn't mean I killed my father. I spent four months in southeast Alaska on a halibut rig out of Sitka. I came back and was going to college when things went bad. As far as I know, Jason never found out."

"Is your aunt still alive?"

He gave me that look again—how would I know? Then, "She came to the trial once or twice but I haven't seen her since."

"Were you close when you were young?"

"My house wasn't exactly like *Ozzie & Harriet*. She and her kids came by when we were young, but by high school, my brother and me were easy to ignore. Cheryl told me about Patricia Lynn when I was fifteen, and left it to me to tell Jason, which I never did."

When I told Jack that there was no birth record at all for Jason, it was either a genuine shock or he was the world's greatest actor. He seemed to stew on it for a minute, then asked, "So what are you saying?"

"I'm not saying anything. You asked for help, I'm looking for answers."

"He's dead, so it's not like it matters. But why wasn't there any record of that in the coroner's report?"

"Small town, everybody knew him? I'm guessing, but given all the authorities had to process in a multiple homicide, the likes of which they'd never seen before, there just may not have been a reason to look it up."

"Other than Jason most likely being born at home, I'm not sure it means all that much. The way the neighborhood was, my dad probably wanted it that way for privacy's sake. It wasn't Tricia's choice, I'm sure of that."

"In terms of the money, you were the only heir after their death."

"I was the last survivor, if that's what you mean. The police thought that contributed to motive. Once I was convicted, inheriting the estate became this big controversy, big enough that the state legislature changed the law after my case. I don't have access to much of anything, but there had to be papers. And if I ever do get out, the value of the house is held in trust with a local bank. I'm still the rightful beneficiary."

Jack asked to borrow more quarters for a third trip to the soda machine. The warden had told me on my earlier visit that Jack was notorious for saving the twenty dollars he received for working each month and using it for postage. Correspondence was much more important to him than a vending machine snack, but at my expense, why not? He'd brought along a note pad and a pencil nub for this visit and while I was pacing, he was drawing an outline of the first floor rooms in the house where the first two murders had occurred. It hadn't occurred to me that Jack might have talents other than his passion for sociology, but he had a genuine skill for drawing. The level of detail and the speed of his craft were surprising.

"I've got a file on my case that I review from time to time. According to the police photos, they found me on the couch right here," he said, as he drew his body into place. The odd thing was that he had a leg up over the armrest and his head was in the middle of the two big seat cushions. It gave the appearance of passing out, not settling in to sleep.

"Jason's body was in the kitchen with his head on the table, but the wounds on his neck had been cleaned up. Police said the way he was killed was almost clinical, like he'd been hit by a professional. And he died quickly. It looked like he'd been killed over the kitchen sink. I have no idea why anyone would do that."

"That's not true with your father?"

"No, his death was violent. Of course, that points to me, especially since I had every reason to hate him for conceiving me by raping my sister."

"Kinda hard to deny that."

"Yeah, well. It's not like I won the trial."

"No anger toward your brother?"

"Why would I have protected him from knowing who his mother really was and then killed him?"

"The money?"

"If it was me, then why didn't I make some effort to hide the evidence? Why didn't I clean myself up? Or run away? Instead, I'm zoned out for days on an acid binge and wind up handcuffed to a hospital bed."

"Can you draw me your girlfriend's place?"

Jack told me that throughout his trial, he'd never once looked at the crime scene photos of his girlfriend's house. He couldn't bring himself to do it. His father's death never bothered him all that much, he said, but he claimed genuine remorse over the loss of his brother and denied any tie to the killing of his girlfriend's mother. In reading the trial accounts, the evidence putting Jack at the scene of his girlfriend's house was circumstantial. The killing had been done with the same knife, and Jack's fingerprints were in the house, but it was also acknowledged that he'd visited often, and as recently as earlier that day.

"You said you saw Dorie earlier in the day. Where was she at the time of the murders?"

"We had lunch at Dairy Queen and we were going to go out that night. We'd been to the county fair two days earlier and it was closing after the holiday weekend, so Dorie and I planned to drop some acid and go do the amusement rides. Fun, right? She got a call about four o'clock from her older sister asking her to sit for the kids at their house up near Neenah. Her sister got called in to the hospital for third shift. Far as I know, Dorie was there all night. The last time my girlfriend and I ever talked was that afternoon. I can't even really remember her voice anymore."

There was a different guard on duty, much more pleasant, and he came by to let us know our time was up.

"Sorry professor," he said to Jack. "Time for you guys to wrap it up."

As much as he'd have liked confirmation of another visit, I knew it was dangerous to set a precedent for seeing him weekly. I told him I'd see him when I could.

||||

After thirty-six years, the last thing Dorie Meeks wanted was a visit from someone interested in the death of her mother at the hands of Jack Degatano. She had no reason to see me except that I'd made it clear I wouldn't bother her at home, I'd only take a few minutes of her time, and I'd never ask to see her again. When she showed up at Pike Place Market, I was standing at a small round table holding a tall latte in a paper cup. It was one of those rare Seattle days when the temperature hits 80 degrees and the Western sky is filled with a few billowy clouds rolling in from the ocean. The market was alive with a festive mix of merchants, shoppers, tourists, street vendors and performers.

As she approached, Dorie went unnoticed by everyone but me. To say there was nothing remarkable about her understates the case. She'd gone out of her way to appear plain, with a pair of light blue tennis shoes, a pastel checkered purse the size of a small backpack, and an oversized Brett Favre T-shirt that fell just above the worn knees of her blue jeans. She had a windbreaker wrapped around her large hips, and there were three small hairs protruding from a mole in front of her left ear. Her long braided hair was the only remnant of the way she'd looked in her 1979 Bristol High School yearbook.

"Some things just don't go away." Dorie didn't respond when I stuck my hand out to shake hers. She just leaned on the edge of the table and asked what I wanted.

"Can I get you some coffee?"

She shook her head with brittle animus.

"I see you're still wearing old number four's t-shirt here in Seattle. You must get booed now and again?"

"Seriously, let's just get to it," she said. "Other than Jack, you're the last person I want to see here, and I'm taking you at your word that I won't hear from you again."

"All we have is our word." I took a sip of my latte without breaking eye contact. "You saw him the day of the murders?"

"Yes, at lunch."

"You were going to drop acid and go hit the amusement rides?"

"That might have been Jack's plan. But I didn't do drugs then, and I don't do them now. I spent the night at my sister's babysitting."

"He claims he doesn't remember anything at all after your lunch."

"If that's true, then he should consider his memory loss a blessing."

"When did you first see him after the murders?"

"In the hospital that next day. He was in a coma, and at that point, I thought he was a victim like the rest of them. The police were still putting things together."

"What did you know about his relationship with his father and mother?"

"What do you mean?"

"Did you know Jack's mother was also his sister?"

Much the way Jack had responded to news of Jason's non-existent birth records, Dorie seemed genuinely shocked by the revelation.

"I never knew her, but that's quite a claim. She was dead by the time Jack was in kindergarten."

"But you did know Jason?"

"Barely. He kept to himself, and Jack and I didn't really start dating until he got back from Alaska the previous autumn. We'd known each other before but it hadn't become serious yet."

"Jason and you didn't interact?"

"No, like I said, he kept to himself. He barely made it out of high school, and I think he was working in a shop or something."

"Jack says you both dropped acid right after lunch."

"There was a lot going on then with drugs. It was a different time. But like I said, I didn't drop acid with him. Not with him, not ever."

"Does your son know that Jack is his father?"

"That's none of your business!" Dorie's face went flush with the notion that I knew anything at all about her son. She turned to leave, clutching her purse closer as if I was an attacker.

"I'm sorry," I said. "He told me your boy was very likely his own. We don't have to go there."

"What is it you want? Really? You don't think he's a killer? I'm sorry, but I closed that chapter a long time ago. He killed his own brother. He killed my mother. He ruined my life and believe me, if I didn't believe in

Our-Lord-Jesus-Christ-Our-Savior, I'd have taken my own life a long time ago."

"I can't imagine how hard this is for you. . . ."

"No one can. You want to know what it's like to raise a son alone in a city two thousand miles from home after your mother has been murdered by someone you thought you loved? No one can imagine that. No one should even try to imagine that."

As badly as Dorie wanted to feel the words she was saying, her body betrayed her. There were no tears, no slump in her posture, no wringing of the hands, no shifting in place. When I didn't come back with another question right away, she made the motion to leave.

"He gave me this. It's for you." I handed her a letter Jack had written and given to me during my last visit.

"I don't want it," she said. "I just want to be left alone."

The market was bustling and neither of us wanted to make a scene. Still, when she started walking, I followed alongside her with the unopened letter in my hand.

"What do you want me to do with it?" I asked. She didn't answer, she just kept moving north toward the parking lot.

When we got to the crosswalk, there was a policeman on foot patrol standing nearby. I knew it would be my last chance to talk with her so I asked the one question I needed her to answer. I leaned in close and spoke in a low, calm voice.

"What about the money? What about the thirty-five thousand dollars from the attic?"

Dorie glared at me, and I was certain she knew about it.

"And you inherited everything from your mother as well," I said.

The crowd around us was wonderfully oblivious. Kids were eating ice cream. Parents were pushing toddlers in strollers. Lovers were happy in each other's arms. A street mime was impersonating Marcel Marceau. It was a beautiful Seattle day.

When I'd told Dorie I wouldn't harass her beyond our meeting, I'd meant it. But even as she walked away, her behavior spoke volumes. I stood watching her. She let the force of the crowd carry her across the street, but still glanced repeatedly at me over her shoulder until she disappeared into the parking garage. We both knew the truth—Dorie Meeks had gotten away with murder.

\\\\

I sat down on the bus stop bench next to an Asian family visiting from Shanghai. The father was checking the bus map and his watch over and over to be sure they weren't missing anything. I assured him I was getting on the same bus and would make sure they didn't miss it. More than once I glanced at the letter, but I couldn't bring myself to open it. Whatever Jack had to say to Dorie after nearly four decades could remain a secret. Whatever he might have confirmed for me would go unconfirmed. When the bus arrived, I made sure the family got on, and then I decided to walk the roughly two miles southeast toward Safeco Field where my travel agent had booked my hotel.

The time change got to me and I fell asleep around 9:30 p.m. I was in the middle of a strange dream when my cell phone rang.

"Yeah?" I mumbled while trying to figure out how I'd gone from the deck of a sinking ore freighter during a white hurricane on Lake Superior to a king-sized bed at a Seattle boutique hotel.

"You're the reporter, right?"

"Journalist, yes," I said.

"But you're bound by confidence, ethics, that sort of thing? I mean, if we're off the record, right?"

It was Dorie Meeks. I sat upright in bed and looked at the clock on my phone. It was just after midnight.

"If someone goes off the record with me, it stays off the record, yes."

There was a fairly long pause during which I could hear the ice cubes jingle in Dorie's beverage of choice. It occurred to me that our little rendezvous might have caused her more consternation that I'd thought at the time.

"You want to talk again, or . . ."

She interrupted me.

"How is he?"

"Jack?"

"He is my boy's father. You can tell him that much. Yeah," she said. "I owe him that much."

"I can't say he's fine, Dorie. He's been locked up and pretty much alone for two-thirds of his life. Frankly, I'm not sure how he's stayed sane. I wouldn't have."

"He wrote to me for a lotta years," she said. "I never once wrote him back."

There was no telling where this might go so I flipped on the bed lamp and grabbed the hotel note pad. According to the *New York Times* quote embossed in fake gold leaf on top of the pad, I was in "Seattle's Finest Boutique Hotel." I knew from city records that Dorie and her son lived in West Seattle near Genesee, so I got up and looked out the window to the west.

"Quite the moon out there tonight," I said. I could see it was near full, and bright enough to cast shadows.

"There was a moon on the night they died, too. My mom used to call it a harvest moon."

"Best time of year in Wisconsin," I said. "In the very late summer, with the ground fog to diffuse the light when the moon rises, a harvest moon's like nothing else on earth."

There was another long pause. I could hear Dorie's breathing, and she was definitely drunk, but it was hard to know what she wanted to say, and I didn't want to lose her with the wrong question.

"Do you want me to tell him anything about your son?" I asked.

"We're talking confidential, right? I mean, just me 'n you and that's it, right?" She wasn't sure of how to ask the question, but I knew that whatever Dorie was sharing with me would have to live in my notebook permanently unless I could confirm it another way.

"Yes, Dorie. I'm like a priest at confession. It's just you and me."

"I called the boy Luke, after the disciple in the Bible. Lucas Matthew Preston. We changed his last name when I got married. There's no reason for Luke to be caught up in this."

"Absolutely right," I said. "I'm sure Jack would want it that way too."

"What's he look like?"

"Well, he still has hair," I chuckled. "And his waist is trim. He claims it's hard to stay in shape with the food they get, but as far as I know, he's healthy. He's done a lot of writing, and by most standards, he's not just a model inmate, he's exceptional."

"Yeah, I read about him getting educated in prison. I got a cousin that sends me clippings from time to time."

"He's not getting out any time soon, Dorie. Even when he's finally up for parole, if he's still alive, it's not likely they'll release him."

"That letter he sent. Is that confidential too?"

"It is if you say it is. It's your mail."

Dorie took another long sip from her glass. I imagined her getting up to look out the window toward my hotel as if reaching for some kind of connection through me to the father of her child.

"Will you read it to me, please? I'd like to hear what he says."

The letter was inside my computer bag, secure in an inner compartment. It took me a few seconds to get it out, and a few more to find my reading glasses. Then I sat down on the uncomfortable chair in the corner of the room near the window. There was enough moonlight coming in to make Jack's handwriting legible. The reporter in me was observing the moment and I had the good sense to hit record on my iPhone before I read it aloud:

Dear Dorie,

Wow. Well, if you're actually reading this, then I'll start by saying that there's no way to know where to start, really. Except that I'm sorry. We had something good back then. You were the best thing that ever happened to me, even now. It's pretty clear I ruined that.

You've probably heard that I don't remember that night, Dorie. I still can't believe I swallowed all those pills. Maybe it was a death wish of my own, I don't know. With you pregnant, with the stuff going on at home, nothing was making sense then. It probably never will.

I'm sorry about our plan, I really am. I know we were supposed to head West together. There was no way your mom should have been any part of it. The police never found the money, they never knew to look for it, so all I've hoped for all these years is that you managed to get away with it, and that you and our son put it to good use. It wasn't my dad's to begin with, so what we did wasn't like stealing it, it was more like we were Robin Hood, taking it from someone who got it unjustly and giving it to someone who needed it. I can live with that.

Much as I'd like to hear from you, I know that after this many years, you'd have reached out if you'd wanted to. With any luck, I'll at least find out that you and the boy are safe. And dare I wish for him to be happy too?

The inmate's life is a sad one, regardless of who did or didn't do the crime. Prison isn't a place anyone should ever be. I wish I'd died that night a long time ago, just like the others. Nothing is worse than being alive in hell. Knowing you and our son are somewhere out there has kept me going. I want to thank you for that small bit of peace.

Love,
Jack

If ever there was a moment for me to sit quietly, this was it. Enough time went by that I had to look at the screen on my phone to make sure we were still connected.

"You understand what happened, right?" she asked.

"I think I do, yes."

"And do I have to say it out loud for it to be confidential?"

"I don't think so, no. But you are confirming it?"

"Yes," she said. "Yes. I am."

\\\\

On my flight home, I made some final notes in my laptop. It was clear, at least to me, that Jack Degatano had what he considered a good reason to kill his father. Some part of him knew it was wrong, even under the circumstances, and my guess is that the moral ambiguity of his actions was cause for his model behavior and academic pursuit. The way Jason was killed showed a kind of warped thoughtfulness not given to Jack's father, so I imagined that Jason was a casualty of bad timing and, perhaps, a killer too stoned to understand the consequences of murdering someone so benign.

Why Dorie Meeks killed her mother is another matter. With her pregnancy, she had plenty of reason for anger with Jack, plenty of reason to take the money, and a great alibi with sleeping nephews and nieces just thirty miles away. With her drunken confirmation, Dorie assumed I'd put it all together, but I hadn't. I could only imagine that she'd found Jack passed out on the couch, grabbed the knife he'd used on his father and brother, then used the same murder weapon to take out her own sleeping mother before driving back to her sister's house in the middle of the night. Seeing her as a frumpy, middle class baby boomer all these years later made it harder to believe, but then Squeaky Fromme didn't look all that threatening when released from prison after serving a life sentence.

It would be a lot of information to share with officials, and it was based on a lot of speculation. There was nothing in Jack's letter to indict Dorie and no record of the money he referenced that she'd taken. The one reason it was tempting to break confidentiality and share the news was that if Jack's case was reopened, he might, at least, have one murder removed from his record and his conscience. But when I played the conversation out, it went something like this:

"So I've been researching the case of Jack Degatano."

"You don't say. Why would you waste your time on that?"

"I believe he's innocent of at least one of the murders."

"Just one of them? How many did he get convicted of again?"

"Three," I say. "But I don't think he killed his girlfriend's mother."

"And the reason you believe this?"

"I spoke with Dorie Meeks. She had Jack's baby. You can do a DNA test on that. And she stole money from the attic above the hallway in Jack's house. Was it stolen money to begin with? Yeah, but then she stole it. Plus, she and her sister were the heirs to the estate of her mother, the same one Jack was convicted of killing."

"Sure. I'll get right on that."

\\\\\

The sun was setting again and I wondered whether Jack could see it from behind the bars of his new cell. The leaves were gone from all but the last few oaks, and the ground was in for a hard freeze. This would be Jack's fortieth winter behind bars. With darkness coming earlier, maybe he could see the last light fade on the pale gray bark of the tree limbs and still make the cafeteria in time for dinner.

DANCING WITH ELLIE

DAD

It was the fourth inning. A journeyman named Jesus Rios was on the mound when Dad tossed out the game changer.

"You have a half sister." As quickly as the words left his mouth, he took a bigger than average gulp of Pabst Blue Ribbon. Dad would only drink Milwaukee beer, and he'd recently had a private meeting with the reclusive San Francisco billionaire who'd bought the brewery, closed it, and pulled the pensions of thousands of PBR retirees.

"Wow. Talk about a tax loss," I said. The "half sister" reference was dropped into the longer discussion about his private meeting.

"Yep. Billionaires are an odd bunch," he said. "Just plain weird. The guy seemed to have no idea that he was punching his employees in the gut." Dad, it seemed, was unaware of his own gut punch.

"A brewery and a half sister?" I said as I gave Dad a pat on his shoulder. "This is definitely more interesting than our usual ball game."

"He's not a bad guy," Dad said. He was making sure we changed the subject back to billionaires. "He's simply misunderstood."

"Aren't we all?" I asked.

Dad gave me his patented half nod, meaning "you might be right, you might not, and besides, what difference does it make?" Dad was as practical as they come. But he wasn't big on transparency. His transition from half sister to beer magnate was an open window big enough for both of us to exit safely. It also wasn't the first time he'd used a ball game as his venue of choice for big announcements. It's the perfect place to sit side-by-side, talk without eye contact, and pay attention to the smallest details of the game when a conversation becomes heavy lifting.

"Another pitch that high and I'd pull him." Dad then relayed a quick anecdote about how Jesus never stepped on a baseline when walking to and from the dugout. "Another superstitious pitcher," Dad said. "Jesus is one of those religious types."

There was a startling quality to his announcement, but I'd come to expect odd things from my Dad, and having a half sister wasn't that much of a surprise. After all, this was the same father who once imparted what he considered profound wisdom about love relationships by saying, "If you ever get caught by your wife while lying naked in bed with another woman, lie." At that point, he said, the last thing anyone wanted to hear was the truth. Very presidential, I thought.

We were eating shredded beef tacos and he took another gulp of Milwaukee's finest to cool off. "Really," Dad continued, "if you're bold about the way you say it, they'll either doubt that you're screwing your secretary right there in front of them, or they'll assume it's their fault. Either way, you'll walk free."

Ah, Dad. Does this really count as wisdom? Of course it didn't, but Dad never gave much thought to the secretary's feelings. In "his genera-tion," (as in, back when our male ilk were still misogynist bastards) they (the secretary) simply moved on with no hint of dismay or charges of sexual harassment. Which is what happened to Liz, the thin brunette who'd managed his company books and who, along with her Leba-nese-born husband Ziad, co-owned a thirty-foot sailboat with our finan-cially strapped family.

Even though I was only sixteen at the time of his affair with Liz, I liked that big boat for one simple reason: I knew where Dad hid the key to his little love nest. On more than one occasion, my Catholic girlfriend and I snuck into the cabin on Saturday nights and explored each other's limits. Desire, guilt. Desire, guilt. It was the age of Gloria Steinem, and despite our adolescent fear, we both wanted to feel libertaed.

"Pull him!"

I know what you're thinking, but Dad was screaming about Jesus, the 34-year-old Venezuelan who'd managed to load the bases with no outs.

"This is why the franchise is in trouble," he said. "It's the commissioner's fault!" Dad wasn't keen on the former car salesman who'd gone on to become the commissioner of baseball.

"So, I have a half sister?" I said. It rolled off my tongue with zero emotion because, let's face it, when it came to Dad, there was a lot of water over the dam.

"It happened a long time ago. You were young."

"How young?" I asked.

"About six months old. Maybe seven months, but who's counting?"

"Does she know you're her father?" I asked in a valiant attempt to make this about anyone but me.

"No. She thinks her father is her father. It's complicated." It always was with Dad. That's why his secretary Liz and her husband Ziad split for Florida. Co-owning a sailboat with the boss made for some cozy weekday afternoons, but it was also "complicated." And expensive.

Two base runners had scored and the Brewers were losing by six runs in the fourth inning. We needed to play the half sister thing out at the ballpark or else we could leave early. I was leaning toward the latter when Stan the beer vendor popped by holding two cold ones in his right hand. It was up to six bucks a beer and Dad tried to pay, but I wouldn't hear of it. The less I owed the guy, the better. Stan asked Dad, a season ticket holder, where his wife had been hiding out. Given Dad's propensity for using the tickets for *business*, I wondered which woman Stan thought was Dad's wife.

"She's in Europe," Dad said. "A business trip to Dublin."

Stan seemed to buy the answer, or in the least, he feigned caring when I handed him a two-dollar tip.

"Do you know her name?" I asked? There was a good chance I had other half siblings scattered around the Midwest, but this one surely had a name.

"Yes. She's in the church choir. She lives in Galena and she's six months younger than you."

"Galena. As in just south of the border Galena?"

"Illinois, yes. Her mother says it's nice."

"So she was born in Iowa?"

"Born in Shenandoah, but raised in Omaha."

Note to self: we were still using pronouns. I wasn't going to get her name before the ninth inning, if at all.

"Her mother and I conceived her as a love child," he said.

"Which makes me?"

I feigned indignation at his reference to "love child." But the facts were piling up. We were both conceived in Shenandoah, Iowa. The boyhood home of the Everly Brothers, the love child, and me.

"It wasn't like that," Dad said. "Her mother and I wanted to be together but it was the late '50s. Nobody got divorced then. You just did what you had to do." What he meant was that you did the neighbor's wife. Or whatever else you had to do.

"I'm sure it was terribly challenging, Dad. I can't imagine the pain you both endured." Did I really say that out loud?

The inning was over and a boyish phenom named Elroy Smart had come to bat for the Brewers. Ballplayers seem to grow up in places like Shenandoah or Galena. But Elroy was a former Mennonite from LaFarge, Wisconsin who played his Double A ball in Helena. Batting .354 with 87 RBI in just four months had earned Elroy a promotion to a challenged major league club. If Elroy couldn't turn the team around, no one could. Not even the commissioner, who, to Dad's chagrin, was "hell bent on keeping the team in the cellar until the owners started sharing revenue."

"So you wanna to tell me her name?" I asked.

"One thing at a time." Dad drank more when he was nervous, and he took two large gulps. "I've been carrying this little family secret for forty-eight years, so I'm not exactly in a hurry. You're the only one who knows."

Forty-eight years was a long time to hold a secret, even for Dad. I couldn't be the only one, I thought. But who else would know?

"I call her mother on June 12th every year," Dad continued. "That's how I know she lives in Galena. She's married and has a ten-year-old daughter."

Why Galena? Why so close to my hometown? What if I know this person? What if we've met on Match.com?

Since it was June 13th I could understand why this half-sister thing was on his mind. I wanted to cut the guy some slack for all the obvious reasons—the big one being that I wasn't walking in his shoes, and I wasn't planning to. There were a few things mildly lovable about Dad, but nothing to put anyone over the top. If he and his soul mate wanted to create a love child back in the day, then who was I to judge it after all these years?

Then, suddenly, it hit me. I have a half sister! And she's just six months younger than me!

"Do Douglas or Joan know?" I was asking about my full siblings now (I'd never thought to consider them "full" before) but Dad claimed they knew nothing. Nor did his second wife, Lindsay. Lindsay was the ex-wife of a suburban minister. She left the good padre after he got caught with a parishioner's husband in the rectory during a time when gay men had very few options. Life after divorce had been difficult for Lindsay, but she eventually found Dad, a man who had been profoundly straight since his late depression-era puberty.

Speaking of full siblings, Douglas is on wife number four, and this one seems like a winner. They met on a dating site for sports nuts where Tippy's profile included a love of early Ann Rice novels, Bavarian beer, and a mild interest in dressage. Douglas owns sixty acres near Scotts Bluff, Nebraska, where he raises horses purchased with his baseball signing bonus. Tippy was running a foundation for pregnant teenagers in Bismarck when she and Douglas tied the knot. Douglas claimed to love her altruism, a rare characteristic among past girlfriends and certainly not a strong sales point for his first three wives. Since Tippy moved south to Nebraska, she's enthusiastically embraced the Sand Hills. I find Tippy refreshing, but it helps that we've rarely conversed until after her first two glasses of Riesling.

"She's as good in the morning as she is at night," Douglas once told me, as if referring to a new colt. I wasn't exactly sure what he meant, but it seemed clear he was his father's son.

Before he threw his arm out and had the "Tommy John" surgery, Douglas made it all the way to Triple A in the Cleveland farm system. He was a magnet for nineteen-year-olds in halter-tops who waited outside the locker room on humid summer nights. In the category of short, shallow relationships, Douglas was the proverbial master, a fact Dad often shared with his country club pals. Douglas had maintained a hero status with Dad long before he'd married Rachel (wife number one). Rachel was a graduate student in physical therapy who met Douglas while icing down his shoulder on a hot August night in Davenport. She'd left behind Amish roots in a village along Highway 1 just south of Iowa City to take up a new spiritual pursuit—barhopping. Her drinking habits were encouraged by my mother, who very much enjoyed Rachel's visits to her home on the West Coast.

We're all close to Mom, but my sister Joan may be her favorite. They practice that love-hate thing as if trying to perfect it for mother-daughter teams everywhere. Joan and her significantly younger lover, Tabitha, live for their Manhattan weekends. Joan didn't discover she was lesbian right away. There were two husbands and three children along the way. Tabitha isn't wild about the family thing so she and Joan live separately, which allows Joan to be with her kids every other week. Husbands one and two, Daryl and Evan, are good fathers, and they give Joan the space she needs for her getaways with Tabitha.

Daryl (husband number two) works as a relationship therapist and teaches dijerido on weekends. His two kids, Madison and Emma, are both experts at circular breathing, and Madison, age 13, competes in bagpipe tournaments. Evan (husband number one) is a yoga instructor and author who remarried shortly after leaving Joan for his stretchy young student, Michelle. Michelle is due in October, and she and Evan have agreed to an underwater birth. Evan and Joan's daughter, Morgan, struggles with asthma, which is why Joan, Tabitha, Daryl, Madison, Emma, Evan, Michelle, and Morgan have all agreed to move to Tucson. It's nice when everyone puts the kids' needs first, even when it makes Manhattan getaways challenging.

The crowd roared suddenly when the big first baseman, Boulder Sims, launched a line drive foul ball into the right field seats just five rows behind Dad and me. Two kids made a diving effort across Dad's lap, and the last two bites of bratwurst with "secret stadium sauce" and sauerkraut wound up on Dad's khakis. The Brewers were down by six in the bottom of the seventh, reason enough for a quick exit. It had been an afternoon of substantial and unnerving (yet not entirely unexpected) revelations, but Dad wasn't inclined to give me much more to go on.

MOM

The reason Mom drinks out of plastic tumblers is that they're quieter than glass. She learned this by sitting up nights waiting for Dad to come home. No one questioned her drinking as long as they didn't hear ice cubes jingling.

There was a brief time back in the fifties when Mom was alcohol free. She was also a routine Protestant, and a devout self-described prude. I discovered her prudishness years later when I brought my college girl-friend home for a visit. I should say "quasi-girlfriend." My high school sweetheart had dumped me during our sophomore year of college, and after a couple of months of broken-hearted depression, I met Sylvie at a drinking party in the southeast dormitories. Love had little to do with our initial attraction, and whether I liked it or not, Sylvie tried to teach me the meaning of mindless sex. She'd taken Gloria Steinem more seriously than most college-aged women, perhaps beyond even Gloria's imagination or intention. Sylvie had at least two guys coming by each week at her discretion for carefully scheduled intimacy. Her terms of engagement were defined by her moods. Never one to think things through too carefully, I wound up with Sunday and Wednesday nights as well as the occasional "date," which included my first and last Neil Sedaka concert. As an open-minded college student unable to fully grasp the meaning of true love, what worked for Sylvie, worked for me. Still, after being dumped by someone I loved, I was anxious for an emotional connection. I thought I'd hit pay dirt when Sylvie agreed to join me for a visit to my folks' house for Thanksgiving dinner.

It was the usual football and feasting, but when Sylvie and Mom went to the kitchen for drinks, Dad nodded his approval. To be specific, he said "she may not be the best looking girl you've dated, but she's smart, and smart women are the best in bed." Dad loved to share his little pearls of wisdom, especially when they were least appropriate.

Mom did a knock-out job on the turkey, including her own unique touch, bourbon-infused gravy. It wasn't long after pumpkin pie that Sylvie excused herself with a migraine and opted for the hourly bus back to Madison. I wasn't so lucky. Mom and Dad spent the late afternoon sipping highballs and probing me with questions about my future. When faced with philosophical questions, Mom's glass was always half full. It helped her think. She'd also make a kitchen run to add an extra ice cube to top things off, her way of sneaking a quick capful of whiskey straight up before stirring. It was early evening when Mom opened up to me with her concerns about Sylvie.

"I'm not sure about that one. You be careful."

There's nothing like parental tutelage to confuse matters for a young man. Did she mean careful as in "use a condom?" Or careful as in "make sure you don't get sucked into that girl's Bohemian lifestyle?" Or careful as in "don't let her wear the pants." As a self-proclaimed career house-wife whose idea of work peaked with the occasional high school bake sale, Mom was not a fan of Gloria. The product of her own domineering mother, Mom seemed happiest in the role of subservient enabler.

Then, suddenly, Mom blurted "She's a slut!" Perhaps it was the bour-bon gravy talking, but she even had one eye squinting at me as if she was a small town sheriff fending off the virginity-stealing vixen who'd just invaded their cozy house in the suburbs. I don't know what she expected, but it wasn't my reaction. I looked her in the eye and repeated "slut, slut, slut," at which point she dropped her cocktail on the patio. I knew a mood swing couldn't be far behind.

"Champ," (Dad liked to call me Champ) "more power to ya. Just make sure you wear a raincoat." Using an expression like 'wear a raincoat' was as close to hip as Dad got in the early '80s. "Your mother and I had sex long before we were married, too."

"That's in the category of more than I need to know," I replied. But it pushed Mom over the edge.

"We did not!" Her voice cracked just a bit, betraying her objection. She refilled her glass and took a gulp to regain her balance.

"He's 21. If he can't hear the truth by now, then Houston, we've got a problem." Dad used clichés with such command that even he believed he'd made them up.

"We did not have premarital sex! Period!" Mom was on a roll.

That's when Dad decided to download his recollection of their high school days back in Nebraska. To hear his version, everyone was having sex. Boys had it easy. But pregnant girls only had two options. The rich ones whose parents owned cattle ranches west of Omaha were sent off to Copenhagen for a Carlsburg tour and a quick abortion. The poor ones went to Aunt Ester's for a nine-month vacation. The conversation was enough for Mom to boil over. She went inside, slamming the door hard enough to show her dissatisfaction but shy of breaking the glass.

But, back to Mom's drinking. I first noticed that things had gone awry when she came to visit Terri (my first wife) and me in 1987, long after Sylvie and college graduation. Neither Mom nor Terri had much interest in me, but they knew a good competition when they saw one. They side-stepped pleasantries and faced off in a weekend-long contest for the top passive-aggressive personality. Given my just-below-the-surface fear of abandonment, I worked the room like a cheerleader fighting my favorite team's losing streak. I couldn't make either woman happy, and by Sunday morning, Terri used my overbearing efforts to placate her as an excuse for an all-day errand.

I hadn't been alone with Mom in years and had no idea what might happen next, so I suggested we go for a ride in the country. Just like the good old days, I said. There was plenty of empty space north of Madison for a hike, but I picked the farm fields just east of the then-vacant Badger Ammunition Factory. The factory is roaring with activity now that America's consumed with fighting a series of losing attempts at nation building. But in the decade after Vietnam, grass grew through the cracks in the miles of pavement surrounding the former icon of wartime economy. The plant had gone offline shortly after the Armstrong brothers were busted for blowing up the Army Math Research Center on the UW Madison campus. As tipping points go, the antiwar movement was crippled, but so was the ammo factory.

Mom needed to talk, and the unsightly skeleton of steel and crumbling brick failed to discourage her. It had only been six years since her divorce from Dad, seven from the time I'd brought Sylvie home for a visit (though I doubt the two events were related). We'd both found time to marry—me to the ever-independent Terri, Mom to a career diplomat from West Virginia who'd had every tropical disease known to man during his tenure as ambassador to Colombia. Mom got it right the second time.

She married her kind, handsome, and monogamous best friend, Earl. Earl was a gentleman. The two weren't without bad habits, including knocking off a cardboard box full of Chablis between four and six o'clock every day. The sugar didn't do much good for Earl's diabetes or the liver problems he related back to a particular strain of malaria. Or maybe it was dengue. Still, the ambassador usually kept his ailments to himself.

So, several years, a new husband, a walk with her son in the hills north of Madison, and a concealed brush-metal flask filled with Makers Mark was all Mom needed to open up on the gritty details of the summer of 1956. It was another blast from the family past. Just like Dad at the ballgame, Mom didn't want to cough up the whole story all at once. Sharing snippets must have made it seem less real to her, as if the life she was describing had happened to someone else.

"When you were six months old," she said, "I took you and Joan, and we left your father. We were living in a house trailer in Shenandoah, I couldn't take it anymore, and we just up and left. Considering I had twenty-two dollars in my purse and no credit cards back then, we didn't have a lot of options. We went to my folks house west of the Missouri River near Fremont."

"Was Uncle Weasel still living at home then?" I asked. It may have been the dumbest question that ever came out of my mouth, but Mom rolled with it as if I was serving up distraction on a silver platter.

"Uncle Weasel was in Galveston with Louisa by then. He'd already bought his first big rig and they were making a pretty good go of it."

Uncle Weasel was bigger than life. Six foot seven, three hundred pounds, and a laugh that could be heard across town. He'd become a legend in Galveston as the first long-haul trucker to have a CB radio. The locals claimed the ground shook when Weasel would fall off his barstool after a three martini lunch. He was a notorious drunk, which even then was a particularly bad habit for a long distance trucker. Still, Weasel had more friends than anyone in South Texas. After serving in the Korean War, he'd met Louisa in a Nogales taverna and they raised two fine kids.

Weasel was a wanderer, and he'd left the family home long before Mom ditched the house trailer in Shenandoah with the hope of finding refuge with her parents. But by that time, Gramps and Lolly had had enough of children, and grandchildren. They were enjoying their life as a married couple for the first time and didn't want it interrupted. Gramps had been heroic in the trenches during WWI, but when he returned from the war he couldn't find the courage to ask a woman to a barn dance. This didn't stop Lolly from trying to win his heart. They were second generation Norwegians at a time when folks still married their own kind. Lolly asked Gramps to marry her and from that point forward, Lolly happily ran their lives, and Gramps let her. It wasn't easy. Gramps was shell-shocked and could occasionally be found in the basement staring at the wall of the rec room. He seemed to manage by staying busy and avoiding visits to the VFW Club. After the wedding, they'd become pregnant with Weasel in a matter of months and settled into the prototypical post-war lifestyle— work, kids, church, Shriner's Club, and a healthy admiration for Herbert Hoover. Unlike Weasel, Mom always tried to please her folks, but they never stopped questioning her choices.

We came to a clearing at a high point overlooking the ammo dump and stopped to watch a hawk as it tracked a field mouse. Mom asked if I wanted a little nip. I declined, but it didn't stop her.

"Lolly thought your Dad was a bastard long before he and I were married," Mom told me. Lolly had masked this well, I thought, because she always seemed perky at family gatherings. But by 1987, she'd passed away and Gramps was long gone, so whatever they'd thought back in '56 was of little consequence.

"Gramps and Lolly took us in that first night," said Mom. "It was a Thursday and we got there just before dinner. I'd driven around all day trying to decide what to do. We'd gone half way up to the Loess Hills and back. We only had one car, a '51 Olds four door. I know you like details but I don't remember what make it was so don't ask!"

I let it go, but was starting to think that a little nip sounded pretty good.

"Driving helped me figure out what to do—I guess I said that already—and what I remember most is that I was worried that your Dad would have had to walk to work that day. How silly is that?"

"Was Lolly pissed off when you showed up?" I asked Mom.

"Stern mostly. She was always that way, except she was always nice to you kids. When we got there, Gramps came out to the car and picked you up right away. That man loved his grandson more than an episode of Milton Berle. You were always a colicky baby and you threw up on him right on cue.

"Nice detail, Mom. And Joan was a perfect toddler?"

"That girl was so cute but she climbed on things, and she had a nasty habit of kicking people in the shin. Believe me, those little saddle shoes can hurt when you take one in the shin. Lolly wasn't big on little kids and Joan challenged her in every way possible. She knocked over everything in her path: house plants, end tables, the Dachshund. I think that's why Lolly made us go back to your Dad so quickly. It was a very brief getaway. We were back in Shenandoah in time for Sunday church."

There was a cool breeze blowing in from the ammo dump and both of us were getting cold. It was early November so the weather changed fast. The few remaining oak leaves rustled, and the farm fields were filled with corn stalks and debris from a quick harvest slotted in between late season rains.

"I always liked Wisconsin this time of year," Mom said. "I miss the change of seasons."

"Maybe you and the ambassador can move back this way. Since you guys missed my wedding, Earl might like to see the . . ."

"I didn't want to see your father," she interrupted with anger in her voice. "I didn't want him to see me happy!"

Now that's a twist, I thought. Mom . . . happy. Yeah, that would have really freaked out Dad and his former preacher's wife Lindsay *except* that he had never truly loved Mom and he was thrilled to be with Lindsay. Dad and Lindsay fought like two pit bulls stuck in Michael Vick's garage, but there was something deeply sexual about the tension they created. Douglas once accused Lindsay of trying to poison the old man with a peanut butter and jelly sandwich, which still brings a laugh at family reunions. Still, Dad and Lindsay had behaved like real parents at my wedding, their display of pride made easier by not having to share their emotional space with Mom and Earl.

In retrospect, what a great choice Mom made by skipping the wedding. Terri and I were doomed from the start, and as the victim of her own failed marriage, Mom probably knew it. Everyone else certainly did. Or maybe I was just holding up a mirror for the family to justify their own botched unions.

"You hung in there much longer than anyone should have," I said. "Life with Dad couldn't have been easy."

"People didn't divorce back then," she said. "This was before Gloria Steinem, you know. It was a different time." There's Gloria again, I thought. This is her story as much as anyone's. She'd enlightened millions in her battle against generations of institutional sexism. She'd added a voice to the dialogue of feminism that society-at-large hadn't heard since Victoria Woodhull took a seat on the New York Stock Exchange back in 1898. It couldn't have been easy for Gloria either, because those who came before didn't want to admit their lies or their failures. Think about it: Mom came to adulthood before The Beatles, before George Carlin, Cassius Clay, MLK, Malcolm X and Bobby Kennedy. She was a full-on adult B.G. Before Gloria. For Mom, change couldn't happen overnight. For her, change really couldn't happen at all. Mom did what she was told.

With tradition and Protestant values on her side, Lolly told Mom to go back to Shenandoah and to heed the will of her husband. Mom was home within 48 hours, and she stayed with Dad for twenty-three more years. She never left again, and it's possible that she never wanted to. Dad went on to become a world class philanderer, but he also provided the basics—food, shelter, security, some money for college, and the occasional westward-ho vacation to the Black Hills or his favorite fishing spot in the Upper Peninsula. By most accounts, theirs was a typical Midwestern marriage, but it wasn't affectionate. I saw my parents kiss only once when he gave her a peck on the cheek after blowing out forty birthday candles. A few years later, on New Year's Eve, 1981, Dad asked Mom for a divorce. Their youngest son had finally finished college. It was time to move on.

HALF SIS

Not long before Dad lost his battle with life as we know it, he'd phoned me from Tucson to share more juicy family details. It had been a year since his announcement at the ball game and Half Sis had certainly been on my mind. And, apparently, his as well. His wife Lindsay had hung on to her father's apple orchard in southwest Wisconsin, and she was there on her annual visit, a trip so deadly boring to Dad that a blazing hot July in Tucson held more charm. Since he was home alone, Dad had time to talk openly.

"She's divorced and moved up to Madison." Dad had a penchant for opening lines, as if the conversation had begun an hour earlier. "She's dating a chiropractor."

"Be careful, Dad. I'm single," I said sarcastically. "What if we meet at the farmer's market? Or a political rally at the capitol building?"

The idea of accidentally dating my half sister would rock Dad's boat, I thought, as I planted the evil seed of retribution. Most families are in the business of punishment, and a night out with Half Sis would be a whopper. But he ignored me, and despite his years of bravado and phony confidence, I heard a twinge of what might have been love in his voice. It wasn't a sound I'd heard before, so I opted to tread carefully.

"In case something happens to me," he said, "I want you to let her mother know I'm gone." Easy enough, I thought. Most of us either have a soul mate or wish we did, though few of us get to spend our lives with them. Maybe deprivation is the secret to keeping the exceptional lover in that cherished place we call our soul. For some people, knowing them too well might break the spell.

"Stephanie," he said. "Your sister's name is Stephanie." We were on a roll, but playing on unfamiliar turf. When Dad blurted something out, it meant he'd been thinking it through for months, even years, leaving the listener largely unprepared for whatever came next.

"Your mom and I used to play bridge with Stephanie's folks—that is, her mom and the guy she thinks is her dad but who isn't. They ran the furniture store. It was a small town, so it's a pretty good bet your Mom knew what was going on."

Knew? I thought. She'd run home to Gramps and Lolly with Joan and me in the back seat of your '51 Olds! I was dying to ask him the make of the car but it was a Friday night and I had a small dinner party happening in my kitchen. We were chopping vegetables for a stir-fry and I had a sharp knife in my hands.

"Dad, I want to know all of this, really I do, but I've got six people here hovering over that electric wok you bought me for a wedding gift twenty years ago. At least three of my guests have had one too many mojitos, and my significant other looked much friendlier when she first arrived. Any chance we can talk tomorrow?"

Timing is everything with Dad, and when I rang him back the next afternoon, he was grumpy. He'd told me too much already, he said. The rest would have to wait. Two months later, Dad's unexpected death was due to the accidental mix of failing health and a lousy hospital. He went in for one thing and died of another—pneumonia resulting from a punctured lung during a routine procedure by a hurried emergency room doctor. According to the fine print, it's "a known complication." Douglas and his wife Tippy thought a malpractice suit would be worthwhile but none of us wanted to front the legal fees. Since my sister Joan and the newly widowed Lindsay had decided to use Dad's death to redefine the upper limits of step-family aggression (accentuated, in Joan's case, by a bad case of panic attacks and an acute case of laryngitis), finding consensus on anything was an uphill battle. I certainly wasn't much help in negotiating because family tension forces me into uncontrollable bouts nervous laughter.

After a few hours of arguing in the hospital lounge, we all agreed that a funeral was out of the question. Religion wasn't Dad's thing. Lindsay, Douglas, Joan, and I did what we could to rally for a memorial service near the putting green on his favorite hole at the Tucson golf club he'd joined after retirement. Three of his golf buddies showed up, and in the spirit of their foursome, they howled with laughter while imitating the way Dad would regularly shank his trap shots. It was show and tell as Douglas and I raked the sand behind them, then asked for one more demonstration (we'd caddied for Dad and knew the importance of golf etiquette).

"Who are those fat slobs ruining my father's legacy?" whispered Joan, albeit loud enough for nearly everyone but the slobs to hear.

"Oh, bite it," said Lindsay. "They're having fun!"

Lindsay, who after years of being restrained in the forced tranquility of her gay minister husband's home on the grounds of St. Matthew the Divine, was always ready for a good time. She had a lot to make up for, and she seemed to genuinely enjoy the golf slobs and their jovial antics. Even Joan laughed when Lindsay slipped off her heels, sank deep in the sand, and tried to punch one onto the putting green with a two iron. Dad, the low-handicap aficionado of Tucson's over-70 crowd, must have helped from on high, because she nearly holed it, leaving it in gimme territory. Slob number one hiked up his trousers and pushed it in with his right foot.

When we finally got everyone sitting down, it was two o'clock. The sun was blinding, and there was no tent cover for the guests. This wasn't world class bad planning as much as our only option—no one plays golf on hot afternoons in Tucson, so the space was available. It was the only time we could seat fifty people near Dad's favorite hole. Everyone raced through their tribute talks as the helpers from the club passed out sunscreen and a few umbrellas. Justin, who played the dual role of assistant pro and gigolo, was extra helpful to Joan's lover Tabitha as he massaged an SPF 30 onto her bare shoulders. It's hard to say what Tabitha enjoyed more—Justin's perfect grip or watching him bend sideways after the elbow Joan gave to his ribcage.

Business had been Dad's power center and outside of the eulogies of the golf slobs, the service was a parade of white men speaking kindly, overblown words they could easily have applied to their own lives. He'd stood up to the left-wing governor, they said. He believed in tax cuts, ignored deficits when he had to, fought government regulations, loved Barry Goldwater, and supported both individual rights and a woman's right to choose. He'd helped build the economic base and bring more manufacturing jobs to the community. Etcetera. Bottom line, we'd all lost another good, albeit godless, Libertarian.

One former female "friend" named Polly had driven in from her retirement home near Sedona. She remarked that Dad had done things differently. He was his own man. He recognized his personal baggage, and he wasn't one to judge others. He was too shy to be an outspoken progressive, she said, but he thought we wasted too much money on useless wars, he worked for civil rights, he fought the glass ceiling, and, to her surprise, he'd been a fan of Gloria Steinem.

I was the last to speak. Like any son, I talked about what Dad had meant to me, what he'd done for me, my feelings of sadness and loss, and the legacy he left behind. Doug, Joan, Lindsey, and I would miss him, I said. He had touched many lives in mostly good ways. Dad was complicated, perhaps more than any of us knew, and yet at his core, he was simply a capitalist who believed in free markets, equal rights, and the power of the individual to overcome obstacles and create wealth. As long ago as middle school, I'd been told that if we had enough Howard Rourk in us, everything would be just fine. He was pragmatic but surprisingly charitable, I said. He didn't seem to need a thing. And, I lied, he was the least romantic person I'd ever met.

As I was about to leave the small podium, a hawk flew in low over the group. It seemed to stall above me, catching the warm breeze as it climbed higher, then moved off toward the desert. It may have meant nothing to Dad's friends, but to me, an unabashed animist, the hawk symbolized my father's transition. He was determined, I thought. His spirit was empowered to glide smoothly, effortlessly, to the time before time, the space before space. Wherever Stephanie was, whomever she had become, I wondered whether my half sister could feel the hawk rising, whether she could sense the updraft that sent her biological father's spirit ascending. Wherever nature was concerned, I'd learned to trust the spirit of the messenger. It was time for me to tell Stephanie's mother that her daughter's father had died. It was up to me to make the journey.

CHOP CHOP

In the days following the service, Lindsay was overcome with grief. She spent the first few nights at their townhouse nestled in Dad's recliner and watching their favorite television show, *Sean Hannity*. Dad loved mindless political banter and cable television suited him just fine. Lindsey wanted to keep Dad close at hand, coveting the smell of his shirts, stroking the nibble marks on the stem of his reading glasses, shuffling across the kitchen in his old leather slippers. Even the cat seemed at a loss. When it couldn't find comfort in Lindsay's lap, it perched in dark corners of the room calling out a haunting, slow meow that rang an octave higher than normal.

During the first few nights after the service I stayed in the guestroom. I was there under the guise of being "good company," but I had a self-serving mission in mind. During the few moments when Lindsay would nod off, I searched for clues about Stephanie's mother. Phone records. Credit card bills. Old files. If only he'd kept a journal, I thought. But Dad had learned the risks of a paper trail back in Shenandoah. When Lindsay was awake, I worked up excuses to examine his personal papers and belongings, but it was too early for her to consent. What I really needed was his old Rolodex. When I suggested that I look it over to see if there was anyone I should call on his behalf, she lightened up. Everyone should know, she said. There were more than three hundred yellowed cards in the file she pulled from the top shelf of their closet. It appeared he'd kept it hidden from Lindsay, but apparently not well enough.

The only thing that stood out was a dog-eared card with a 402 area code—Omaha—and the name "Ellie" in Dad's handwriting. It was my first clue.

\\\\

Years ago, I learned it was best to visit Mom in the late morning. The alcohol from the night before was as flushed out as it would ever be, and there was still some productive time for conversation before cocktail hour.

"Remember that empty book I gave you?" I asked. "The one where I was hoping you'd fill it in with your version of the family history?" The book was sitting on Mom's credenza with about half of the first page filled in. I could see where she'd erased things and started over.

"There's still time," she said. But writing family history wasn't Mom's thing, so if I was ever going to get details on what, if anything, she knew about my half sister Stephanie, now was the time. It would be up close and personal, I thought.

"I filled in half a page about my Aunt Eunice who died in the house fire." Mom sounded enthused, so it was important to placate the one person who knew what I needed to know.

"I do remember that story," I said. "Wasn't the basement filled with propane or something?"

"Natural gas. Blew Euny to smithereens." Mom gestured big, as if she could see pieces of Aunt Eunice flying through the air. "Thank God she was a spinster."

"You think it was an accident?" I asked.

"I think she was a disgruntled lesbo!" Eunice may have been playing for another team, but she wasn't the real target of Mom's irreverent dismissal. Mom had been disappointed in her own offspring since Joan's coming out party, a point she made with every opportunity.

"Suicide?" I asked.

"Suicide."

I wanted Mom to be comfortable with the note taking I'd perfected on my day job, so before switching subjects I showed her my list:

Aunt Eunice.

Natural gas fire.

Lesbian . . . suicide.

Blew her to smithereens.

Mom nodded as if she was impressed with my journalistic talent. She even seemed to enjoy being the subject of one of my all-too-frequent interviews.

"Eunice was Gramps' sister, right?" Mom nodded her head yes. Mentioning Gramps brought her back to the death of her own father and for a moment, she had a far off look in her eye.

"I took that one hard," she said. "Gramps was like a rock for me. An inspiration, really. Quiet. Determined. A strong man who didn't let evil destroy him ever after that horrible war. Had some bad days with the shell shock, as you know. Lost his hair from the gas. But he treated people the way he wanted to be treated, and they were loyal to him."

A story for another time, I thought, and made a few more notes:

Gramps.

WWI.

Poison gas.

Shell shock.

Destroying evil.

"What can you tell me about 1956?" I didn't want to get hung up on pre-me events so I opted to dive right in.

"1956?"

"You took Joan and me in the '51 Olds, left Dad, went to Fremont."

"Who told you that?" Mom had killed a lot of brain cells along the way, and this memory escaped her.

"You did. When you visited Terri and me in Madison back in '87."

Mom stared into space for some time, then got up from the table. She opened the refrigerator and pulled out two cold bottles of Miller High Life.

"Beer?"

"Why not." I wasn't about to let my dislike for cheap lager get in the way of information gathering.

Mom opened the bottles like a pro and took her time draining them into a couple of tumblers she'd picked up at the Dollar Store. Whatever database she was mining didn't seem too corrupt. She just needed time to pull the pieces together and a cold beer would help.

"Your father wasn't coming home at night," she said. "I'm not sure where he was, but you were six months old and puking like a champion. Joan was climbing on everything she could find, kicking people in the shins, and I was alone."

Mom took a long pull on her beer.

"The sad thing is, that was normal. Sometimes he said he slept at the office. Sometimes he was on business, though I don't think that was the truth. But in June of '56, his being gone mattered. There was just me, two small kids, a trailer with a bad screen door, and windows that wouldn't lock."

Mom got up and walked slowly to the closet near the front door. She put a small footstool down and then, very deliberately, pulled a box of gloves and old hats off the top shelf. Behind them was another box, wooden, with a small metal clasp. She carried the box back to the couch and set it down in front of her, justifying the corners along the horizon line of the table. When she blew on the top of the box, particles of dust floated through a beam of sunlight from the kitchen window. When she leaned back into the beam, her frail shadow followed on the back wall.

"This belonged to my father," she said. "And his father before that."

I ran my hand along an engraving with the letters H.S., then opened the box slowly.

My questions were being answered before I asked them. There were several small items inside, her personal collection. A pocket watch. Jewelry. Old dog-eared letters. Some 19th century coins from Norway. She leaned forward into the light, pulled out her first wedding ring and looked at it closely.

"This is the ring your Dad gave me. The diamond was from his Scottish grandmother, Neela Mc-something. I wanted to give it to Terri for your wedding but it didn't happen. Sorry. I just couldn't make that one."

If pulling up the old memories was painful, Mom wasn't showing it. Instead, our discussion provoked a few moments of clarity that I'd rarely seen from her.

"Some of the letters are from your great-grandfather. He came here from western Norway, near Stavanger. He became a coachman for a wealthy family, and that's how he met your great-grandmother."

From the corner of the box, she removed a handful of neatly trimmed newspaper articles from the *Des Moines Register*. She looked each one over, then handed them to me one at a time. They were all dated from early June, 1956. I spent an extra moment on a birth announcement for a girl named Stephanie Marie Baltus, born to parents Eleanor and Ralph Baltus, owners of a furniture store in Shenandoah. Stephanie was the 17th child born in Shenandoah that year.

There was a broken rubber band on another tight pile of clippings. Mom slipped it aside and rubbed the residue off the indentation. No one had looked inside the box for years. She unfolded an article and handed it to me—a page one report about an escaped convict from the state prison near Marshalltown. He'd been on the run for a week, and the residents of western Iowa were panicked.

Mom's fears were well founded. A World War II hero from Council Bluffs named Tommie Boston had killed four female coeds on the college campus in Ames during the fall of 1948. He was sentenced to life in prison with a parole date in 2010. But Tommie Boston, whom fellow inmates nicknamed Chop Chop, had managed to sneak his way out of the joint in the prison laundry truck. He was nowhere to be found, but the local folks in southwest Iowa were nervous because Tommy's former wife still lived close to the Missouri River. The whole county was on edge.

Dad may have been staying out late with Eleanor Baltus, and if they were soul mates, who could blame him. But he was also leaving his wife and kids alone in a dirt-poor house trailer on the north side of US Highway 6 just west of Shenandoah. I'd imagined so many reasons why Mom had escaped to her parents' home with Joan and me in tow. But none of them had included saving us from a late night visit by a murderous fugitive named Chop Chop.

ELLIE

Some things are meant for dreary days. My quest to locate Eleanor Baltus was one of them. In the obsession to find my half sister's mother, I'd played out our first encounter hundreds of times. I'd have the element of surprise on my side. I'd be bold, matter-of-fact, even a bit cocky, impervious to anything, or everything. But when it was finally time for me to speak, nothing came except the obvious.

"You don't know me," I said.

In the pause that followed, I wondered whether she'd ever considered a phone call from her former lover's son, whether she'd prepared things to say, whether she'd hang up, faint, fake a coughing fit, or suggest a meeting. It was new terrain for both of us, and Eleanor Baltus played to my weakness with a very long pause. I imagined my father sitting next to me at a ballgame, a proud grin on his face. In my fantasy, he nodded, admiring the courage it took for me to reach out to his soul mate, admiring her for standing ready, fearless.

"You're his son?" she asked.

"I'm sorry, I know this must be a shock. But he asked me to call you when he died. It was important to him."

I pictured Eleanor on the other end of the phone just as she'd appeared in the *Des Moines Register* photograph from the 1949 Adair County Corn Festival. Dad had quite an eye back then, and when Eleanor was crowned Corn Queen, she'd worn her hair just like Lauren Bacall's.

"It happen recently?" Her voice stayed calm, as if she already knew he'd passed.

"About three months ago. He'd had health problems for years but pneumonia and a lousy doctor killed him."

Another long pause.

"Which son are you?"

"His first. My brother Douglas raises horses about 200 miles west of where you live."

"Who else knows?"

Was this the big question—as in, who else knows the truth about Stephanie? I took the easy way out.

"It was in the papers in Tucson, and back in the Midwest. And the family of course."

"I'm sorry. I didn't mean his obituary. I was wondering who else might know what you know about me?"

I wondered if she could hear me take a deep breath.

"I'd say it's a good bet my mother knows," I said. "She's still alive down in San Diego. My dad's second wife doesn't know."

"And your siblings?"

I laughed, and the tension seemed to ease a bit. "Joan would kill the messenger. And Douglas is, well, he's Douglas. I'm pretty sure he'd be fine either way. I don't think they know."

The pauses were killing me. I have trouble not multi-tasking so giving full attention to the call required patience I hadn't used in a while. I was calling from a street corner on what had to be the last pay phone in America, and I found myself pacing in place. The cold drizzle had matted my hair flat against my forehead. With my free hand, I popped open a cheap black umbrella, the kind that magically appear on the carts of big city street vendors with the first sprinkle of rain.

"I'm sure you're wondering about your half sister." It wasn't a question, and I couldn't tell whether she was apprehensive or relieved. Either way, we'd moved from the facts to a moment of truth.

"He told me about her a few months before he died," I said. "Apparently she and I are almost neighbors."

"I raised four children with Ralph. Stephanie was number two. I say 'raised' because like your mother, Ralph had figured out that Stephanie wasn't his during my pregnancy. Still, he was a good father to her."

"Does she know?"

"Ralph died about twelve years ago." Eleanor avoided the question. "Cancer. To the end, he loved that girl almost more than the other three." Eleanor paused, then took a deep breath. "Do you believe in God?"

"Why are you asking?"

"It's a yes or no question."

"Yes, I believe in a god I guess. I'm not exactly religious but . . ."

Eleanor wasn't looking for a big explanation and she interrupted without missing a beat.

"I think God played a trick on all of us," she said. "Do you think God has a sense of humor?"

"A sense of humor? It's hard to say, but I'm not big on personifying the god thing."

"Stephanie has that same thing," she said. "The girl can't answer yes or no. Maybe it's a good thing you don't know each other."

"No, if there is a god, I don't think he has a sense of humor."

"Well if he does, and I happen to think he does, then what a beautiful thing he's done for Stephanie, and what a joke he's played on your father and me. Because she's always been more grounded and happy than either your dad or I could ever be. She is everything we could have hoped for."

"Mrs. Baltus, I don't know Stephanie, or you. I just wanted to tell you he's dead."

"You can call me Ellie, but with what I know of you from your father, you probably choose your words exactly the way you want to."

"Maybe when I'm writing," I said. "Or asking questions in an interview. But conversation makes me nervous, especially when it's someone I've never met."

"True enough. I haven't seen you since you were 18 months old."

I did the math. Ellie had known me. I'd probably shared a playpen with my half sister. Maybe we'd barfed on the same blanket. Maybe we'd cuddled during naptime. Maybe we'd played with the same toys.

"We moved away just before I turned two," I said. "But you probably know more about that than I do."

"I might. Your mother and I were friends too. Good friends for a time."

"Interesting choice of words. With friends like you . . ." I didn't have a manual to follow, but the sudden defense of my mother with sarcasm against a betrayal that happened decades ago didn't seem to fit the occasion.

"I don't expect anyone to understand it, really. Your father and I had an attraction we couldn't understand, let alone manage. We were like magnets. We did things we shouldn't have, things no one should do. Even half a century later, I still feel bad for Ralph and your mother. They deserved more. We deserved more."

"So you're telling me you have regrets?"

"No, actually. That tractor left the shed decades ago."

"Dad used to say that too. It must be an Iowa thing."

"What I'm saying is that we couldn't help ourselves. We didn't have fancy words for it then like 'soul mates,' but I loved him like I've never loved anyone else. There was an irresistible force when we were together. So no, I didn't mean to hurt people, but I have no regrets."

I imagined Ellie sitting in a favorite chair, a very old woman, waiting to surrender. The rain began to fall harder, tapping back the years. I pictured her like Lauren Bacall again, and suddenly I had them in my mind—Dad and Ellie on a deserted country road in western Iowa. They were in the back of a pickup truck on top of a thin army blanket thrown across a bed of straw. A cold bottle of Schlitz sat in the hub of the spare tire that was chained to the floor.

It was late August, the sun was floating low in the harvest haze, and Ellie was wearing a print sundress that accentuated her tiny waist and round bottom. She and Dad couldn't unbutton things fast enough. Magnetic force. Her hair fell full across her shoulders, and her hands pushed against the back of the cab as his fingers ran the length of her neck and breasts. It was much more passion than play, and Ellie's kisses turned to licks, her tongue lashing his cheeks and eyelids. Dad's mouth explored parts of her he never allowed himself to imagine with my mother. Their bodies took control in a breathless frenzy of sweat and contortion that sent waves of soft wind across the prairie. Their innocent sounds, their giggles and moans, their wishes, mixed with the low buzz of crickets and the occasional sound of night birds.

"And you?" She interrupted my fantasy. I'd never thought of Dad that way before, and hearing Ellie's voice put me right back on the street corner outside her house just in time for a UPS truck to splash water from the curbside puddle.

"What was your question?" I was sure she'd heard the splash but she said nothing.

"Do you have a partner?" she asked. "Someone you love?"

"I'd like to know where Stephanie was conceived?" I wanted to confirm my pickup truck scenario, and there was no way we were talking about my love life.

"Stephanie was conceived in a small conference room behind your dad's office. There were no windows, only old florescent lights hanging from the ceiling. It takes a lot of nerve for you to ask that question."

"I'm sorry, I don't mean to be rude. I just had a different idea. I thought it would be more romantic, I guess."

"We never had a place for romance. It was a small town, so it wasn't like we could visit a hotel or have a picnic in the park. We both had families, jobs, and a lot of responsibilities. I had church. My brother coached your dad's softball team. It was complicated."

"And the trick you were talking about, the one from God?"

"It was simple, really. Your dad and I wanted to create a child. It seemed innocent, like something we were born to do. It was as if a child could embody the dreams we'd never be able to achieve as a couple. And in many ways, Stephanie represents that for both of us. But we were naïve about what it meant to bring a child to life outside of a marriage. We were naïve about the people we would hurt. We couldn't leave our spouses to be with each other, but staying meant burying a passion neither of us would ever feel again. I was the lucky one because I was able to see Stephanie become the woman she is now, and that's a beautiful reward for my bad behavior. But I've never been able to look at her without seeing your dad. The joke from God is that she's her own person, she's her own soul, and she's nothing like either one of us. She didn't seem to need your father or me to be happy, just Ralph. She and Ralph were inseparable."

"He said you talked on the phone every year on her birthday."

"We did," she said. "At first it was a way to stay in touch. Then it was just painful, but I thought he had a right to know."

Ellie could hear the low rumble of thunder to the west.

"You really should come inside. You'll catch your death of cold."

I looked toward the brick bungalow across the street—244 Lincoln Avenue. When I squinted, I could see someone peering out at me through the blinds.

"How did you know?"

Huge drops of rain began to ricochet off my umbrella.

"Just an old woman's hunch. Please, come inside."

I hung up and ran across the street. Before I could knock, Ellie opened the door, and for the first time in my life, I froze.

"You were expecting someone else?" She was right. I was imagining Lauren Bacall circa 1956. But 81-year-old Ellie Baltus waved me inside.

Ellie was a small, thin woman who bore more resemblance to an aging Audrey Hepburn than Lauren Bacall. Her voice was softer than it had been on the phone. She wore a sweater Stephanie's daughter had knit for her the past Christmas. I'd imagined her tall, but even with heeled shoes she only came to the middle of my chest. Her hair was cropped short with rough edges, as if she'd cut it herself. The only thing that fit from the photo I'd seen was her string of pearls. I wondered whether they were a gift from Dad.

"I lost my hair last year with the chemo," she said. "Nasty stuff. Sit, sit."

Still speechless, I took a seat. I noticed the music for the first time. Henry Mancini. I was a mess from twenty minutes standing in the rain and Ellie brought me a roll of paper towel from the kitchen. She studied me as I dried my face, then rubbed the water from my hair.

"You look like him," she said. "The same narrow face, the thin frame. And your eyes."

Whatever I came for, it suddenly seemed wrong.

"Would you like something? Coffee? Tea?" She seemed anxious to be a good hostess.

"Nothing, really. I was driving to Colorado and had to pass through Omaha. I thought I should stop. Dad had asked me to tell you when he died and . . ."

"Yes, so you said. Would you like scotch, perhaps? Your father liked scotch."

"I'm more of a gin guy, I guess. Bombay. But really, I should go."

Ellie went to a small table and filled two small glasses of sherry. She took her time, careful, but also lingering. I noticed her shuffle as she walked back with the glasses.

"What about your stepmother Lindsay? Did he find any happiness with her?"

For the first time, I could see a tear in the corner of Ellie's eye.

"I'm sorry, Ellie. I didn't come here to stir things up."

It was a lie, of course. It was exactly why I'd come. We're all drawn to those things in our past that we think can heal us. But my visit was at Ellie's expense. There was so little foundation between us that I used the awkward silences to look around. I wanted to know my father's lover. I wanted to know him. Her furniture was older but stylish. She didn't appear to be much of a reader. The newest books I could see were *The Purpose Driven Life* and a Laura Bush biography. But Ellie sure could dust. There wasn't a spec to be found, even on the old stand up piano. The two carpets on the hardwood floor were from the East.

"Himalayan carpets?" I asked. "I see you must have traveled far and wide."

"Ralph did. He sold aircraft parts in Turkey and Iran. He went to Egypt a couple of times."

"They're silk?"

"Yes, silk. You seem to like details."

"You're a Laura Bush fan?"

"It's an old book, but my oldest son's a Republican. He lives in Ohio and worked for that rich governor before he fell from grace. I can't bring myself to throw the stuff out, so it sits there."

"You're not political?"

"I vote. But your dad was the political one. The politicians all say the same thing if you ask me. I do like Michelle Obama, if that helps you."

"The pictures near your hallway, those are—." I stopped short and stood up to have a closer look.

"Your half sister is the second one on the toboggan." Ellie sipped her sherry, thinking. "She loved to sit right behind Ralph. That one was taken before we had our fourth. There used to be a sledding park near Aksarben, the old amusement park."

From an end table, Ellie picked up a family photo of a middle-aged woman and two kids. They were on a dock, a northern lake lined with white pine and sugar maples stretched out behind them. One of the kids was sitting in a rowboat anchored alongside the dock, the other held up a string of fish.

"That's Stephanie from last summer," she said. I stared at the photo looking for some familiarity, but there was nothing. Stephanie's face was round like Ellie's. And she didn't appear to have my dad's high metabolism.

"The girl on the right is your niece. That's her friend Sophia next to her."

My niece. Another brick in the wall I hadn't known was missing. Suddenly, for the first time, I was holding back tears of my own. It didn't help listening to Henry Mancini, I thought. Yes, love is blue. It was like Henry had composed the original score for my parent's demise and denied my dad his true love. I stood up, uncomfortable, and moved a bit closer to the door.

"My niece's name?" I asked.

Ellie couldn't talk anymore. I'd never imagined any of this—a tired, short, aged woman collapsing in my arms. She was someone I didn't know wanting something I couldn't give.

"Forgive me," she said. Ellie looked at me through her tears and I felt a sense of panic as she moved toward me. I thought about how tiny she was, how her skin folded tight against her bones. I saw how the years of sadness had made it hard for her to smile, how they'd left her sloping forward, how her shoulders seemed to lead her as she moved.

I was in the center of her living room with no way to turn back. My half sister's mother, my father's lover, took my right hand in her left. Her bent, arthritic fingers barely fit into my palm. When Ellie folded my left hand behind the small of her back, she could feel my resistance.

"Forgive me," she repeated. The whisper of her voice trailed off until all I could hear was my own long, deep breath as I exhaled my father's guilt.

Ellie put her free hand against the small of my back but kept a respectful distance.

"Will you dance with me?" she asked. "Will you dance with me."

CHIP DUNCAN is a writer, photographer, and filmmaker with a penchant for overseas assignments. His professional journeys have taken him to many extraordinary lands, including Afghanistan, Bhutan, Ethiopia, Sudan, Colombia, Peru, and Myanmar. A life-long Midwesterner, Duncan lives within earshot of the Great Lakes and enjoys both Alaska and Peru as regular stomping grounds. His previous work includes the book *Enough To Go Around: Searching for Hope in Afghanistan, Pakistan & Darfur* as well as numerous films broadcast worldwide. He can be reached through ChipDuncan.com.